MIDN[

GILLIAN HARVEY

B
Boldwood

First published in Great Britain in 2025 by Boldwood Books Ltd.

Copyright © Gillian Harvey, 2025

Cover Design by Alice Moore Design

Cover Images: Alamy and Shutterstock

The moral right of Gillian Harvey to be identified as the author of this work has been asserted in accordance with the Copyright, Designs and Patents Act 1988.

All rights reserved. No part of this book may be reproduced in any form or by any electronic or mechanical means, including information storage and retrieval systems, without written permission from the author, except for the use of brief quotations in a book review. This book is a work of fiction and, except in the case of historical fact, any resemblance to actual persons, living or dead, is purely coincidental.

Every effort has been made to obtain the necessary permissions with reference to copyright material, both illustrative and quoted. We apologise for any omissions in this respect and will be pleased to make the appropriate acknowledgements in any future edition.

A CIP catalogue record for this book is available from the British Library.

Paperback ISBN 978-1-80549-978-7

Large Print ISBN 978-1-80549-979-4

Hardback ISBN 978-1-80549-977-0

Ebook ISBN 978-1-80549-981-7

Kindle ISBN 978-1-80549-980-0

Audio CD ISBN 978-1-80549-972-5

MP3 CD ISBN 978-1-80549-973-2

Digital audio download ISBN 978-1-80549-974-9

This book is printed on certified sustainable paper. Boldwood Books is dedicated to putting sustainability at the heart of our business. For more information please visit https://www.boldwoodbooks.com/about-us/sustainability/

Boldwood Books Ltd, 23 Bowerdean Street, London, SW6 3TN

www.boldwoodbooks.com

for Jackie

...but what about us?
    We'll always have Paris.

— CASABLANCA

PROLOGUE
TWO WEEKS AGO

Sophie leant on the cool stone of the bridge, her toes flexed, lifting her a little higher so that below she could see the water froth and whirl. She tried not to think about whether he would come.

The Seine continued at a rapid pace, the peaks and troughs of its surface thrown into light and shadow by the sun's rays, which sprinkled it like glitter. A boat passed, packed with tourists leaning against the railings, photographing the view, taking selfies. Their clothes were a riot of colour against the turquoise-brown water, and their chatter broke through the other sounds of Paris – the buzz and growl of traffic, the hum of pedestrians, the fizz and whorl of the passing river – then drifted away on the wind.

It was busier than it had been the first time they'd stood here, but other than that the view had barely changed in the years that stretched between then and now – the sandstone buildings topped with grey tiles, the majestic lines of windows gazing down on the trees in their uniform, clipped lines. They'd always loved standing here on the Pont du Carrousel, gazing out over this very patch of the river. If he was coming, he would know to find her here.

Soon enough, as she turned her gaze from the water, she saw him approaching, recognisable even at a distance with his habitual swaggering walk. 'I wasn't sure you'd come,' she said as he drew closer.

He chuckled warmly, the sound sending shivers of memory through her. 'And miss this?' he said with a mischievous grin. 'Never.'

Sophie didn't answer. She turned towards him, trying to keep her expression neutral. 'You know it has to be the last time?' she said. 'I have to move on, we both do.'

'You've said that before.'

'Yes, but Tom, this time I mean it.'

His eyes danced with laughter, as they so often did. 'You've said *that* before, too.'

He was closer now, almost touching her. She raised her hands slightly as if to stop him. 'I'm getting married, Tom,' she said.

'I know.'

'To Will.'

He nodded, the smile not leaving his lips. 'I know, Soph.'

'You love Will. *I* love Will. I can't hurt him, Tom. I can't come again.'

'To Paris? You love Paris!'

'*We* love Paris,' she said, dipping her head. 'It won't be the same without you.'

He shook his head. 'You flatter me,' he said. 'People have been coming to Paris for centuries and as far as I know, they're here to see the Louvre and the Eiffel Tower. Not Tom Gardner.'

She gave a small laugh, then turned back towards the water, watching the last of the light shimmer on its surface as the day began to give way to dusk. 'It won't be the same for *me*,' she said. 'Paris is ours. And this...'

'...has to be the last time,' he finished for her. 'I know. Can we not talk about it?'

'What else do you want to talk about?' she asked.

He lifted a shoulder. 'Pretty much anything else.'

She looked at him. 'Remember when we met?'

1

THE FIRST SUMMER – 2011

The first trip to Paris had been Tom's idea.

He'd given her the envelope when she'd been sitting on the edge of his bed, slipping her trainers on, ready to disappear to class. Reaching past her, he'd pulled it from a drawer at the bedside and handed it over.

'What's this?' she said. 'Exam results or something?'

'Open it.' He grinned, confident of her reaction.

She hated opening presents in front of the giver, hated feeling their sharp, discerning eyes on her face, judging her reaction. She never got the expression right – the surprise of the gift inside, the shock of it, adjustment – it took time. 'Are you disappointed?' people would say, or 'I've still got the receipt if you want to return it.'

This time, drawing out the tickets, she snorted. 'Eurostar?' she said.

He shrugged. 'Why not?'

'It must have cost a fortune!'

He laughed and lay back on his single bed, under a black poster with white lettering emblazoned with the words

'PARENTAL WARNING: EXPLICIT LYRICS'. 'But do you like?' he asked.

'Well,' she coloured. 'Of course. It just seems...'

'What?'

'A bit extravagant?'

'They're just train tickets.'

'Yes, but to Paris.'

'Yes. You said you wanted to go one day.'

'They're first class!'

'Only the best,' he said, a lazy smile crossing his features. She couldn't get used to his relaxed stance on money. His parents *had it* apparently – she wasn't yet sure whether that meant they lived in some elaborate country pad, or just that they were doing OK in middle-class suburbia. She suspected the former – it was something about his ease about money, the way he spent it, the way he talked about it as if it were no big deal.

She – attending Anglia Ruskin, the former polytechnic, rather than the 'real Cambridge' university in the same city – felt herself to be an ordinary student, living on beans and pasta and watching every penny. Poor. Budgeting. Counting out change to see if she could get chips on the way home from the uni bar. But it didn't matter because she was the same as everyone else in her circle.

When she was with him though, things felt different. She was somehow reduced. He wouldn't automatically order the cheapest thing on the menu, didn't baulk when he went through the till at Sainsbury's. Got two scoops on his ice cream in the park. It wasn't that he was off buying expensive luxuries, but to her – in her third frugal year of an English degree – the carelessness with money felt foreign.

He got an allowance, whereas she topped up her student loan with two shifts a week at The Anchor. When he was short,

Midnight in Paris

he rang his dad for a bung. When she was short, she rang her parents for sympathy – the only thing they had plenty of.

It shouldn't make her feel inferior – her almost certainly first-class English degree would set her up in a way his half-hearted philosophy third (albeit from 'real Cambridge') might not. But somehow, she always felt on the back foot.

'I can't... pay for mine,' she said.

'Soph. It's a gift.'

She nodded. She knew that, really. But something inside her twisted. They'd been together for two months – it was early for this kind of gesture. But maybe in his world that's what couples did. She felt him watching her. 'Thank you,' she said at last.

'It's nothing,' he said casually.

She wondered whether it really did feel like nothing to him. Or whether he'd stressed over giving her the tickets. Whenever she bought something for a new boyfriend, she worried it might seem 'too much'; that she might scare them off. She couldn't imagine for a second that Tom had felt this way – would ever feel this way.

She showed them to Libby later as they sat in the fifteenth row of the lecture hall, watching an academic in an ill-fitting suit lecturing on seventeenth century poetry. Libby opened her mouth in an expression of surprise. 'From Tom?' she whispered.

Sophie nodded.

'Lucky.'

She shrugged her response. She didn't know how she felt about it yet.

'He must really like you.'

She wasn't sure about that either.

Sophie had barely remembered Tom when they'd bumped into each other in the small Internet cafe on Mill Road a week or so after the infamous party. She'd been sitting at a table reading

Middlemarch and he'd joined her without even asking if it was OK, opening his own book and ordering a coffee before saying, 'Oh, you don't mind do you?' in a way that gave her no real recourse to say that she did, that actually she was reading a set text and it was difficult to concentrate with his constant slurping and spoon-stirring.

'Just trying to read,' she'd said.

'I won't distract you, don't worry,' he'd said before proceeding to distract her constantly – especially frustrating as she was already struggling to get through the enormous tome and had come to the cafe in the hope it would help her focus.

By the end of the hour, he had her number and she wasn't 100 per cent sure exactly how it had all happened.

'Smooth operator,' Libby had said when she'd told her. 'Are you going to see him again?'

'He probably won't ring.' She'd shrugged, embarrassed that she desperately wanted him to. Even though he was annoying. Even though he'd made her even more behind with her work with his incessant (albeit charming) chatter. Even though she resented him for making her feel something when she was so determined not to.

He'd called her that evening. And now, somehow, they were in this fledgling relationship where all her newly acquired, near-adult confidence seemed to disappear. He had an aura about him, something about privilege maybe, and it was hard to fully read him sometimes. She wasn't sure exactly what they were to each other even now, whether it was a fling to him or something more. And she hated that he had her wondering like this – like a lovelorn schoolgirl rather than the woman she was determined to be.

Being at different unis, they had no friends in common whom she could ask about him, no ex-girlfriends in her circle

Midnight in Paris

whose ears she could whisper into. The students from the two universities – and within them their colleges and departments – seemed to cluster together, sharing halls and houses and lecture notes with their own and forming tight-knit groups with friends who had become, over the short, intense years, like family.

Their first date had been to the theatre – a rather tired, student-led production of *The Importance of Being Earnest,* followed by drinks at The Anchor, sitting on a little bridge over the Cam and watching the river sparkle below. 'So, what made you choose English?' he'd asked her.

She'd shrugged. 'I love reading. Books. Language. What about you? Why philosophy?'

He'd laughed. 'I'm a whore for Socrates,' he'd told her. Then, 'Nah. Just didn't know what else to do, if I'm honest. And there was a place, so...'

'Right.'

He was fun, she'd decided after he'd kissed her goodbye and she'd walked home along the back streets of Mill Road. He'd sent a text message asking her out again and she'd typed 'OK'.

Their second date had almost been their last. A picnic on Parker's Piece – a large area of green that stretched between her university and the city centre. He'd brought sparkling wine and two glasses, she'd brought some 'nibbly bits' then felt embarrassed when he'd laughed at her calling them that.

But they'd got on well, again, and she'd begun to feel herself relax in his company. He was funny, told a good anecdote and she found herself laughing freely. Until he'd said it. 'You know your laugh reminds me of something?'

'What?' she'd asked, almost priming herself for a compliment.

'A pig.'

'What?'

'Yeah. You snort like a pig when you laugh.' He'd told her this as if she would take it as – what? A compliment? A joke? But she'd flushed – she knew she had an unusual laugh, a tendency to draw air through her nose and snort when really amused. But she hated any attention being brought to it.

'Oh, come on, Miss Piggy!' he'd said. 'I think it's cute.' He'd nuzzled against her, making snorting noises, opening his eyes wide and trying to appease her.

'It's not funny.'

'Sorry.' He'd sat up then.

An awkward silence had come over the pair of them as they had sat together, tearing bits off the French stick, sipping at their wine. And she'd thought to herself that if he asked her out again, she wouldn't say yes.

Then he'd shifted closer to her again, put an arm around her shoulders and pulled her to him. 'I really am sorry, you know. What an idiot!' he'd said. 'I just... I was trying to make you laugh. I love your laugh. I do, honestly.'

It wasn't his words that had soothed her as much as his touch. The smell of him as she nestled closer. And she realised that when she was in his arms, she'd forgive him almost anything.

Now they spent most nights together in his digs, went for drinks or food in the town several evenings a week. Spent far too long on the phone when they weren't together. At twenty, it was the most serious relationship she'd ever been in.

Even so, going away on holiday together seemed significant.

She'd tucked the envelope back into her rucksack, pulling it out later in her bedroom – slightly curled after being caught under her lunchbox – and smoothed it on her desk. *Don't overthink it*, she told herself. After all, she had always wanted to go to Paris.

2

TWO WEEKS AGO

The trip to Paris – her tenth visit but her first alone – had seemed easy, logical, from a distance. Meeting Tom one last time, in the city they'd both loved, and drawing a line under part of her life. A place she probably wouldn't want to return to in the future after everything that had happened; it was steeped in memories of them both, synonymous with her love for Tom.

Now she was here, booked into a room at Hotel Cler – a cheap place they'd stayed in before, right at the start of things – it felt almost silly; dramatic. And somehow terrifying, too. Worse for the fact that she'd lied to Will about coming; he knew she was here, but not that Tom would be here too.

She let herself in to the small, clean room with its chocolate-brown floor and cream walls. Beige curtains hung from the windows and on the walls, there was a scribbled artist's impression of Paris – an attempt, she supposed, to make the room look arty.

She'd decided on the train that she'd take it easy when she arrived, get a coffee, make her way to the bridge without rushing, but found that as soon as she'd unpacked and drunk one of the hotel's gifted water bottles, she was too restless to simply sit. She might as well do what she was here to do. And though she wasn't even certain he'd be waiting, she felt something inside her stir – as if some unconscious part of herself knew that he was close.

Her phone buzzed. A message from Will. And suddenly the bubble she was allowing herself to inhabit here was burst, its delicate structure pierced by memories of saying goodbye to Will at the station, inhaling the fragrance of his clean clothes, and the unmistakable scent of *Will* beneath. His arms, strong and dependable, had laced behind her and she'd held him tightly in return. It was evolutionary, wasn't it? This need for closeness, contact. Ridiculous but when she was in Will's arms, she felt as if nothing bad could touch her; that they formed this impenetrable circle of safety from the rest of the world. She'd drawn back, looking at his face, and had opened her mouth.

'Stop it,' he'd said.

'Stop what?'

'I know what you're going to say. You feel guilty about leaving me, going off to Paris on your own.'

'Well, yes,' she'd admitted. 'How did you know?'

'Oh, you know. Psychic powers. Plus the fact that you've said that about ten times this morning already.'

She'd grimaced. 'Sorry. I just feel bad about leaving you.'

'Well, don't,' he'd said firmly. 'We talked about it, and decided it was for the best. I'd only get in the way. You know that. You'll be grand on your own.'

She'd shrugged, not wanting to admit it. 'Still,' she'd said.

'I'm a big boy,' he'd grinned, 'I'll cope.'

'You mean you'll live on takeaways and spend the entire weekend sitting around in your pants,' she'd teased, grinning.

His eyes had met hers. 'How did you know?' he'd joked in

return, then kissed her firmly on the forehead. 'Now go. Before I change my mind and whisk you back to my lair.'

'Do you promise?' she'd said, pushing herself up on tiptoes to kiss him back. 'Because from where I'm standing, your lair looks pretty darn tempting.'

He'd laughed. 'Even though I'm going to be wearing nothing but my pants?'

'Especially because of that.'

On the train, she'd fingered the silver heart locket at her throat and felt the heaviness of guilt settle on her again. Sure, Will knew about Tom. Knew all about their history, their connection with Paris.

What he didn't know was that Tom would be there to meet her. Didn't know that part of the reason Sophie had persuaded Will to stay at home was that she needed to be alone with Tom in the place that had become theirs.

She'd wanted to tell him; opened her mouth to several times. But if she'd been completely honest, he might have wanted to stop her going. And she had to see Tom; had to say goodbye properly – in a way that would draw a line under everything.

Now, a woman in a navy shift dress, her hair tied up in a sensible bun, served her yoghurt and a Danish pastry, offered her tea or coffee. She chose coffee, knowing as she did so she'd probably be unable to stomach it. A white cup and saucer were set in front of her on a tray, the black surface of the steaming liquid wobbling and reflecting the light. 'Thank you,' she said, and smiled.

'No milk?'

'No, thank you.'

And at last, the woman moved on along the half-empty carriage. Sophie found herself dipping the silver teaspoon into the bowl of white, creamy yoghurt, with its dash of raspberry coulis, but she couldn't bring herself to eat. Was it guilt, or excitement, or the fear that even after all she'd risked, maybe he wouldn't even meet her when she got there?

It would be her tenth time in Paris; and every year she'd been, she'd left a little of herself behind. Would all those Sophies – the ghostly past versions of herself shed like snakeskin – be there too? Would she be able to gather up some of their optimism, stoicism? Capture some of who she'd been before it had all happened?

She wasn't the same person, she knew that. Knew she'd changed for the worse. Always cautious, she was now almost neurotic at times. But who could blame her after everything she'd – they'd – been through.

Tom. Lovely, carefree, jokey, loving Tom. It was OK for part of her to still love him, wasn't it? Didn't everyone carry a tiny torch for their first love?

She dipped her spoon into the yoghurt, half-heartedly bringing it to her lips, before setting it down and turning her attention to the windows as the train journeyed under the Channel and emerged in the place where she'd finally see him again.

3

THE FIRST SUMMER – 2011

When she arrived at the station that first time, nervous and excited, clutching their tickets, the last thing she thought Tom would do was laugh at her. But as soon as their eyes locked, she could see that he was amused by something.

'What?' she said, once she was in earshot. She tried to smile, but actually it was a bit insulting, considering how much thought she'd given to her outfit and hair. She'd taken at least half an hour trying to tame her shoulder-length mane into what a magazine had called 'beachy curls', and had been relatively happy with the result. She'd spent ages on the kind of make-up designed to look like you weren't wearing any make-up, and when she'd glanced in the mirror before leaving, had felt about as satisfied as she ever would be about her appearance.

And he was laughing.

'Nothing,' he said, tilting his head affectionately. 'Just wondered how many outfits a girl needs for two nights away.' He nodded at her wheeled suitcase.

Ah, so it was the suitcase. She felt relieved, then embarrassed. 'I didn't know what we'd be doing,' she said, only to have him laugh again.

'Oh, I think I've got a few ideas,' he said, drawing her to him. Then it didn't matter suddenly whether he was laughing at her, teasing her. Because something about his touch made everything else seem irrelevant.

'It's not *that* big,' she added as she pulled away, only to have him cock an eyebrow.

'Excuse me?' he said with mock hurt.

She slapped him lightly on the arm. 'Tom! The suitcase!'

On the train, she settled into the seat and looked out of the window, conscious of not wanting to seem too excited to be going to a place she'd always dreamt of but so far never made it to. Tom had been to Paris about eight times, he'd told her. Mostly with family. She hadn't liked to push him on the 'mostly.' Probably with other girls too, then. She'd rather not know.

But he was so blasé about it, she was a little embarrassed at her own excitement and tried to keep it under wraps.

Two months together and he was still a bit of a mystery to her – this boy with his posh accent and strange intellectual friends. They'd first met when she'd drunkenly crashed the after-party for some sort of am-dram production by Cambridge students. She'd been wearing a black dress, short. Her friend Libby had been in hotpants. They'd been en route home from Ballare – their favourite nightclub – slightly worse for wear from cheap vodka and erratic dancing, when they'd seen that one of the heavy wooden doors leading into the old stone building had been left slightly ajar, revealing a sliver of light within.

'Come on!' Libby had said, grabbing onto her arm as they'd half walked, half stumbled through the gap and into the stone-tiled corridor inside. 'Let's see how the other half live.'

While essentially studying in the same city, there had always seemed to be a divide between 'town and gown' – the students of Cambridge University, and her more ordinary ex-polytechnic. Students travelled in packs, easily distinguishable somehow by their attire, their conduct, often their accents. Few managed to bridge the strange social divide between the two institutions, and on the rare occasions Sophie had found herself chatting to Cambridge students in a bar or club, she'd always felt a sense of detachment on their part, as if they had no real interest in getting to know her.

Of course, she reasoned, it could just be that she was shy, that she looked for the negative, for reasons not to connect with people when things seemed different.

That night, she'd had no such inhibitions; alcohol-soaked and high from a night of dancing, her legs aching and the back of her shoe rubbing painfully against her foot, she'd clung to Libby as they'd giggled up the corridor and followed the sound of laughter to a small room, in which they'd discovered a group of people decked out in what appeared to be fancy dress.

'I like your outfit,' Libby had said to a man close to the door who'd haughtily looked down at her as if insulted, despite donning a strange flouncy shirt, a leather waistcoat, and sporting what looked to be a narrow tail on the back of his trousers.

'Who are you?' he'd asked them, top lip curling. 'This is a private event, you know?'

'Don't be a dick, Michael,' another voice had said; a tall man with an easy smile had appeared, wearing some sort of weird cream tunic and what appeared to be glitter on his cheeks. 'Is that any way to greet our guests?'

'Yeah, come on, Michael, the more the merrier, right?' someone else had said.

Michael had snorted. 'They're wasted. And it's after midnight.'

'Don't mind our friend Michael.' The first man had somehow managed to wrap an arm around both their backs at once, and guide them towards a table covered with scattered beer bottles and what looked like a dubious bowl of punch. 'He's had a rough night.'

Libby had laughed and enquired, 'Why's he got a tail?' and had been treated to a single raised eyebrow.

'He's Puck!'

'And you are...?'

'Demetrius,' he'd bowed deeply. 'At your service.'

'No, you nob. Your real name.'

'Oh! Tom.'

'Well, Tom, you might like to know that your tunic's tucked in your underpants at the back.'

Tom had appeared unfazed, pulling the material down into place. 'Hazard of the job,' he'd joked.

'And this guy is...?' Libby had pointed at the other man. He was thicker-set, stronger-looking than Tom, but his face was open and friendly.

'Oh, this is Will.' Tom had laughed. 'I'm afraid that Will was not in *A Midsummer Night's Dream,* he's just his usual, fashion-challenged self.'

'Whoops!' Libby had seemed delighted with her mistake. 'Thought you might have been Lysander or maybe Bottom?' She'd given a drunken wink.

'Libby!' Sophie had admonished. Will was wearing a white shirt, blue jeans. Nothing out of the ordinary.

'Ah, she speaks!' Tom had said, making her blush. Then turning to Libby, he'd remarked, 'She's quiet, your friend.'

Libby had shrugged. 'Yeah. Only cos she can't get a word past me.'

Sophie had felt her face get hot.

'Don't worry about Tom,' Will had then said conspiratorially at her side. 'It's actually a compliment. He's flirting.'

She'd looked at him incredulously. '*That's* flirting?'

'He has a pretty high success rate, believe it or not.'

It had been a strange evening of too much red wine, a combination of welcoming banter and borderline flirtation from some of the boys, and haughty disdain from others. At some point, someone had brought out an ancient karaoke mic, inserted a DVD into a small TV in the corner, and soon they were laughing, dancing and cringing to the sounds of outdated nineties hits being belted out by posh boys with mediocre vocal skills.

A few of them had started to dance, a couple more girls had found their way into the party and soon the tiny room was hot, sweaty, filled with a fug of forbidden cigarettes and alcohol. Libby had started dancing with Michael who'd mellowed after a couple more whiskies, and Sophie had found herself sitting alone, sipping dubious punch on a beanbag that had seen better days.

'Sure you don't want to dance?' Will had asked her, sitting down heavily on the edge of the beanbag.

She'd shaken her head, embarrassed. She'd barely touched her drink and had started to sober up, could feel the ghost of a headache throb at her temples. Earlier, a drunken lad had sat next to her and begun talking about quantum mechanics enthusiastically, and she'd found herself nodding along without understanding a word. This was not the kind of party she was used to.

Just when she had been considering how to get Libby's attention and suggest they got out of there, a plastic cup had been thrust at her. 'Come on,' a voice had said. 'Have a bit of wine. That punch is toxic.'

She'd taken the cup and looked up, seeing Tom, a wide smile stretched across his glittery face. 'Thanks.'

He'd put out a hand and she'd instinctively put hers out to meet it, then before she knew what was happening, she had been pulled to her feet and into Tom's arms, rocking away to some half-forgotten hit by the Spice Girls. She'd looked back at Will guiltily as she was tugged away.

Close up, she could smell the clean scent of Tom's aftershave, the slightly musty cotton of his costume, a touch of cigarette smoke. She'd never been a big fan of dancing, but here in this private and crowded space, the most they could do was rock a little to whatever song came on next. She'd caught Libby's eye across the room and her friend had given her an enthusiastic thumbs up. She had shaken her head emphatically. No. She had not pulled.

The party had passed in a blur of music and drunkenness until one by one, people had drifted off to their rooms or back to the street. Eventually, close to three in the morning, it had been just Sophie, Tom, Will and Libby.

'Well, thanks for letting us crash your party,' Sophie had said.

'Hang on. You *crashed* our party?' Tom had said in mock surprise.

'Ha ha. Very funny.' Libby had given him a gentle smack on the arm.

Sophie had clambered to her feet. 'We'd better go. It's like 3 a.m.'

'OK, see you!' Tom had waved tiredly without moving from his position on the sofa.

'Can I get you a taxi?' Will had offered.

'No, it's fine,' Sophie had said. 'We're not far. Come on, Libby.'

'Can't we sleep here?' Libby had whined. This was typical Libby – the first few drinks of an evening seemed to energise her, but she'd hit a wall on drink six or seven and simply want to lie down and go to sleep. Sophie had come down one morning to find her out cold on the kitchen floor, propping her head on a tea towel and completely oblivious to the rest of their housemates tiptoeing around her and brewing coffee before morning lectures.

'Lib, no!' Sophie had said, grabbing her friend's arm. 'They might get into trouble, you know we're not meant to be here. Come on.'

Reluctantly, Libby had acquiesced.

'Taxi?' Will had offered again, following as they half stumbled towards the door. 'Honestly, my treat.'

'We're good,' Sophie had said, 'thanks though.'

'See, they're fine!' Tom had exclaimed, appearing behind his friend and throwing his arms wide. 'They can take care of themselves, mate.'

But Will had persisted, until eventually Sophie had allowed him to walk to the taxi rank just outside with her – both of them now supporting Libby – and hand the driver a twenty-pound note on her behalf. Taxis were something she shared with friends now and then on an emergency-only basis (if one of them broke a heel, or was ill) and although she hated the fact she'd let him pay, she really didn't have enough to cover the fare home.

At least she'd probably never see him again.

Tom had come out at the last minute, looking at Will, confused, before waving at them enthusiastically.

'Bye, Will! Bye, Lysander!' Sophie had joked out of the window as he waved them off.

Tom had looked at his legs protruding from his tunic as if just realising that he was now on a street at 3 a.m. wearing what was effectively an ill-fitting dress, and he had made a face before giving her a brief wave and trotting back across the road towards the wooden door.

'He was nice,' she'd said to Libby who was leaning heavily against her shoulder.

But Libby was asleep.

4

TWO WEEKS AGO

The hotel lift was a little smaller than she remembered and as soon as she stepped into it to make her way down to the reception, she regretted not using the stairs for the four flights. Two young French men, or boys perhaps, were in there and as the doors slid closed, she realised how close together they were all standing.

The taller of the two had brown hair, thick and wavy, curling to the nape of his neck, a shadow on his top lip which might be the beginnings of a moustache. The other sported a goatee and had short hair gelled into a neat point at the front. Both were dressed in jeans, band T-shirts, smart loafers. The lift interior smelled of enthusiastically applied aftershave and teenage hope.

One of them motioned at the buttons. '*Rez-de-chaussée?*' he asked.

She had limited French but knew at least what this meant. '*Oui, merci.*'

'You are English?' the other man enquired, a smile breaking across his face like a wave. 'On holidays?'

'Yes,' she said, not willing or able to explain that this wasn't quite a holiday. What else could she say it was? A mission? One last moment with Tom before she finally let him go?

'Well, you must let us show you around!' he enthused. 'Evan and I, we know all the best places!'

'Thank you, but no. I'm meeting someone.'

'But of course!' he said with an exaggerated eye-roll. 'A beautiful woman like you will already have someone waiting, especially in Paris. It is not a place to come alone.'

She smiled thinly and waited as the doors slid open on the second floor to reveal an empty hallway. They were silent as the doors slid shut again and the lift shuddered into life and continued its descent.

'Well, have a good holidays.' The man bowed slightly as she left the metal container and stepped onto the thin carpet of the reception.

'Thank you. You too.'

She silently walked the familiar route, seeing how little had changed over the years since they'd first come. She was only thirty-five – hardly old. But imagining the younger version of herself walking these well-trodden streets full of hope and life and excitement, she felt a strange sense of wanting to protect the younger woman. Of wanting her to know how things would work out.

Or perhaps that former her with her wide eyes and ready smile would be better off just enjoying the moment while she could.

She meandered along the Parisian streets, feeling something buzz inside her as she always did when she was here in this eccentric, artistic, historical, beautiful city. It was early August and hot, the sun beating on the pavements; people dressed in shorts and sunglasses, summer dresses and hats. In August, she knew, many of the residents made their way to their country houses, preferring to spend the holiday month away from the city.

But she'd almost always come this time of year – mainly because she'd always been in education (either studying or working), so her summers were free months. She enjoyed the heat, the warm evenings, the sparkle of sunlight on water. There was always shade, always a fountain to drape your hand into. Always ice-cold white wine or enormous jugs of water to pour. Plenty of sunshades on outdoor tables to take the edge off while you rested.

And although she didn't have any way to compare, she wondered whether Paris was friendlier, more open, at a time when many residents disappeared but tourists flooded in, making an eclectic, friendly and vibrant temporary population of their own.

Once in a while, her hand would creep up to the silver locket at her neck, and she'd finger the cool metal, close her eyes and think back to a time when life was simpler, when her future had looked obvious and she hadn't imagined the kind of curveballs life could sometimes throw.

Her phone rang and she smiled: Sam, her younger sister. 'Hi,' she said, bringing it to her ear.

'Hey. So, how's Paris?'

'Ah, you know. French. Hot.'

'Sounds pretty good to me,' her sister said, her voice bright. 'You know it's going to rain all weekend here? Might actually come and join you.'

'Next time, eh,' she said gently.

'Yeah. So have you done it yet?'

'Sam! I've only just got here.'

There was a pause. 'Sorry.'

'It's OK.'

'Are you all right, sis? Because I don't like thinking of you being there on your own. All that shit going through your head.'

'I'm good,' Sophie said firmly. 'Anyway, aren't I meant to be the older sister, taking care of *you*?'

Sam laughed loudly. 'I'd like to see you try!'

Sophie smiled, moving closer to the wall of one of the buildings so as not to block the way of any walkers.

'Anyway, I'm keeping my phone on all weekend. So just call if you need to, OK?' her sister added.

'Thank you.'

She ended the call and, while she thought of it, sent a quick message to Libby.

SOPHIE
Here safe.

A green dot lit up next to her friend's name and an ellipsis appeared in the chat box.

LIBBY
Good. And you're feeling OK?

SOPHIE
I'm OK.

LIBBY
Glad to hear it. Just, you know… Get it done. Don't overthink it, Soph.

SOPHIE
OK.

LIBBY
Soph?

SOPHIE
What?

LIBBY

You're overthinking! I can sense it!

SOPHIE

Damn! Rumbled! OK, how about this? I'll buy myself an enormous millefeuille to numb the pain?

LIBBY

Atta girl!

She slipped the phone back into her bag and continued to walk, wishing she felt half as upbeat as she'd tried to appear to the two most important women in her life.

5

THE FIRST SUMMER – 2011

The train pulled away and she sat opposite Tom sipping sparkling wine and looking out of the window as the scenery flashed past: the apartment blocks with balconies full of washing or children's toys; the graffitied walls and tunnels; the rows of tiny terraces stretching away – then they moved farther from London and she watched the view transform from green and natural to built-up and back again, and people's lives ebbed and flowed past her like a river.

Tom, uncharacteristically, had his nose in a book – disinterested in what, for him, was quite an ordinary journey, she supposed.

In her bag, the brand-new passport she'd had to borrow money from Mum to buy, the photo embarrassingly recent. She'd never left the country before, never been farther than Cornwall. Now she was racing towards the coast on a train that ran under the water and would take her to the city she'd dreamt about seeing for years.

'Have you never been on a train before?' His voice broke through her thoughts.

She blushed. 'Of course I have! Just not this one, is all.'

He laughed as if it were cute that she was so untravelled, folded down the corner of his page and moved across to sit next to her, nuzzling against her neck.

'Get off!' she said, laughing, nudging him with her elbow.

He laid his head elaborately on her shoulder. 'I just want some attention,' he said. 'What have those buildings got that I haven't?' He widened his eyes in a way that he clearly hoped was appealing.

She looked at him, amused. 'Seriously?' she said. 'You're jealous of some buildings?'

'I'm jealous of anything you look at like *that*,' he said, flashing his trademark cheeky smile and straightening up. He drew a tiny MP3 player from his pocket and offered her one of the earphones. 'Soundtrack?' he said.

She'd actually have preferred to sit quietly, lose herself in her thoughts. But instead, she took the small, plastic, foam-covered bud from him. The Black Eyed Peas began playing in her right ear, the sounds of the train continued in her left. Tom reached and grabbed her hand, giving it a squeeze, and she settled back against the headrest, enjoying the closeness of him, the music, and allowing herself at last a little excitement at what was to come.

What was to come, it turned out, was a bog-standard hotel, a three-star establishment in a building that was majestic on the outside but tatty inside. She was rather relieved when they walked in, although Tom's face flushed a little when he saw the size of the room.

'It looked better on the website,' he said.

'Don't be silly, it's lovely. We're in Paris, for God's sake!' She walked to the window and fiddled with the catch, eventually finding purchase and opening the windows, flinging them wide then standing, looking down on the narrow street, the people meandering or striding along, the bicycles, the chatter, the sound of distant music. She breathed deeply. She was *here*.

'We can check in somewhere else if you like,' he said, kicking the leg of a dressing table.

'Why?'

'It's a shithole.'

She looked at him. Was he serious? 'Tom, it's fine. It's clean, it's got a bed. We're in Paris. It's good.'

He lifted a shoulder, reluctantly acquiescing. 'I guess.'

He seemed childish, suddenly, and she felt a flash of annoyance. 'Come on. Let's not waste time on the room.'

'I guess I'm just...'

'What?'

'Nothing.'

'Tom, what were you going to say?'

He shrugged, embarrassed. 'I'm used to better things?' he said, an inflexion in his voice now.

'Whereas I'm used to crappy hotels at best? Is that what you mean?'

'I didn't mean it like *that*.' He sighed, running his hands through his hair. 'I just wanted to treat you, is all.'

'You have.' She swallowed down the insult; he hadn't meant it. 'It's fine. We're together, that's the most important thing.'

Tom's features relaxed then and he walked towards her, wrapping his arms around her waist, the movement bringing, as it always did, a shiver of pleasure. She wished sometimes that she wasn't so attracted to him. Because it would no doubt end in tears.

'You don't date Tom, you borrow him,' one of Tom's friends had joked when they'd met briefly in a bar. 'The minute you feel settled, he'll be on to the next.'

Tom had laughed it off, but something in the back of her mind had recorded this and she had filed it away in a box marked 'Danger' in her brain. She couldn't allow herself to fall for this man because he simply wasn't someone who fell for anyone back.

But she turned to him and let him cover her with kisses; felt her body respond until she no longer cared about his past or their future but simply the moment; she forgot about everything other than him, and her, and the both of them together in this tiny fourth-floor hotel room in Paris.

* * *

'Is it worth it?' he asked two hours later when they stood in the square outside the Louvre, tourists milling around them.

'Are you kidding me?'

He shrugged. 'You've seen the outside. And we can get pictures...' He trailed off, sensing he wasn't going to win this one. 'Maybe we could come back later? The queue is totally insane.'

She was too taken with the sight of it to mind the queue, this building she'd seen many times before in guidebooks and online but never in the flesh. The traditional, sombre buildings that hugged the square, and the pyramid of glass and light that rose up in the centre, both at odds with – and somehow complementing – each other. The Louvre had been her first choice, the first place she'd wanted to come when he'd asked, and she couldn't quite believe what she was hearing.

'It'll be just the same later,' she said. 'Maybe we should just wait.' She hated the hesitancy in her own voice – knew it was, in part, because he'd paid for the trip. He owned their time in Paris.

'You don't know that. Maybe people stop coming at teatime or something.'

'Tom, we're in Paris.'

'Yup.'

'It's not going to stop for teatime.'

'OK.' He looked sulky, boyish. 'I just hate queues, is all. And there are loads of other galleries.'

'It's the Louvre, Tom.'

'Yes, I'm aware.'

'And you must have known. The website said most days you'd have to queue.'

He sighed and suddenly it felt as if he was half her age. A small boy frustratedly waiting at the window of the ice cream van.

'Look,' she said. 'Go, if you want. I'll queue. We can meet up later? Or I can call you when I'm nearer the front or something.'

'Your phone won't work here, remember?'

'Well, maybe you could just pop back and check from time to time. I'm staying, but you don't have to if you don't want to.' She almost stamped her foot with frustration, but managed to contain the impulse.

His eyebrows shot up at her tone. 'What?'

'Well, you're clearly not that bothered so...' she shrugged, meaning it.

'Don't be silly,' he said. 'You want to see the *Mona Lisa*, we'll see the *Mona Lisa*.' She bristled a little at his sing-song tone, but when he smiled and rolled his eyes, she couldn't help but smile in return. Damn it, the boy was good-looking. No wonder he seemed to get away with everything.

'Thank you,' she said.

'Even though she looks a bit like George Harrison.'

'What?'

'Yeah. You wait. The spit of him in his longer-haired days.'

'Beard and all?'

He grinned. 'Well, no. But actually, I think one might suit her.'

She shook her head and laughed. 'I'll bear it in mind. So we're staying, yes?'

'Looks like it. Even if I pass out from boredom or dehydration or something in the queue.'

She stood on tiptoes and gave him a quick kiss. 'My hero.'

'But don't say I didn't warn you,' he added. 'The *Mona Lisa* is a massive disappointment. I've seen it four times and each time it looks a little bit more crap.'

She slapped him with her guidebook. 'Don't. You'll spoil it. I've never seen her.'

'Seriously, I have no idea why people think she's gorgeous. I'd rather look at you.'

'Oh! Praise indeed,' she joked.

'Well, it's true.'

'Well then, Tom, you can look at me and I'll look at her. We'll all be happy.'

As it was, the queue moved quickly and they were inside the glass pyramid in just over half an hour, their voices hushed as they moved from work to work, reading the information cards. She absorbed, taking in every detail. He, impatient, wanting always to move forward, forward, forward, occasionally sighing audibly, leaving her embarrassed.

'Don't leave me behind!' she said at one point when she almost lost sight of him. Her voice echoed more than predicted in the high-ceilinged space and a man turned, regarding her with a frown.

'Sorry,' Tom said, returning to her side. 'Ants in my pants, my mum always says.'

She looked at him, softening. He really wasn't in his element here. 'Look, thanks for this. I know you're not really an art guy. Your choice of venue next.'

'You promise?' They fell into step and he reached for her hand. 'We'll look at it all though, if you like.'

She snorted. 'Did you know that if we spent thirty seconds looking at each piece of art here, it would take us over six months?'

'You're kidding.'

'There are thirty-five thousand of them.'

'Oh. Never did get around to reading that guidebook.'

'So we'll stick to a couple of rooms this time.' She reddened at having used the words 'this time', although he appeared not to notice.

'OK, let's make a deal. See the *Mona Lisa*, look at the paintings on the way, then coffee,' he said hopefully. 'We'll look at more next time we come.'

She raised an eyebrow at the thought of next time, how he said it so casually as if it were a foregone conclusion, then nodded, 'Deal,' turning back to the guidebook she'd brought and then looking intently at a picture of a woman sitting on grass, her hand on a tiny rabbit. There was something almost transcendent about seeing the painting in the flesh, something she couldn't put into words. To be as close to the painting as the artist had been, to see the grooves of his brushstrokes, the places where the paint was thicker, masking indecision and mistakes; to feel so close to someone whom you'd never met but whose work made your heart race all the same.

When she looked around again, Tom was gone.

The *Mona Lisa*, when she finally reached it, was a tiny bit disappointing, she had to give him that. Somehow less vibrant and so much smaller than she'd imagined. It didn't help that she was surrounded by people craning their necks for a closer look.

'Do *you* think she looks like George Harrison?' she asked a woman on her left who gave her a sharp look and turned away.

It was hard to stay enthusiastic on her own, and eventually she wandered towards the exit and the gift shop where she found Tom peering at a stand of postcards.

'Where've you been?' she said, trying to keep the annoyance from her voice.

He shrugged. 'Got bored.'

She shook her head. 'I thought you were meant to be the intellectual.'

He looked at her then, amused. 'Yes, but I'm selectively intellectual. I like music, but art... well, it's OK but it doesn't fascinate me.'

'So no more galleries?' she said, hoping he'd laugh and say they'd go anywhere she wanted.

'No more galleries.'

Instead, they'd walked – Tom pointing out landmarks from Notre-Dame to La Défense and clearly in his element being tour guide. She'd tried to keep her responses muted – not wanting him to realise how excited she felt every time she recognised a monument she'd only seen before from photographs.

Dinner was in a pizzeria – something that disappointed her a little, considering where they were – but she didn't say anything. It had been delicious in any case – fresh, thin-crusted and dripping with piping hot cheese, and they shared a bottle of rosé.

By the time they left the restaurant, the sun had disappeared and the sky was bright and star-sprinkled. She checked her watch: 11.30 p.m. 'Oh,' she said.

'What?'

'It's nearly midnight!'

'Oops. Past your bedtime?'

She slapped him lightly. 'No. Of course not. Just thought it was earlier.' She stifled a yawn that she wasn't sure came from actual tiredness or from her acknowledgement that it was so late. Yes. Maybe it *was* past her bedtime.

He grabbed her hand. 'One more stop,' he said.

'Seriously?'

'Trust me.'

He walked quickly, she making little running steps every few paces to keep up. And then they made their way onto the Pont du Carrousel, its arched stone length stretching across a Seine whose dark water twinkled with starry reflections. At the centre, he rested his hands on the edge of the thick balustrade and leant over slightly towards the water.

'Tom!' she said, instinctively grabbing a bit of material on the back of his shirt.

He laughed. 'I'm not jumping, you know.'

'Yes, but...' She felt embarrassed, but he had looked like he might slip, and he'd been drinking. The Seine passed choppily below, ready to gather anything that fell into it. 'Can we go?' she asked.

He stood and put an arm around her. 'In a minute.'

'Why?'

He sighed, but not in frustration; almost as if taking it all in. 'Memories, I guess.'

'Memories?'

He looked at her, his eyes enormous pools of black reflecting the light. 'Mum brought me here once. I was eight. Sure it was going to be a carousel. You know, a real one.'

She laughed. 'Oh no!'

'Yeah. I made such a fuss.' He was quiet for a minute. 'But then Mum kind of lifted me up, sat me on the stone, held me of course. And it was late. And she made me look at the stars.'

Sophie wrapped an arm around Tom's back, rubbed it briefly.

'It's stupid,' he said. 'It's just I had the feeling in that moment... that everything was kind of magical, timeless. And I was an eight-year-old idiot, but I felt something. As if the lack of a proper carousel didn't mean anything. Because I was with my mum looking at the stars, and it felt...'

'Felt...?' she prompted after a moment.

'If you tell anyone how pathetic I'm being...' he said, grinning embarrassedly.

'Just between us.'

He sighed. 'I've never told this story to anyone. But I suppose in that moment, in my tiny mind, it felt as if I could see heaven. As if I were part of this enormous universe, but that it was safe, magical, and we would all go on together. And Mum told me it was midnight, which when you're eight is, like, mind-blowing!'

'Aw.'

'Yeah,' he glanced at her. 'So I try to come, when I'm here. At midnight. Usually on my own. Just to... It's never felt that magical again. But...' he looked up at the sky. Somewhere she could hear a bell chime. 'It's kind of become special; a ritual.'

And they stood together, looking into the deep navy of the night sky, studded with jewels, and she imagined for a moment that she could feel it too. That sense of eternity he'd felt all those years ago.

6

TWO WEEKS AGO

'So where to?' he said finally, as they turned from the Seine and began to negotiate the busy pavements. 'The Louvre?'

'Ha ha. Very funny.'

'I mean it. Why not?'

She looked at him askance. 'Seriously? You actually want to go to an art gallery? I had to literally drag you there almost every time I wanted to go before.'

He shrugged. 'For old times' sake. Plus, we've probably only seen about fifteen thousand pieces there; that makes – what – just twenty thousand to go. We ought to try to see a few at least.'

'Wow!'

'What?' He looked at her. 'Things can change. People change.'

'Not you,' she said, her tone a mixture of sadness and fondness. 'And you know... this trip is about you, really. I don't mind where we go.'

'Then we'll go to the Louvre,' he said. 'I spent too many years complaining about it. But I've become somewhat fond of it and its motley inhabitants. Anyway, if this really is the last time.' He looked at her, eyes full of mischief.

'Tom. You know it is.'

'I know. But a man can dream.'

She laughed. A woman passed her and shot her a look, as if her laugh had seemed odd. It hadn't been that loud, had it? She covered her mouth for a moment, then decided that it didn't matter. This was the last time, after all. Paris wouldn't remember her.

Her feet were rubbing against her shoes and she could feel the sting of skin on leather. She thought about suggesting they take the metro, but decided she'd prefer to stick to the familiar routes, to the places where their memories merged and she could picture them – every year for almost a decade, through all sorts of things she'd never imagined, bad and good – together in the place that had somehow become *their* place. Heels be damned.

Instead, she slowed her pace and Tom immediately matched hers, staying close to her side. She remembered that first time, the way he'd been so energised – always racing off, hardly thinking about her.

He was looking down, concentrating on the ground in front of them, but as she watched, he lifted his head and gave her the full force of his brilliant eyes.

'What's he got that I haven't got?' he asked, half smiling, half serious.

'What?' She looked at him, not understanding.

'Will. What's he got that I haven't got?'

She almost laughed, but there was something so desperate in his asking. Where had this come from, this question? 'Don't, Tom.'

He was silent for a minute. 'But I suppose what I'm trying to say is, if it were different... If things were... If we could still be together, would you choose me? Would you choose me over him – even now?'

'What kind of question is that?' she said, her voice louder than intended. She felt heat rise in her, realising what she'd said. 'For God's sake, Tom. I've moved on. Changed. I'm not the same person. After you left...'

'But what if I hadn't?'

'But you did!' She was exasperated now. 'You left me. YOU left ME. And I am who I am partly because of that. You can't take it back, you can't turn time back. So stop!'

'Stop what?'

'Torturing me!'

'What? I'm only wondering?'

She shook her head. It was too much. Perhaps she shouldn't have come. 'Everything changed,' she said, her voice quieter now. 'I've changed. Maybe we'd have changed together if things had been different. Become one of those older couples who finish each other's sentences. But we'll never know.'

He nodded, just once – a finality about it. 'It would have been nice,' he said.

'What? Getting old?'

'Getting old with you.'

They were silent for a moment, and she looked across the Seine, the sun still on their left, glittering; the boats still making their slow and silent way along its length. Across the way, more people, colourful dots on a Monet painting in front of buildings she'd passed so many times and would never see again. It was too much. She touched the diamond ring on her left hand and twisted it slightly, the metal still cool against her finger.

'I'm sorry,' he said quietly.

'It's OK.'

'You still miss me though, right?'

She almost laughed.

It was three o'clock, but as they moved away from the ancient municipal buildings towards the cafes and shops on the Quai du Louvre, the tables set out on the street were still full as people sipped tall glasses of ice-cold beer, or after-lunch espressos. Some wore suits, others sundresses, some still sported jumpers, others had vest tops and T-shirts. Everyone somehow belonged to the scene – tourists, locals, people here on business, sightseers – each had a sense of permanence, each always formed the backdrop to this place. It was one of the things she'd always liked about Paris – yes, it was different, foreign, but you felt part of it the minute you stepped off the train at the Gare du Nord. Part of some essential whole.

'Can we stop for a sec?' she said, suddenly gasping. 'I could do with a drink.'

He looked at her, gave a single shoulder shrug. 'If you want. It's not like we have an itinerary, is it?'

She smiled, although there was still something a little sulky about his voice. 'Table for two?' she said to the waiter, and he nodded half-heartedly towards a small table under the awning still covered with glasses and plates from the previous clientele. She thanked him and sat down, as he cleaned and cleared in front of her. '*Voilà, Madame,*' he said at last. 'What can I get you?'

'Just an orange juice, please.'

'And for your friend?'

She shook her head. 'Not right now.' She caught Tom's eye.

'Of course,' the waiter said with a nod before disappearing.

'God, I could murder a beer,' Tom said, more to himself than to her. He watched for a moment as a couple opposite sipped from sparkling glasses.

Sophie didn't respond.

Her drink arrived quickly and she sipped the iced orange liquid through the paper straw and sighed. Tom regarded her steadily, a half-smile on his face. He looked exactly the same as he always had. No, better in fact. Younger somehow than when they'd last been together. She was conscious that time had faintly sketched lines under her eyes and at the corners of her mouth – an artist planning a canvas to which he'd add detail later. In contrast, Tom's skin looked smooth, almost translucent.

'What?' she said at last.

'Just looking at you.'

'I know. Stop it, will you?'

He shrugged. 'Can't help it.'

She smiled, trying to remind herself that this was the last time; that before this, there was a time when she was sure she'd never see him again. How, back then, she'd have given anything to spend a day or two with this infuriating, bewitching man.

'Just don't go making me fall in love with you again, Tom,' she said quietly, shaking her head.

He smiled that slow, confident smile of his and she knew exactly what he was thinking.

Whatever she'd convinced herself of, where Tom was concerned, there would always be something there. That was why she was here. To cut it off. To say goodbye to him, to the past version of herself who loved him, and to step into her future.

7

THE FIRST SUMMER – 2011

'Hang on, hang on,' Libby said, sitting forward on the rather saggy sofa in their shared house. 'Let me get this straight. You have decided, after four months and a romantic trip to Paris, that you are going to dump Tom Gardner?'

'I guess I have,' Sophie said, shrugging, taking a sip of her water.

'*Tom Gardner*. The boy that pretty much every girl at Cambridge is lusting over? The boy whom you told me was *the* best sex you'd ever had?'

'To be fair, he's only my second, so...'

'Still.' Libby shook her head, incredulous. 'Well, I did not see this coming.'

'I know.' Sophie gave a little half-smile. 'I know, he's great. Good-looking. Kind.'

'So, you're dumping him because...?'

'It's not really dumping. We're only dating.'

'Sounds like dumping to me.'

'OK. Well,' Sophie shifted, slightly annoyed. 'I'm just not sure we fit, that's all.'

'In what way?'

She shrugged. 'Just a feeling. He's great. But I'm pretty sure he's not that into me. Take Paris for example.'

'What about it?'

'You know. In the Louvre. He clearly didn't want to come.'

'So you're dumping him because he doesn't like fine art?' Libby arched an eyebrow, but her tone was light, teasing.

Sophie laughed. 'No, of course not!'

'Because he *did* go with you, didn't he? Even though he's not a fan. That means something, surely.'

Sophie looked at her friend who seemed to be a great believer in love and fate and romance – provided she wasn't the recipient of it herself. 'Yeah, but he whined the whole time. I felt like his mother.'

'Oh. Not a great turn-on.'

'Exactly. Oh, Libby!' Sophie flung herself back against the worn material of the decades-old sofa. 'I don't know. I just – we're never going to maintain things, are we? Summer, then we're off doing different things. And it's Tom. You borrow him, remember? He's not for keeps!'

Libby laughed. 'Who told you that?'

'Not sure. Some random idiot in a bar. It might even have been you!'

'Oh, God. Don't listen to *her*,' Libby joked. 'She'll say anything.'

'I'm going to miss you, you know,' Sophie said quietly now. 'Living with you. This...'

'Me too,' she said. 'Loads.' For once, her friend didn't make a joke. 'Do you want me to talk to him for you instead?' Libby said then, looking at the envelope in Sophie's hand. 'Or you could call him? Send a text?'

'Come on, nobody dumps anyone by text, Libby?'

'True.'

'And, yes, the letter's a bit... lame. But I wanted to explain it properly and I know if I talk to him...'

'You'll end up in bed?'

'Something like that.'

She'd written the note the night before – it had taken ages even though the final letter was only three paragraphs long. Thanking him for the time together, for the trip. Asking whether they could still be friends. Breaking up with Tom Gardner, while things were still OK between them.

'And it's not, you know... eighteen pages – front and back?' Libby grinned, referring to the *Friends* episodes they'd been bingeing over the last month.

Sophie laughed. 'No. He'll get through this one without falling asleep, I think.'

'Well, I still think you're borderline insane. But if that's what you want, I'll help.'

'Thank you.'

It wasn't that the trip hadn't been wonderful – it had. Almost too wonderful. She'd adored Paris, loved everything about it, in fact. It was just that... the more she'd fallen in love with the city, the more she'd realised how different she and Tom were. He wanted to go to restaurants and for the odd walk but otherwise, spend all day in bed together. She – although she'd enjoyed herself – couldn't waste the opportunity like that. She wanted to look at the art; wanted to admire the buildings. Wanted to soak it all in.

'Are you sure that it's not just that he'd been there before, so he'd seen it all?' Libby said, voicing one of Sophie's own fears. 'Most people would be bored going round the same gallery for the twentieth time. Maybe you didn't give him a proper chance?'

Sophie turned the envelope over in her hands, studying it.

'The thing is, it's not just Paris. It's not just that we're different. Obviously, I knew we were different when he asked me out. That can be nice sometimes, can't it? It just seems silly to try to keep something going when everything is going to change.'

Libby nodded. 'I suppose.'

'Can you actually imagine Tom waiting for me? Having a long-distance relationship with me? With anyone?'

Libby laughed. 'OK, I admit he's not the type. But there's a first time for everything. And you know, people find ways. Can't one of you change your plans or something?'

'Well, he's off to London for that internship – and for the record, I've no *idea* how he managed to land that.'

'Knowing people in the right places?' Libby suggested.

'More than likely. Anyway. Good for him. But,' she shrugged. 'I've got my teacher-training course. It's a good one and it's near Mum and Dad. I can't afford to live out again 'til I get a job.'

'Even with that massive bursary you're getting?'

'It's a few grand, Libby.'

Libby nodded. 'True.'

'Anyway,' Sophie said decisively. 'There's no future in it.'

'Teaching?'

'Tom and me,' she said firmly.

'You're probably right.' Libby pursed her lips together.

They were silent for a moment, then Sophie said: 'Do you think he'll be all right?'

'Tom? Yeah, pretty sure he'll find a way to move on.'

'Don't sound *quite* so confident about it.'

'This is Tom we're talking about. He's basically got a huge reputation as a slag.'

'Libby!'

'Well, he does. You know that.'

Sophie remembered the lingering kiss they'd had on the

Midnight in Paris

bridge, the second night of their trip. How something had shifted inside of her; how Tom had seemed different in Paris – more attentive, somehow more grown-up. But Libby was right. He'd soon move on to the next girl in any case.

'So really, it's sensible,' she said, running her finger along the seal of the envelope to make sure it was properly stuck.

'Yep. Sensible Soph.'

'Hey!' she laughed. It was an ongoing joke in their group that if anyone did all the recommended reading, it would be Sophie. And she was the only one who would be up and ready for every early class, every lecture. But she didn't think that made her boring, just driven. Sometimes all she could think about at night was the amount of debt she was accruing simply by being here. She had to make it count somehow. She didn't have an allowance or friends in industry who could give her a job, her parents earned modestly in their little kitchen-table bookkeeping business, but they couldn't support her and she wouldn't want them to. Besides, there was her sister Sam, too, at home, still ploughing through her A levels.

She had her place on a teacher-training course and there would be a bursary to keep her going through that. But she was under no illusion that it would be easy. For her, there would be no gap year, no travel, no internship on astronomical pay. She wanted to squeeze every bit of value out of her degree as she could – and if that made her boring, so be it.

The conversation moved on, Libby not realising how momentous the decision was to write Tom a letter, pop it through the door of his shared digs and run, half terrified, half giggling around the corner before anyone opened the door. It was juvenile. People were meant to talk about this stuff, at least make a phone call. But whenever Sophie was with him, she couldn't find the words. Something about his easy smile – those eyes – defeated her every time.

Tom, at least, wouldn't be too bothered. He'd roll his eyes and shake his head. Maybe he'd feel sad for a day or two. But he wasn't an idiot. He must know as she did that this wasn't a love story for the ages. Just a little fling between two bored students making the most of the last weeks in student accommodation before they were spat out into the world.

* * *

The cocktail bar was buzzing with life – not the affluent customers it was probably used to, but with groups of snickering students poring over its sticky menus and laughing at the names of some of the drinks on offer. On Mondays, they did a buy-one-get-one-free hour and it never failed to attract the crowd from the ex-polytechnic.

The barmen duly pretended to smile every time a giggling eighteen-year-old requested a 'Sex on the Beach' with barely suppressed amusement, or nodded as if impressed when a second-year necked a couple of shots, slamming the glasses down on the counter in triumph. Only a few noticed the glazed expression in the eyes of most of the staff as they tolerated this lucrative – but extremely taxing – time each week.

The moment the hour was up, the bar would clear and the staff would quickly make the rounds with cloths and trays, gathering discarded drinks and wiping sticky surfaces. A sense of calm would return and only those who could afford the usual prices would remain.

Sophie had treated herself to a Brandy Alexander – usually a bit too calorific for her to enjoy without residual guilt. 'Drowning your sorrows?' Libby had said, cocking an eyebrow.

Sophie had laughed as if it were a joke but in reality, she supposed she was – a bit.

This summer was going to be full of goodbyes and lasts, and scary new horizons. Nothing that had seemed fixed in her life for the past three years was going to stay in place. Friends would scatter home and they'd all be ejected into adult life, like baby birds nudged from a nest. She took another sip and felt the creamy, decadent liquid with its reassuring afterburn slide down her throat. There were a lot of sorrows to drown.

Libby had started talking to a boy at the table next to them when the hand grabbed Sophie's. She started at the unexpected touch and looked up to see Tom, clutching at her wrist, his face serious.

'Hi, Tom,' she said, trying to stay neutral. She raised her glass. 'Can't beat happy hour!'

He took the glass from her hand and set it on a table, his expression unreadable.

'Hey, I was drinking that!' she said, half laughing, half annoyed.

'I'll get you another one,' he said, gently tugging at her arm and pulling her towards the exit. 'Just come. Please.'

'What are you doing?'

She allowed herself to be led.

It wasn't aggressive, more insistent, and as usual her skin responded to his touch with a series of tingles that shivered over her body. By the doorway, he paused. 'Just hear me out,' he said, as if she hadn't already let herself be dragged out of the bar, leaving her expensive drink, to do just that.

'Sure,' she said.

It was still light outside. After the gloomy, electric-lit atmosphere of the bar, it was a shock. She became aware that her make-up, now no doubt punctured by beads of sweat, would look horrendous in the daylight. The day had been warm, but had cooled in readiness for evening; her shoulders, in a thin vest top, felt somehow vulnerable.

He led her opposite, out of the way of the queue of people waiting to be granted entrance. 'I got your letter,' he said.

She nodded, feeling herself flush.

'I don't get it.'

'Oh, come on, Tom,' she said lightly. 'It was never going to be a long-term thing. It makes sense.'

His eyebrows furrowed. 'What do you mean? How do you know if you never gave it a chance, Soph?'

He must be joking. This attractive, self-assured young man with a choice of bright futures ahead of him, no matter which way he turned. 'Well, we're leaving in a couple of weeks,' she said. 'Everything's going to change.'

He raked a hand through his hair. 'But you said...'

'Tom. Come on. Is this just about being dumped?'

He flinched slightly at the word. She wondered whether she was the first woman ever to break up with him. That might be it. A pride thing. 'No,' he said at last. 'I just thought... Well, things were going OK, weren't they? Did I miss something?'

She shook her head. 'No... I just... it's going to be impossible. Seriously, I'm going to be teacher-training in Bedfordshire, you'll be in the city swaggering around in a suit. What are we going to do? Meet up at weekends?'

He looked down. 'We could,' he said.

She touched his arm. 'Tom, you're a great guy. But come on. This was fun, but we're not compatible long-term.'

'How can you say that? You don't know that!'

'I can say that because it's true. Take Paris for starters.'

'You *loved* Paris!'

'Yes, I did. And thank you so much. But we wanted different

things even then. I suppose it made me realise that we are different. Different worlds, different ambitions...' she trailed off.

'Is this about the fucking *Mona Lisa*?' he said.

She snorted – a loud, single burst of laughter. 'Tom. Of course not!'

'Soph... you're the only one I can... talk to, you know. Properly.'

'You can talk to anyone! You barely draw breath.'

He stepped back, hurt. 'Not like that. You know what I mean. I thought we meant something.'

Her head spun slightly as the drink began to fully hit her bloodstream. Was he being facetious? It just felt so... odd. To have someone fight for her. And he was so far above her league. It was as if it was all an elaborate joke.

'We can still talk,' she said. 'We're still friends, aren't we?'

He nodded. 'So that's still a no then?'

'No to what?'

'Me. As your boyfriend.'

She laughed. 'Seriously? You really want to be a couple like that? With me?'

He misread her incredulity. 'Forget it.'

'Oh, Tom. Don't take it like that! I mean...'

'No. You're right. Incompatible,' he said, turning.

'Oh, come on. I just meant...'

But he was too far now, his long pace carrying him quickly along the chequered pavement.

Moments later, a breathless Libby appeared at her side. 'Was that Tom?'

'Yeah.'

'You all right?'

'Been better.'

'You didn't finish your drink.' Libby handed her a plastic beaker with a light brown liquid. 'I got a plastic glass for you.'

They looked at the rather unappetising contents. 'Thanks,' Sophie said, taking a tiny sip.

'Come on, let's go to Ballare. It's nineties night. We can dance it off.' Libby linked an arm through hers and Sophie pushed any thoughts about Tom to the back of her mind. He'd get over it, and so would she. Life was only just starting, unfolding before them like a treasure map, and she wanted the chance to explore it fully.

8

TWO WEEKS AGO

She finished the last of her orange juice with an unexpected slurping sound as the straw met glass, ice cubes and air. Tom, opposite, grinned at her. 'Finished?' he asked, amused.

Sophie nodded.

'In that case, I think those women want to take our table.'

She looked over her empty glass to where he was indicating and saw two women in neat skirt suits pointedly watching her. She felt annoyed to be rushed, had wanted to finish up the ice from the bottom of the glass. It was a bad habit, but she loved the squeak of the freezing cubes between her teeth before they finally yielded and cracked; loved the way it cooled her. Loved, if she was honest, getting her money's worth, even now.

'Time to give it up?'

'Fine,' she said standing, nodding to the women and leaving a five-euro note on the little metal receipt tray the waiter had slipped in front of them a few minutes ago.

'What's the matter?' he said as they resumed their walk.

'Nothing. Just feel weird, that's all.'

He slipped into a rhythm at her side and they walked like this for a bit. 'It's nice though, isn't it? Seeing each other again. I've missed you.'

'Me too,' she managed.

'Do you think...' he began, then trailed off.

'Here it is!' she said in a voice that was almost too loud, too relieved to break the current direction of the conversation.

The first time she'd seen the Louvre, she'd been astonished at the size of the enormous glass pyramid, the way the unashamed modernity of the spotless structure contrasted with the traditional buildings that surrounded it. She'd loved walking on the glass floor panel and looking down into the space below.

She still had it, that sense of wonder, despite having been here time and time again; but now it was richer, tinged with emotion as she thought of all the different versions of herself; the different versions of *them* that had pushed open the doors and walked inside, queuing, buying tickets, seeing the same paintings with new eyes, a new perspective each time.

And the last time they'd been here. It was impossible not to think of it. How she'd had to hide how broken her heart had been seeing what Tom had become; the contrast with his former self.

'Don't go getting emotional on me,' he said now, looking at her. 'It's just a massive greenhouse.'

She laughed, despite herself. 'Only you would come up with that description.'

'I'm serious. Alan Titchmarsh would probably kill to have this space for his tomatoes.'

'Want to go in?'

He shrugged. 'Might as well. For old times' sake.'

'Come on then,' she said, feeling lighter, reminding herself that she was here with him, that he was OK, that the past was safely behind them now. 'Race you to the *Mona Lisa*.'

* * *

'She's beautiful, isn't she?' a woman said, noticing how Sophie seemed absorbed in the famous painting.

Sophie smiled. 'Someone once told me they thought she looked a bit like George Harrison.'

The woman looked at her, slightly disapproving. 'Well, you can tell that person he is an idiot.'

'"He"?'

'Ah, it is always a "he",' said the woman. 'All they want these days is red lips, come-to-bed eyes. They cannot stomach a woman who looks intelligent, interesting.'

Sophie laughed. 'I'll pass it on,' she said, glancing sideways at Tom.

They were silent for a minute. Around them the crowd of tourists ebbed and flowed, always at least twenty of them packed in to view the tiny painting.

'I do think she's beautiful, for the record,' Sophie added, turning to the woman again. 'But it's something else about her that makes me keep coming back. I think... she looks kind of wise. Like she knows something.'

The woman nodded. 'I'm sure it is true.'

Tom chuckled quietly in her ear. 'She looks kind of wise,' he joked.

'Well, she does! Like she can look right through me.'

She felt the buzz of her mobile in her pocket and put her hand to it, knowing without looking that it would be a text message from Will, asking how it was going, whether she was OK. She'd ring him later when things were quieter. She couldn't be the person who broke the rules and started talking loudly in an art gallery.

She saw Tom looking at her. 'Will?' he asked.

She nodded. 'Sorry,' she said, not really knowing why.

* * *

'I want to ask you something,' she said quietly later over a glass of rosé at an outdoor cafe.

He leant back, his eyes amused, looking at her steadily. 'Fire away.'

'Did I ruin it?' she asked, amazed that she'd finally got the words out.

'Ruin what?'

She took a deep breath, not sure whether he was being kind or whether he genuinely didn't know what she meant. 'Ruin us.'

He shook his head softly. 'You couldn't.'

'But I wasted all that time being... well, fucking miserable, for want of a better word. The baby stuff.'

'You weren't that bad.'

'I was! And I made you miserable too!'

Another shake of the head. 'You didn't, Soph. And even if you had, it wasn't your fault.'

'I didn't know. If I'd known...'

'Neither of us knew.'

She swilled the wine in her glass. 'Kind of feels like it was my fault.'

'All of it?'

'Some of it at least. I was so focused on myself, I didn't notice *you*. And maybe if I had...' She took an enormous, shuddering breath. 'Maybe if I had, things would have turned out differently.'

His hand moved towards hers over the table's wine-ringed top. 'No,' he said firmly. 'None of it was your fault.'

'Not intentionally, no. But I'd do it differently if I could,' she said. 'If I could go back...'

He looked at her, eyes glistening. 'Me too,' he said. 'If I could go back, I'd make sure I'd never have to leave you.'

9

THE FIRST SUMMER – 2011

She was chopping carrots in the kitchen of her student lodgings when the doorbell went. 'I'll get it!' she called, wiping her damp hands on a tea towel and walking to the front door. 'Oh,' she said, opening it to find Tom there.

He was looking down when she first answered and from her raised position inside the house, she was slightly above him Then he looked up and she saw something in his eyes she hadn't seen before. A steeliness, perhaps.

'I've come to give this back,' he said, handing her a torn envelope. Her letter.

'Tom, that's nuts. I mean, throw it away or something if you want...'

Their eyes met. 'No. I'm giving it back because I don't accept it.'

Was he joking? 'You don't accept what?'

'I don't accept you breaking up with me.'

She let out a small laugh, then felt mean. 'I'm not sure it works like that, Tom. Pretty sure both parties have to agree that they're in a relationship.'

'I know that,' he said. 'Obviously. I mean that I think your logic is flawed.'

'Now you're grading my writing? Who are you? A professor?' The teasing was light, something that came naturally between them. She felt herself begin to relax. 'Look, come in. Have a cup of tea, if you want?'

He nodded and walked past her into the kitchen, putting the kettle on as if suddenly she were the guest and he, the host. He leant against the counter and looked at the chopping-board, its white, scored, plastic surface stained orange.

'So my logic is flawed?' she prompted, getting a mug out.

'Yes. You reckon it wouldn't work – that we wouldn't see each other. And I think we would. And if that's the only reason you're calling things off, don't you think you should at least give me a shot?'

It was flattering, his fighting for her. But in some ways, she felt like his mum, having to explain to her son how life worked – that while he might *think* he would want to keep things going, that actually, both of their lives were going to change dramatically and they were going in different directions. That breaking off now would save a great deal of pain – hers probably – later on. 'Tom, I just think it's for the best,' she said, putting teabags in the mugs and looking up at him. 'Come on, you'll meet someone else soon, I reckon.'

He gave a laugh, but it was humourless. 'Oh, right, because I'm Tom Gardner, the boy who sleeps around and is never going to settle down.'

'Well, yes. I thought you were quite proud of that.'

'I was... but then I met you. It's different with you, Soph. It doesn't make sense, but it is.'

He was so earnest, not realising that the *doesn't make sense* sent a flurry of questions through her. Why not? Her looks? Her background? Was she not good enough for him on paper? She kept the questions inside, turning instead to pour boiling water into the mugs, watching the tea begin to mix in the heat.

'Thank you,' she said at last, passing him his mug. 'It's nice that you feel that way.'

'But...' he prompted.

She indicated with a tilt of her head that they ought to make their way to the living room, sit on the rather saggy sofas. He took a seat opposite her, and for a minute she wanted to laugh – it was as if she were in a formal meeting rather than sitting with a friend who wanted to be more.

'I'm not convincing you, am I?' he said, setting his tea down on the tiled surface of their second-hand coffee table.

She shrugged. 'It's a bit of a surprise, if I'm honest. I mean, I like you, Tom. Really like you. But...'

'But you want to be *sensible*,' he said, emphasising the last word as if it was an unfortunate flaw rather than... well, sensible.

'And what's wrong with that?'

Maybe he just didn't like to lose, she thought. She wondered again if she was the first person to break up with Tom Gardner. She didn't know everything about his background, but everything about him oozed privilege. He was good-looking, almost criminally so, with his deep blue eyes, dark hair and the kind of lashes that she could only dream of having. He'd never wanted for much as a child, never had to economise. Now he was at Cambridge where he'd been spectacularly lazy with his work, yet he'd still managed to land the kind of internship many of her contemporaries dreamt of.

Was she the first hurdle he'd fallen at?

'Everything,' he said, after a pause. 'Come on, Soph. We're twenty-one! If you can't take a few risks now, when can you?'

'So you admit it's a risk?' she teased, hoping to make his

Midnight in Paris

earnest face break into a smile. But he caught her eye and held it.

'Everything is,' he said. 'And even sometimes the sensible option can be a risk. Depends how you look at it.'

'Oh, Tom,' she said. 'Look, it's so sweet that you feel that way. But I really think...'

'That I'll be off with a new woman the minute my feet touch the ground in London?'

'Well, yeah,' she admitted with a shrug. 'I don't want to go through that. And nor do you.'

He nodded and she felt a sudden pang of rejection.

'It's for the best,' she said again, not sure why she was prompting him to speak, only knowing that she might give in if he tried just a little bit more. Something about his presence, his proximity. Those eyes.

'OK, how about this,' he said, more decisive now, his voice more like his old self. He drew an envelope out of his pocket. 'You go and sow your wild oats or whatever you're hoping to do at teacher-training college...'

'Get my PGCE?' she suggested. 'Learn stuff?'

'Yeah, all of that,' he said. 'And I'll do my internship. But we'll stay friends, right? You did say you wanted to be friends?'

'Yeah, of course,' she said, eyeing the envelope, wondering what it could possibly bring to the equation.

'And the only reason that you want to break up is that you don't believe I'm serious. Don't believe I know myself, right?'

'It sounds horrible when you say it like that. I just think we've both got so much ahead and...'

'Well, look...' He drew what looked like a ticket out of the envelope. 'I bought these. Two tickets to Paris. You know, after our last trip I thought it could be kind of a tradition.'

'Oh,' she said, looking at it. 'For next year.'

He nodded.

'I'm so sorry. Can you get a refund?'

He laughed. 'I'm not worried about the money. I only booked them yesterday. But I thought – doesn't this show you how serious I am? I'm planning something for in twelve months' time. Something for *us.*'

She nodded. But she'd never thought he'd been lying to her about how he felt, what he wanted. Just to himself. He was naive, not a liar.

'So,' he said, holding one ticket out to her and waving it slightly to encourage her to reach for it. 'Take it. No strings. You loved Paris, right? All that art...'

'Well, yeah.'

'All the sex,' he added, raising an eyebrow.

She laughed. 'I suppose it had its moments.'

'Well then,' he said, as if this solved everything.

'Well then, what?' Was he buying her with a ticket to Paris? Because although that obviously cost a bit, she was pretty sure she was worth more.

'Keep the ticket. Do your training. Then, in a year, come to Paris. I'll be there too. I mean, friends can go away together, can't they?'

'Right.'

He shuffled forward slightly, reached for her hand. She put down her tea and let him take it. His fingers were smooth and warm against her perpetually cold skin.

'And if I still feel the way I feel, and you feel – well, the way I think you might feel... Then we'll give it another go,' he said. 'Call it a test, if you want.'

'You're serious, aren't you?'

He shrugged. 'Even idiots like me have got to be serious sometimes.'

She held his gaze. Then, 'OK.'

'OK?'

She nodded. He leant forward and pressed his mouth to hers, his lips soft and warm. She put her hands up around his neck and allowed him to lift her to her feet.

'Seal the deal?' he said, a little breathless already.

She nodded. 'Handshake?' she joked.

'Oh, I think we can do a little better than that.'

10

TWO WEEKS AGO

Half a day had already passed and now Tom was next to her on the hard bed of her hotel room, leaning up on an elbow as they talked.

'Can't believe you booked the Cler!' he said, shaking his head. 'I thought we agreed it was a complete shithole.'

'For old times' sake, of course!'

'Yes, but... why not one of the others we stayed in? That posh place off the Champs-Élysées, or the one with the glass lift. This is... well...' he shook his head, '...beneath you.' He grinned, looking at her, his tone light.

She laughed. 'Beneath me! Well, maybe I'm not used to living in the lap of luxury like you, but it suits me fine. Anyway, it's the first place we went. It seems...'

'A good place to say goodbye?'

She nodded, touching the place where he lay just lightly. 'I guess so,' she said, suddenly sombre.

'You don't want to recreate any of the memories of that hotel stay... you know, for old times' sake?' He raised a suggestive eyebrow.

'Tom!'

'Worth asking.'

'You haven't changed a bit, have you?' she said, catching his smile. 'You're exactly how I remember you.'

'Well, obviously. Evolving is so overrated.'

They'd always had this ease when they'd spoken, always this back and forth, a blend of jokes and hard truths, made palatable by their shared humour. It was different with Will. But that wasn't a bad thing, she told herself. There were so many different ways to be close to another person.

Thinking of Will made her suddenly sober. She lifted her phone off the bed and looked at the screen. She hadn't heard it buzz, but there was a message there.

WILL
All OK?

SOPHIE
Yes.

WILL
Not too lonely?

SOPHIE
No, it's fine.

WILL
Miss you.

SOPHIE
Miss you too.

Looking up, she saw Tom watching her and tried to smile. 'Sorry,' she said.

'It's OK. I love Will!' he said. 'Say hi to him from me.'

'Very funny.'

'I take it he doesn't know?'

She stiffened. 'Not everything. I just don't want him to worry.'

'About me?'

'About *me*. I tried... I wanted to explain that I need to see you. Paris. Talk to you about things. Say goodbye properly – and this is what it is, Tom. But I couldn't... saying it sounded so...' She looked down, then back up at him. 'I didn't lie to him,' she said. 'I just didn't tell him everything.'

'Talk about what things?' It was as if Tom had only paid attention to the bit that involved him. Which was, actually, typical.

Suddenly animated, she stood up. 'Let's get out,' she said. 'I can't stand it in this tiny room. Let's go for a walk, eh?'

She grabbed a jacket, her bag, and made her way down in the lift to the foyer. There were a few people milling about, and the woman on reception smiled as she passed. Then she was outside, in a street still flooded with bright sunshine. She hadn't waited for Tom, but a moment later there he was, emerging from the hotel reception and jogging over to her.

'Slow down!' he said, bending over, hands on knees, as if exhausted from hurrying.

'Yeah. Sorry about that. Claustrophobia.'

'Not Tom-ophobia?'

She lifted a shoulder and let it drop. 'Maybe a little.'

They smiled at each other, then fell into step together. Sophie felt the tension leave her body as she inhaled the fresh air and let the Paris scenery transport her. They didn't have long and while she knew nothing could be perfect, she wanted this to be as close to it as possible.

Her phone rang again with a call from Sam but she sent it to voicemail. She'd talk to her later.

'Where're we off to, anyway?' he said moments later, as they turned the corner and found themselves caught up in the flow of pedestrians, some smart, some dressed-down, some suited, some in summer holiday mode.

'I thought I might just get a drink.' She looked at him. 'Oh, sorry. I keep forgetting.'

He gave a short nod. 'Doesn't matter. But let's not go to a bar, eh. Get something from one of the shops. Maybe grab a bench?'

'What, a whisky bottle in a brown paper bag?' she teased.

'It's a look,' he said. 'But maybe something a little more sophisticated.'

'Bottle of champers?'

'Maybe a small one,' he grinned.

'And you don't mind...?'

'I can't have you dying of dehydration just because I don't touch the stuff any more,' he said, smiling. 'Don't worry, I'll just try to remember what it tastes like.'

Tom had tried to give up drinking a few times over the years, never successfully. Each time she'd tried to join him, finding it a little easier than he did – the drive to drink less compelling. Perhaps it was cruel to drink in front of him now. But she needed something to help her relax, to get through this time. And she was pretty sure he understood.

She was a different person with Tom, she realised, as they sat side by side on the bench, her sipping from a small can of red wine – *the height of sophistication!* they'd joked – and him simply watching her looking out over the Seine. It was as if she had tapped into a younger version of herself, for better or for worse. She was less confident in herself, more in awe of him. And this time, on the cusp of a final goodbye, sickeningly aware that time was always slipping past.

'So, is everything set for the wedding?' Tom asked her.

'Do you really want to know?'

He shrugged. 'Kind of,' he admitted. 'You know, Will and I always said we'd be best men for each other.'

'I know. Will said that too. You could always come.'

She'd been joking, so was surprised to see his brow furrow, considering. 'I don't think I could make that work. Anyway, you need to concentrate on each other.'

She nodded. 'Don't want me to do a Ross from *Friends* and say the wrong name at my wedding!' she quipped, trying to lighten the mood.

'Will would literally kill me!'

'You know that's impossible, right? Anyway, as far as he's concerned, you're still his best friend.'

They were silent for a moment. Thinking.

'It won't be the same as our wedding,' she told him. 'I mean, it's going to be nice, but not as... well, lavish as ours.'

'Lavish?'

'You know what I mean.'

Their wedding had been funded entirely by Tom's father, who'd insisted they must have whatever they wanted. It had been an incredibly generous gesture, although looking back, she wondered whether she'd really have chosen the stately home with its cool, stone staircase and high-ceilinged dining hall if she hadn't been thinking a little of her father-in-law's preferences when she made her choices. Her dress had been a one-off, stitched especially for her. And in it she'd felt like – well, it was corny to say it, but she'd felt like a princess.

This time, she'd chosen off the rack – a dress made of satin that swung at her calves and nipped in at the waist. The venue was a converted barn in the Hertfordshire countryside, close to where Will's parents lived. They were paying for it all themselves.

'Is it enough?' Will had asked her one night when they'd

snuggled together in bed, talking into the darkness. 'We could do more?'

'It's perfect,' she'd told him. And she'd meant it, too. She hadn't chosen the venue, the dress, the cheapest of the offered meals on the menu because it was the second time around for her. This would be just as much of a celebration as the first. It was more because she felt freer to choose what she wanted, without fearing judgement. And perhaps, although it was depressing to think it, because she was growing up. Fairy-tale weddings belonged in fairy-tale books. She wanted a marriage that was built for the real world – and this time, one with a happy ending.

Tom nodded. 'I hope it's good,' he said.

'You're being very generous about it.'

He shrugged. 'What else can I do? I can't pretend I'm thrilled about how things turned out for us. Hardly the dream. But it is what it is. The more time passes since... you know... the more I've had to accept I can't change anything.'

She gave him a small, sad smile.

'And you deserve happiness, you know,' he said softly.

She looked at him. 'Thank you,' she said. 'It doesn't always feel that way.' She took a sip of her wine, felt it warm her throat.

'Yes, well, you've always had a problem with that,' he said. 'Thinking you don't deserve things. But after what I put you through, you must be due an enormous amount of good fortune.'

'That's ridiculous! It wasn't your fault,' she said, echoing his earlier words to her.

'I know,' he said. 'But you still went through it, didn't you?'

She nodded. 'Yeah. I suppose we were both just unlucky. Especially you, obviously.'

'Sometimes I think maybe I had it too good, you know? You

were always saying it. Laughing at my upbringing. My privilege. To me, it was just how things were. I didn't know what it was like to want anything I couldn't have, to not be able to fix things by asking my parents for some cash. I took it all for granted and bam!'

'Seriously? You think what happened was... what, some sort of divine counterbalance?' she said, half laughing, half horrified. 'Come on, Tom, that's not like you.'

'I don't know. Sometimes I think you have a certain amount of luck – each of us do – and if you use it all up too early... Well, maybe you run out.'

They watched silently as a riverboat passed them. Passengers leant on the front railing, watching the water lap against the front of the vessel as it cut through the water. Others, inside, sat and took in the view through the windows. There was something about the boats, she thought. A sense of peace that being on the water brought.

It was the one thing they'd never done in Paris – Tom suffered from seasickness and she didn't fancy going on one by herself.

'Well, luck or no luck, you were one of the best decisions I ever made,' she said. 'And you know I don't believe for a minute that you brought it all on yourself, everything that happened.' She shifted, turned to him slightly. 'I'm happy with Will, you know I am. But if there were a chance, even a tiny one, to do things differently...'

He put his hand lightly on hers and she felt a thrum of energy pulse in her. 'I know,' he said.

They fell into silence again, each imagining the decade-younger versions of themselves on the same bench, with a very different sort of future ahead.

11

THE FIRST SUMMER – 2011

Sophie stood back, almost tripping over some of her textbooks, and looked at herself, her lips pursed uncertainly. Her reflection in the half-length mirror they'd propped against the wardrobe wobbled uncertainly back at her.

'You look great,' Libby said. 'Very classic.'

'And classic is...?'

'Classic is good! We're talking about a place with hundreds of years of tradition here; classic is the kind of look you should be going for.'

'I'm not even sure if I *should* be going,' she said for the hundredth time.

'Oh God, not this again.' Libby stood up and placed a hand on each of Sophie's shoulders, looking into her eyes, half serious. 'You, Sophie Baker, are going to the Christ's College summer ball. And you are going to be fabulous.'

'Says who?'

'Me!' Libby laughed throatily. 'I'm your fairy godmother.'

Sophie laughed. 'So when's the pumpkin arriving?'

'I think we'd be better off getting a taxi on this one.'

When Tom had asked her to the summer ball as they'd lain in bed together after making their pact, her first instinct had been to say no. But then he'd said it could be as friends, and she'd decided that maybe she could do it this one time. They had a ball at Anglia university too, but she hadn't been to one of the Cambridge ones and it would certainly be an experience. She'd seen dishevelled revellers making their way home in the early hours after their events last year, and had wondered what all the fuss was about. Now she'd get to see for herself. Besides, she didn't like the thought of Tom taking anyone else.

She'd chosen a simple, silky white dress with thin straps, paired with silver sandals, had added mousse to her hair for extra volume, and slicked on some red lipstick. Libby was right, she did look pretty good.

Not that it mattered. Because they were just friends, of course.

'It's got a theme,' he'd told her excitedly when he'd asked her.

'Which is?'

'*L'Esprit Nouveau*. We're creating Paris in the college grounds.'

'Seriously?'

'Seriously. Well, we're going to give it a good try.'

'And it's in June?'

'Yeah.'

'But you call it the May ball?' she'd said, her lips lifting into a smile.

He'd shrugged. 'Who am I to question tradition?'

'All right, I'll come.' And she'd been rewarded with one of Tom's dazzling smiles.

Before she could think any more, there was a knock on her bedroom door and Tom stepped in, bearing a bunch of white roses.

She started – embarrassed at the mess of discarded outfits, underwear, her silly photos on the pinboard, the towels on the bed. 'Oh!' she said.

'Sorry.' His eyes were steady, fixed on her. 'You look great.'

'Thank you, *friend*,' she told him, taking the proffered flowers and smelling them, because that's what people always did on TV when they received flowers, and this was her first bunch.

He slipped his hands into his pockets and watched as she poured some water from a half-consumed bottle into an empty mug and shoved the bouquet into it. 'Just until we get back,' she told him. 'I'll get them in a proper vase tomorrow.'

It was a lie, and they both realised that. But it seemed wrong to stick the flowers in the little bear mug she'd bought as a lucky mascot from Clinton Cards at the start of her course. Not least because it was stained dark with tea on the inside.

She left her room, gratefully closing the door on the chaos, and made her way along the corridor and down the communal stairs. They emerged into the early evening, the day still bright and summery, the sun warm on her skin. There was a taxi waiting, the driver reading a book and whistling like a caricature of a cabbie.

'Christ's, please!' Tom said in a faux haughty voice as they slipped into the back.

The guy gave him a look that suggested his patience was already wearing thin this evening, put the car into gear and drove the short distance to the front of Christ's College. As they stepped out, Tom offering her his hand, her accepting it, she could already hear the strains of a string quartet. Other couples and small groups were making their way through the stone archway, and the air was buzzing with excited voices.

'Here we go,' he said, nodding at one or two people as they made their way in.

She laughed when she saw the model of the Arc de Triomphe that had been constructed in the ball's honour. 'You don't do things by halves do you, you Cambridge lot?' she said.

'But didn't your ball have decorations?'

'We had balloons, Tom. Fairy lights. Not a reconstruction of a famous landmark.'

He snorted. 'In that case, wait until you see the Eiffel Tower.' He grabbed a glass of Buck's Fizz from a table and gave it to her. 'Chin-chin.'

She laughed as she sipped, feeling already quite surreal.

They rounded the corner only to see marquees, a stage, an enormous Ferris wheel. 'Wow,' she said.

'Yeah, fancy a ride?'

Her stomach, empty of anything other than fizz, curdled at the thought. 'Nah, I don't think so,' she said. 'But you go ahead.'

He nodded and dropped her hand, calling out to a couple of lads in the queue who let him in, and soon he was being strapped into a chair next to a girl she didn't recognise. He waved like a small child to his mother as the mechanism started to turn, and she lifted a hand in acknowledgement.

'Hi,' said a breathy voice at her side. 'I'm Caitlyn.'

'Sophie.'

The girl was wearing a black dress in a silky material which flared out at the knee. She had on a pair of flat, strapped shoes which looked both cute and eminently sensible. Sophie was already regretting her sandals, the three-inch heels of which were sinking into the soft turf of the lawn.

'Which college are you at?'

'Oh, I'm just at… the other uni. You know?'

'The poly?'

'Actually, it's a uni now.'

'Right.' There was something sneery in Caitlyn's voice, or was she reading too much into it?

Sophie smiled thinly and returned her eyes to the Ferris wheel, willing it to hurry up and finish. Without Tom, she was simply in a place full of hundreds of strangers – there would be nobody she recognised, nobody she could really talk to when he wasn't at her side.

'So how do you know Tom?' Caitlyn persisted.

'Oh. Well, we used to date.'

'*Used* to?' Caitlyn arched a pretty eyebrow and looked pointedly up and down Sophie's body in its flimsy dress.

'Yeah, we're just friends.' It was more complicated than that, but Sophie certainly didn't feel like explaining herself to the unfriendly Caitlyn.

Caitlyn nodded. 'But you're here?'

'Yes.' Sophie said bluntly. 'I'm here.'

The wheel stopped and crowds of students, some already slightly worse for wear, were expelled onto the grass. Tom, laughing with his companion, walked towards them. He slid an arm around Sophie's back and gave her a squeeze. 'All right?' he said. 'Hey Caitlyn!' He gave her a nod.

She fixed her eyes on him. 'I was going to see if you wanted to dance. There's lessons.'

He crinkled his nose. 'Maybe later. Not really my thing.'

'That's not what you said last year.'

He laughed. 'It's amazing what too much punch will have me doing.'

'Guess I'll catch you later then.' Caitlyn shot a look at Sophie, her animosity quite visible, then walked off, raising her hand in an elaborate wave at a group of girls in the distance.

'She seems nice,' Sophie said.

Tom looked at her. 'Caitlyn? Well, she's...' He relaxed suddenly. 'You're joking,' he said with a chuckle.

'I've seen friendlier axe murderers.'

'Ah, she's all right.' He gave her a squeeze. 'What now. Want to watch the band? Or apparently there's a casino somewhere around here?'

'Could we just get another drink?'

It was around midnight when she lost him altogether. She'd popped to the ladies' – queueing and pushing past girls who were clustered around the mirrors correcting their make-up – and returned to discover he hadn't waited for her. She was slightly dizzy and her head ached.

She walked around the grounds, in and out of the marquee, past the buildings, excusing herself as she pushed past raucous groups, exchanging tight smiles with other guests as she made her way. She suddenly felt utterly, utterly ridiculous in her flimsy dress – everyone else seemed to be wearing fitted designs, with thick satin that looked made to measure. Hers looked like a nightdress in comparison.

Laughter filled the air around her and – as she was excluded from all of it – it felt like the loneliest sound she'd ever heard. She'd even dialled Tom's phone a couple of times but it had gone straight to voicemail.

Tom, she was sure, was somewhere having the time of his life. He seemed to know everyone and people seemed drawn to him like wasps to jam. Groups of lads had passed, asking him along for a beer, girls fawned over him. She'd felt like a spare part even when she was on his arm – and felt, too, that she had no recourse to complain. After all, she was just a friend.

She knew that he wanted to stay until 5.30 a.m. when they'd gather together for the 'survivors' photo' – a badge of honour for those who made it through the night, but in all honesty, she just wanted to get out of there, get home.

It was dark now and the air had cooled. Other girls had wrapped themselves in pashminas or borrowed their dates' formal jackets. The queues for all the activities showed no sign of abating, and everyone seemed in high spirits.

She began to push her way through the crowd, the dizziness increasing – made worse by the fact she'd been nervous and hadn't eaten enough – her heels now hazardous against the uneven stone of the paths and the treacherous kicked-up turf.

'Excuse me,' she said, making her way through. 'Excuse me.'

'Is it Sophie?' a voice said. She looked up into the catty eyes of Caitlyn. 'Are you all right, darling? Have you lost your *friend*?'

She ignored her, heading for the gate, wanting more than ever to simply break out into a run and get home as quickly as she could. The voices, the laughter, the music, the joy of other people felt suffocating, and she just wanted to be alone in the cool dark street, away from it all. She never should have come.

As she made it through the final fifty metres, her heel turned and she fell onto her knees, mud staining her dress. 'Oops,' she heard a male voice say, 'someone's had too many!' There was laughter but no move to help her to her feet. She got up, her knees stinging with pain, her eyes stinging with tears. 'Fuck you!' she wanted to yell at them. But they'd probably just find this funnier than ever.

Someone appeared in front of her as she stood, trying to adjust the strap on her shoe where it had slipped to one side. 'Sophie?' a male voice said.

She looked up. It was Will.

'Oh. Hi,' she said, suddenly embarrassed, aware that her hair was dishevelled, her mascara smudged. The mud on her dress and the dress itself, so insubstantial and cheap.

'Are you OK?'

'Yes. I'm just calling it a night.'

'Right. Tom not with you?'

She shook her head.

'Typical Tom.' Will seemed annoyed. 'I'll find him for you if you want.'

'No! No,' she said. 'Please don't. He's having a good time. And it's not as if... We're not together or anything. I was just...' She felt her shoulders slump. 'I just want to get out of here to be honest.'

He laughed. 'That bad?'

She nodded, trying to keep the tears at bay. Because of course she wanted Tom to be there. Only his friend shouldn't need to drag him out for her. He should be here anyway. Whether they were together or not.

He looked at her. 'Shit,' he said. 'That bad. Come on.'

With Will's large frame alongside her she was able to make her way more easily through the last of the people and finally burst through the gate onto the lamp-lit street. It wasn't empty, there were people walking home, taxis making their way to the rank. The club along the street was throbbing with the beat of music. But she was out. In familiar territory.

'Thanks,' she said, turning to him.

'It's OK. Let me walk you home?'

'I'm good. Honestly. I...'

'Soph. I'm walking you home,' he said firmly.

He was right of course, she thought as she nodded. She liked to think that the streets were hers at night, that the familiarity of them somehow kept her safe. She'd walked them hundreds of times – probably – by now at all times of the day and night. But in that dress, on darkened streets, she wasn't safe, not really.

She hated that fact, but it was what it was. She was a woman; she had to risk-assess even a walk home.

It wasn't far. They started out, their footsteps echoing on the pavement. The sound of the ball – its music, its chatter, the busyness of it – faded as they walked and she entertained herself with thoughts of Tom running up after them, full of consternation and apologies. But there was nothing. She felt her shoulders stiffen.

'So, what's next for you then?' Will said. 'Tom told me you're doing a course?'

'Oh, yes. Teaching.'

'Noble profession, so they say.'

She snorted. 'Maybe.'

'Well, look. Good luck. Are you on Facebook?'

'No.' She'd resolved never to go Facebook, to make her life public.

'Well, if you do go on... I'm on there, now. Not posting a lot.'

'OK.'

'Or get my email off Tom. Stay in touch,' he said. 'It's weird leaving everything, everyone behind.'

'It is.'

They fell into companionable silence, their bodies close but not touching as they moved side by side.

'I'll tell him,' Will said as they reached her road at last. 'Tom. That you've gone.'

'Thanks,' she said. Although she doubted he'd be bothered either way. 'And thanks, Will. You really... well, saved me.'

'Anyone else would have done the same,' he said.

They stood for a moment looking at each other, both knowing that it wasn't true. Then she watched him walk away, back to that other world where she'd felt so out of place. Nobody else had seen her at all.

12

THE SECOND SUMMER – 2012

'It's very *An Affair to Remember*,' Libby remarked on the phone as Sophie carefully packed her small, wheeled suitcase. 'You know, when they arrange to meet on the top of the Empire State Building.'

'Well, I hope not,' Sophie said, holding the phone between her shoulder and cheek to free up her hands. She held a yellow T-shirt up, and deftly reduced it to a tiny square, neatly slipping it inside the satin-lined case. Packing for this year's trip – *had it really been a year?* – she'd felt odd not speaking to Libby who'd always helped her choose her outfits for a trip when they'd lived together. She'd had to make do with a call instead. Sophie knew it was normal to move on into adulthood; that living in a student let with friends wasn't forever; but sometimes she missed her friend so fiercely her heart hurt.

'I mean, because it's romantic, you idiot,' Libby laughed. 'Arranging to meet, hopefully getting back together. And in Paris! I'm not saying that you're going to get mown down by a car on your way to meet him. Although do look both ways when crossing the street, won't you?'

'Libby! This is nothing like that film. I know he's going to be there, for starters. And we're meeting at St Pancras, not at the top of the Eiffel Tower.'

'Oh my God, you *should* have made it the top of the Eiffel Tower! That's a story for your grandkids right there.'

Sophie snorted. 'Now who's getting ahead of themselves?' she said. 'I don't even know if he'll still be interested.'

'Well, he's going to be there, isn't he?'

'Yeah. But he's not giving anything away.'

'Have *you* given anything away? Given him any reason to hope?'

'Well, no.'

'Well then. I bet you anything he still wants to be with you,' Libby said decisively.

Sophie zipped up the suitcase. 'You really think so?'

'Come on, you two are destined to be together. I can feel it.'

'Since when did you become a hopeless romantic?' Sophie asked, ignoring the surge of hope in her chest as she listened to her friend's words. 'I thought you were a cynic.'

'Well, maybe I've mellowed.'

'Ha. I highly doubt it.'

They both laughed. Libby was probably the most discerning person Sophie knew when it came to dating. Which meant she rarely ever did it.

'Did I ever mention that the night we first met, I had Will down for being more your type?'

'Will? What makes you say that?'

Libby shrugged. 'I could just imagine you together right away. Tom seemed... Well, you two are really different, aren't you? But sometimes that works, I guess.'

Sophie smiled. 'Here's hoping.'

'Anyway,' Libby continued, 'I just have this feeling...'

Sophie smiled. She also had a feeling. But she forced herself to be pragmatic. It was a holiday to Paris with a friend. That's all they'd promised each other. Tom had been true to his word, his promise not to talk about anything more between them until this trip – which could, as Libby said, be completely and utterly romantic, but could also mean he'd forgotten what he'd suggested and had simply moved on with his life.

They'd stayed in touch, pinging off the odd email, letter and phone call over the twelve months, but both had been busy. Tom hadn't mentioned any other girlfriend, but then it didn't mean he wasn't meeting people. He wasn't one for social media, and rarely seemed to post anything. Not that she looked. Often.

'Do you regret turning him down?' Libby asked, almost out of the blue. 'Wish you'd stayed together the whole time?'

'No!' she said instinctively. Then, 'Well, maybe a bit. But for all I know I could have been right. He might not be interested in me like that any more. And if that's the case, well, I've saved myself a lot of heartache.'

'There she goes again. Miss Sensible.'

'Why does everyone say that as if it's an insult?' She *was* sensible. Sensible and proud of it. It meant that she showed up to lectures and lessons on time, that she got her work done without a last-minute rush. Being sensible meant that she'd spent the last year at home, living with her parents, rather than try to find the money for a rental. It meant that she had a little money saved as a backup. And that she'd already secured a new post for September. That was sensible. And it looked OK from where she was standing.

'Ah, it's not,' Libby said. 'But maybe...'

'Maybe what?' she said, putting down the pair of jeans she'd been folding and holding the phone with her hand.

'A little bit... boring?'

She was genuinely hurt. 'I'm boring?'

'No!' Libby laughed. 'You could never be boring. But you might just create a boring life for yourself if you're not careful. And you deserve more.'

She was silent for a moment. 'Thanks – I think,' she said at last.

'Anyway, this is exciting. The Paris meetup.'

'The St Pancras meetup.'

'What are you going to do? Run into his arms? Tell him how you feel straight away?'

Sophie felt a frisson of anxiety. 'I'm not actually sure. I might just see how it goes. Maybe on the bridge...'

'What bridge?'

But of course, she wasn't meant to tell anyone about that.

'Oh, I don't know. Just somewhere romantic, I suppose.'

'OK, well like I said. Be careful.'

'Hang on, I thought you said I should throw caution to the wind – take a risk?'

'I meant be careful when you're crossing the street. These romantic liaisons don't always have a happy ending, you know!'

'Idiot.'

As they said goodbye and ended the call, Sophie felt her good mood fade. It was terrifying, the thought of meeting up, not knowing what Tom was thinking, what he wanted. She was rubbish at expressing herself, she knew that. Always left it up to the guy to make the first move – not because she was traditional, but because she was usually frozen with fear at the thought of being shot down.

Hopefully Tom would take the lead.

She looked at herself in the mirror. Her hair looked OK; it had grown quite a bit over the past few months – largely because her teaching course had kept her so busy that she hadn't had time to arrange an appointment, but it quite suited her. She'd tried to scatter a few loose waves through it with a curling tong, and was pleased with the result. It had darkened to a mid-brown, due to the lack of time spent outside, so was quite different from when he'd last seen her. She wondered what he'd think.

But there was no time to worry about that now, she realised, checking her watch. She took one last look in her bag – purse, travel money, her new mobile phone. Not that she could afford to use it in Paris. Would it even work? She kept it on her anyway.

Almost on cue, the taxi pulled up outside.

'Taxi's here,' her mum called from the kitchen which overlooked the road.

'Thanks, Mum!' She grabbed the handle of her suitcase and began to lug it down the stairs.

Mum came out into the hallway, rubbing her hands on a tea towel. 'Well, have fun!' she said.

'Thanks, I will!'

'Say hi to Libby for me.'

'I will,' she said again, feeling a little guilty but reassuring herself that she wasn't lying exactly. When she'd mentioned the trip, Mum had simply assumed she was going with her best friend, and she'd decided not to mention it was anyone else.

Her parents weren't prudes, she knew that. But she still felt sort of awkward admitting she was holidaying with a boy. There'd be too many questions before and afterwards that she might not know the answer to. It was easier this way.

Sam knew the truth but had been sworn to secrecy.

'Bye!' Sophie pulled the door closed behind her and wheeled her suitcase to the waiting driver.

Two hours later, she was feeling (and no doubt looking) overheated and dishevelled as she made her way through the glass doors into St Pancras station. As always, the space teemed with life; everyone in a hurry, streaming towards or out of trains, running to platforms, walking while talking loudly, mobile phones clamped to ears.

The statue caught her eye as it always did, the bronze of a couple, clasped together, noses touching, lips close – the perfect piece of art for the space. A scene that had perhaps been played out many times over the years in St Pancras – a place where people reunited and said goodbye hour after hour, day after day. She paused briefly, the rumble of her wheeled suitcase on the smooth floor stopping, and looked at the pair. Their foreheads were touching and their eyes stared into each others' intensely. It was impossible to tell if it was a scene of relief or sorrow – reuniting or parting.

'For God's sake, woman, it's not the *Mona Lisa*!' came a voice at her ear.

She jumped, then turned around and beamed. 'Tom!' she said.

He was altogether the same and yet different from when they'd last seen each other in person. Gone were the baggy jeans he'd favoured at university and in their place, smarter, more fitted trousers in grey cotton, and a simple T-shirt – white with a single navy stripe. His trainers looked new – a world away from the battered pair he'd often donned back in the day. Had he smartened up his look for her? Or was this how he dressed now? What else had changed?

She saw in his eyes that he was appraising her in the same way. She'd definitely been more casual – bordering on a complete and utter mess – at university, squeezing the life out of her favourite jeans and trousers, wearing plain T-shirts and cheap jumpers. Other than at the ball, he'd probably never seen her in a dress, let alone the smart, belted one she'd picked out from New Look.

'I like your hair,' he said at last.

'Thanks.'

They fell into step together and there it was, that feeling of comfort that always seemed to settle over her when they were together. But behind that, this time, was something else. A feeling of being desperate to ask: *So? Do you still want to be together?* But an inability to express that.

She glanced at him as they walked towards the Eurostar check-in. But his expression was unreadable.

13

TWO WEEKS AGO

'I thought you were going to dump me again, you know,' Tom said out of the blue. 'Back in the day.' He leant back on her bed, arms behind his head, and not for the first time Sophie wondered what Will would say if he knew. But they'd done nothing wrong. And there wasn't anywhere else to sit, really, in the hotel room.

'Dump you?' She repeated, incredulous. 'What? After uni?'

'On that second trip. You know when we'd agreed to go as friends, to see what happened? I was terrified the entire time.'

'You didn't *seem* terrified. Anyway, can you even dump someone when you're not officially together?'

'Well, shatter my dreams, then.'

She laughed softly. 'So dramatic.'

'Everything *did* feel quite dramatic in those days. All or nothing.'

'We were kids, really.'

He nodded. 'Yeah.'

He'd turned up at her hotel room this morning after she'd returned from breakfast, and was now lying on her bed as she brushed her hair and added a slick of mascara to her lashes. She was glad – relieved even – that he'd decided to come back.

Closing her eyes now she pictured that day, so many years ago. When she'd taken him to the bridge and he'd looked at her. And they'd both just known. The kiss under the stars, the water running beneath. That magical midnight hour where heaven had seemed to come down to earth and they'd felt part of something enormous, bigger than themselves.

Last night she'd been uncomfortable on her basic mattress at the Cler, and had woken with the realisation that either she had got used to slightly better things, or her body was a decade older than when she was last here and felt the bumps and hard areas of the mattress more keenly than its younger self.

Tom hadn't tried to come in when they'd returned, just after midnight. And she hadn't felt able to ask. Instead, they'd said goodbye chastely outside the double doors, and she'd been left to return to her room and sink into sleep. She'd been both glad and disappointed at his absence – feeling better when texting Will, but also being aware of the emptiness of the room with its impersonal beige and brown colour theme and basic, laminated furniture, without Tom's easy smile to make it seem like the best place on earth.

There was only one more day before she left – one more night to sleep. And then she'd be home, two weeks away from becoming Mrs Will Baxter, and it would all be over.

She was ready for this new time in her life, to walk down the aisle towards a man who'd not only been there for her as a friend, but had literally saved her in recent years.

But saying a final *au revoir* to Tom? It was too soon. It would always be too soon. Yet what choice did she have?

She smiled now. 'But I had come to Paris with you, that must have given you a clue that I was interested.'

'Not really. I thought you might just be in it for the art galleries.'

She shoved him playfully, her hand missing its target and making her stumble. She felt her cheeks get hot.

'I see your aim hasn't improved,' he said, laughing.

'I thought the same,' she said, more serious, as they left the room and made their way down the beige corridor. 'I really worried you were just being a nice friend.'

'It's not that long ago, really. But I can't imagine being that...'

'That *what*?'

He shrugged. 'I just remember it being really difficult, in those days. To say the right thing, to know what I was meant to do or say.'

'The perils of your twenties.'

'Yes, probably.'

She pressed the button for the lift and he waited at her side as it made its way to the fourth floor. The doors hissed open to reveal an elderly woman with a suitcase. She looked at both of them and they stood to one side as she wheeled it past.

A man pushed past them and got into the lift, and Tom raised an eyebrow at Sophie as they made their own way in. 'No, no, after you,' he said quietly into her ear.

She tried not to giggle as she stood in silence next to the rude man who strode off the minute the doors opened on the ground floor.

'Weren't you tempted to say something?' Tom asked.

She shook her head. 'It's not worth it. Men like that.'

They walked across the foyer and emerged into the sunlight.

'It's funny,' she said as they began to walk together, seemingly on the same page, 'when I think back to that trip. I mean I don't feel like I've changed much over the years. But I can't imagine why I just didn't ask you outright.'

'What, like, *Look, are you going to shag me or not, because I've been waiting long enough?*'

'Yes,' she said, mock-earnestly, 'something subtle like that.'

He laughed. 'Well, it would have saved me a huge amount of heartache if you had.'

She was silent for a moment. Around them, crowds milled and moved back and forth along the ancient streets – blood in the veins of the city, giving it life.

'What will you do after?' she asked him, her face serious.

'After?'

'Tom, you know. You *know*.' She couldn't find the words to say it out loud.

He shrugged. 'I literally don't know,' he said. 'I guess I'll just take one step at a time, see what comes my way. I don't feel... it's not really up to me. What happens next.'

'Oh Tom, I...'

'No,' he said, turning to her. 'Stop it.'

A man with a backpack stumbled behind her as she suddenly halted, turned to look. Huffing and cursing, he pushed past her and continued, glancing over his shoulder at her from time to time. She barely registered it.

'Stop what?'

'If this really is our last day, then I don't want to fill it with *sorry*s and *I wish*es and worry for the future,' he said. 'Whatever happens next will happen; there's nothing I or you can do to change that. I just want to spend the day with you. With the real you. The you that you are when you're not worried about tomorrow. Otherwise, what's the point?'

She nodded. 'Sorry.' Then, realising what she'd said, 'Oh! Sorry. I mean...'

He laughed. 'That's more like it. Much less apologetic.'

She found herself giggling too. 'Perhaps we're not as good communicators as we gave ourselves credit for, even now.'

'So what's the plan? Eiffel Tower, Montmartre and then, at the end, the bridge?' he asked.

She nodded. 'OK. Yes.'

'It'll be OK, you know; "all things come to an end" and all that,' he said.

'Yes, they do.'

'And you know, if things go tits up with Will, maybe there'll be a chance for me in another life.'

'Tom!'

'Well, can't blame a bloke for trying.'

The day gradually came into itself as they walked, Sophie trying as hard as she could to take in all the sights and sounds of the city she'd come to love and associate with love. Of the city that had seen some of her happiest times, and her worst too. She looked at the buildings, the balconies, shutters flung open to let in the light. The cafes with their colourful awnings. She took in the scent of coffee, of cigarette smoke, the chatter and the buzz of it all. She looked up at Tom by her side, sometimes with his eyes fixed ahead, sometimes turning to look at a riverboat, or a passer-by; always beautiful, always her Tom. And better now. Not drawn and pale as when they'd last been here. Not grey in his face and hollow in his eyes.

Whatever happened next, she'd had this time with him. And she was going to commit as much to memory as she possibly could.

* * *

For some reason, seeing the Eiffel Tower again, looking exactly as it always had, almost took her breath away. The structure so familiar, so shockingly enormous each time, so strangely beautiful despite the fact it looked a little like scaffolding with its hard lines and unyielding metal construction. But it wasn't the tower itself that made her feel this way, although seeing it always felt special; it was the memories it instantly evoked in her – as if in her mind there were a folder marked 'Tower' where the emotions from all her previous visits were stored and tumbled out as she stood at its base.

She thought back to that first, magical time when they'd been determined to take the stairs and spent the next day hobbling, their aching muscles protesting; about the last time, that awful last time with the lift and the grim knowledge hanging over both of them that everything was about to change. The tower had witnessed her highs and her lows, her excitement and disappointment. And now she was back – how would this memory be filed in her mind in the future? As something she thought of fondly? As a terrible betrayal and mistake? Or as something that ended so painfully she wanted to lock it away and never access that file again? She put her hand on the locket. It felt cold against her fingers.

'Cheer up love, it might never happen,' came a voice with a strong cockney accent in her ear. She jumped and put a hand to her chest before giggling.

'Tom!'

She'd told him in the past of the men she'd encountered who'd called out at her to smile, or cheer up, or the hundred other versions of the same phrase, and how annoying she always found it, how she'd wanted to retort each time and say it was none of their business how her face looked. From him, though, it was somehow hilarious.

'Can't have a pretty thing like you looking down, can we sweetheart?' he continued.

'Come on,' she said. 'I booked online. Let's go up.'

He nodded and turned towards the snake of tourists heading for the lift.

'Oh no. Not so fast,' she said. 'I booked the stairs.'

'Seriously?'

She shrugged. 'Old times' sake.'

'You know that not everything that happened in the "old times" has to be repeated for nostalgia's sake, don't you? I know our trips have been brilliant, but sometimes there's a reason things have... evolved as they've gone on. I mean, I won't be buying a sandwich from that dodgy street vendor near the station either.'

'Well, no. Me neither. But come on, when we visited the Eiffel Tower – the time we took the stairs – it was one of the best days.'

'You're looking back with rose-tinted specs,' he told her. 'You've forgotten the pain of it. My legs took about six months to recover.'

'Ah, don't be a lightweight,' she said. 'Come on!'

'I'm not worried for me,' he said. 'But you're getting on a bit now, aren't you?'

She opened her mouth in mock horror. 'How dare you!'

'It's your funeral,' he quipped, following close behind as she strode towards the door leading to the staircase at which, unsurprisingly, the queue was far shorter.

In the end, they only made it to the first floor. Enough to see Paris spread out below them, looking almost, at this distance, identical to the Paris all those years ago that had fallen forward from their view like a sea of possibilities. Back when they could have chosen to do anything, both for that holiday and with their lives. They hadn't realised, at that age, how many doors would shut over the next decade, how each choice they made would seal something else from their future until they were left in a situation they'd created, but would never have chosen outright.

I'm only thirty-four, Sophie reminded herself. *There's still time to do whatever I want.*

Except this, she thought. She looked at Tom in profile, his brow furrowed slightly, his skin almost iridescent in the light. Her funny, upbeat, loving man. For many years, her perfect partner. His loss had been the hardest thing she'd ever had to bear.

Then she thought of Will. The way he had of making the rest of the world fall away, of cocooning her in his arms and allowing her to let go of the chatter in her own mind and finally be calm. She hadn't survived the last decade-and-a-bit unharmed – she'd endured and got through and endured before she'd got to this point. Like a muscle, she'd been broken down, but rebuilt herself – a new version, stronger. Maybe no longer the Sophie that Tom loved. Maybe a Sophie who was brand new.

14

THE THIRD SUMMER – 2013

She'd always imagined that one day Tom might propose to her in Paris.

Although when she'd pictured it, they'd been twenty-five at least, thirty maybe. A few years more into their relationship. But she knew that Tom was planning it on this, their third holiday in Paris, and the fact of it hung over everything they did.

It was farcical almost, she thought.

She knew he had a ring in his pocket.

He knew he had a ring in his pocket.

And she was pretty sure that *he* knew *she* knew he had a ring in his pocket.

It seemed they were going through the pantomime of it anyway. Both acting as if he didn't have a ring box at all, but was just especially pleased to see her.

It was her third time in Paris, a year since they'd got back together here. And it had been a good one. His internship had morphed into a managerial position (perhaps thanks in part to his dad having a word in the right ear at the right time) and she'd passed her gruelling NQT year and become a proper teacher.

They'd managed six months of long-distance dating – train and car rides to and from London almost constant – before he'd found a leg up that got him into an office in Cambridge. Then there'd been his flat, the top floor of a Victorian house in a gorgeous central location. She'd done all the relationship commuting after that. Taking a Greyhound bus from the local town which wound around every backroad en route, or convincing her mum to drop her at the station in Ashwell, from which there was a direct link.

She'd stayed over so frequently that she'd started to think of it as *their* place, rather than his. But she'd never admit it; not unless he said something first.

And here they were. The stresses of the classroom left firmly behind her, the office – other than the odd phone call – barely interrupting his thoughts. Back in the city that had become *their* city, on a yearly trip that was starting to become a tradition.

'We'll do a proper holiday too,' he'd told her when he'd suggested the trip. 'I just thought it would be romantic to go again. An anniversary thing.'

'It's not a *proper* holiday?'

'No. It's Paris. Proper holidays have sunshine, beaches, cocktails, that sort of thing,' he'd said, as if going to Paris were just an appetiser and the Maldives a main meal.

But she'd learned to laugh at his assumption that everyone must have had childhoods like his, that holidays were only holidays if they were ten days long or more, and involved tans and fancy meals and very little else.

'If you insist,' she'd joked instead.

In reality, even though he could definitely afford it – *they* could, actually, with her salary too – she still felt a little uncomfortable looking at the cost per night of the hotel off the Champs-Élysées he'd chosen, where they were the youngest guests by a country mile and where they earned slightly suspicious looks, as if they'd just wandered in off the street and were chancing their luck.

She'd seen the proposal coming a few weeks ago, when he'd started trying to subtly find out about her favourite jewels, and she'd caught him going through her jewellery box looking for a ring to size. The day he arrived home late from work with a bulging suit pocket and the fact she later saw an Ernest Jones bag stuffed in the recycling had left her in no doubt about what he was planning to do.

Poor Tom. He'd tried so hard to be subtle, but he clearly didn't have it in him.

She almost felt sorry for him. Like she should have put him out of his misery by saying: 'Look, I know you're going to pop the question. The answer's yes. Now can we just go to the little place around the corner for a pizza rather than the special restaurant you said you'd booked – I'm not going anywhere where they serve foie gras.' But she hadn't. Because while it might relieve him in some ways, it might ruin something he was trying to build up to.

And she was going to say yes. Even though, in her gut, she felt it was far too soon. That she'd have preferred to give it another year or more before breaking out the jewellery. She'd thought about it over the preceding weeks and realised that if she wanted to be with Tom, she really had no option. He'd never recover from the humiliation of a 'no', or a 'not yet'.

Instead, she'd decided to do the delighted squeal – or as near to it as she could bear – that he was probably hoping for. She'd take photographs of her left hand to show her parents and friends later. She'd... well, she'd find a way to tell her parents that wouldn't lead to them trying to convince her she was too young and making a mistake.

They'd just have to have a long engagement, was all.

Mum and Dad liked Tom; they'd met him several times in recent months. The most recent, at the flat where she'd tried and failed to cook duck à l'orange and ended up buying Chinese. They'd made polite conversation with him, and everything on the surface had seemed completely fine. It was only because she knew them so well that she could read between the lines of their behaviour, and see their occasional glances when Tom mentioned his slightly-righter-than-theirs political views, or talked about investment schemes, or asked them where they liked to holiday each summer and had seemed amazed that they'd visited the same cottage in Cornwall for the past twenty years.

'Don't you ever fancy going farther afield?' he'd said, biting on the end of a spring roll. 'Doing a safari or something?'

'Um, not really,' her dad had replied politely.

Because they couldn't afford it! Sophie had wanted to say, but hadn't.

She was confident that her parents would come to love Tom the way she did. To see through their differences and find the man inside who, while a little misguided sometimes – mostly on account of his upbringing – meant well and loved her fiercely and protectively and with a passion that sometimes took her breath away.

Things with his folks were odd too. She'd seen more of them than her own parents in the past year – they met up for meals regularly, sometimes at his family home which seemed to her the kind of place that gets featured on one of those property design shows – and sometimes in restaurants. And each time she felt herself trying to become the sort of girlfriend they'd probably hoped for for their son.

She liked them – of course she did. But she'd cringed a little at his dad's rather loud, sexist comments, at his tendency to treat wait staff in a haughty manner; tried to ignore the fact that Tom seemed completely unaware of the way she felt about the kind of world his parents inhabited.

She looked at him again, as they walked quickly towards the Eiffel Tower – his pace betraying his agitated state of mind – and reminded herself that she wasn't her parents any more than he was his. And she wasn't marrying his extended family, just him. And not yet, in any case.

What she was doing now, when he finally got around to dropping onto one knee, was making him happy in the moment, securing their relationship right now. Because she didn't want it to end. And if that changed, well, she could always give the ring back.

She jumped a little when she realised he was looking at her.

'What are you thinking?' he said. 'You look miles away.'

'Sorry. Just... you know. It's nice to be here again. It feels like it's *our place*, doesn't it?'

He laughed. 'Sophie conquers Paris. I love it.'

'You know what I mean,' she said, giving him a dig in the ribs with her finger. He twisted out of her way and grabbed her hand.

'Sorry, Your Majesty,' he said, eyes twinkling. 'Queen Sophie of France. I'd be careful if I were you, the French don't take kindly to being ruled.'

'Good point,' she said with mock sincerity.

An hour later they were at the top, her breath taken away by the view, her mind inundated with a mixture of wonder and the slight fear she always had in high places that she might have a sudden temptation to jump into the void for no particular reason.

She stood as close to the edge as she dared – despite the criss-crossed metal barrier, she was still irrationally afraid of the drop – and gasped as the city lay before her, its tall buildings and mismatched architecture seeming more uniform and map-like than on the lower level.

'Two hundred and seventy-odd metres,' Tom said, his mouth close to her ear. He wrapped his arms around her. 'Better hang on tight.'

'Any excuse,' she said, leaning one of her arms around his neck, but not taking her eyes off the view.

There were more people here with them than she'd bargained on and the area felt a little claustrophobic. Soon they'd take the lift down and she'd look at the tower from her preferred angle – feet clamped firmly to the ground – she decided.

His arms seemed to drop from her waist and he moved away slightly. At first, she thought he'd gone to look at the view from the other side – see another area of Paris as it fell flatly away from view. But then there was a cough, and she noticed one or two heads turned her way.

Although she'd been onto him for a while, she'd got one thing wrong. The restaurant tonight was meant to be the after-party. The real event was happening right here, right now at the top of the Eiffel Tower in front of delighted tourists, some of whom had already snapped pictures of Tom kneeling, looking up at her with his earnest eyes and holding an open box in which she saw an almost comically large diamond ring.

'Oh!' she said.

'Sophie Baker, will you do me the honour of being my wife?'

She smiled. 'Yes, Tom Gardner, I will.'

She was no longer in her body, but playing a part for those around her, imagining how each of the people here would go and tell their story about the proposal at the summit of the Eiffel Tower. The good-looking, earnest boy, the enormous diamond ring. Her delighted, emphatic 'yes'.

As he slipped the ring on her finger, she felt slightly shaky. 'Shall we go?' she said quietly, and he nodded.

He held her hand as they made their way to the lift and put his arm around her. 'Are you happy?' he asked her.

'Yes,' she said. And she realised that she really was.

15

TWO WEEKS AGO

It had felt odd asking Tom to leave for a bit, all things considered. But he'd nodded and allowed her to return to the Cler without making a fuss of it. Bit different from back in the day; he'd been childish in his neediness sometimes – annoyed or threatened when she'd wanted a bit of Sophie time. But she'd had to get away, just for a moment; needed to call Will and also spend time getting her head straight.

She'd wanted to ask Tom where he was going to go, but held her tongue. It wasn't her business to know everything about him, not any more.

In their years together, they'd gotten over the initial reserve that comes at the start of a relationship when you don't want to put the other person off by letting your guard down too early (*I want a big family! I'd love to get married one day! I have a third nipple!*) and they'd developed an openness with each other; had known each other inside out. Now she wasn't so sure, so easy around him. It was hardly surprising after not seeing him for so many years.

She picked up her phone and answered a text message Libby had sent yesterday.

LIBBY
How's it going?

SOPHIE
OK.

A green dot appeared by Libby's name, accompanied by a moving ellipsis; her friend was online, typing.

LIBBY
OK? Is that all I get after 12 hours of wondering why you hadn't replied? How is Paris? And, more importantly, HOW WAS THE MILLEFEUILLE!

SOPHIE
Glad to see that you have your priorities right!

LIBBY
Precisely. And pictures next time or it didn't happen.

SOPHIE
Hard to find my appetite with… well, you know.

LIBBY
I know. But seriously girl you are in IN PARIS. It's criminal not to at least come back a few pounds heavier.

SOPHIE
OK. I'll get to it.

LIBBY
Love you, you know.

SOPHIE

I know.

LIBBY

Wish I was there.

SOPHIE

Because of me? Or the pastries?

LIBBY

Well, both. I have a lot of love to give to both of those things.

SOPHIE

Idiot *smiley face*

LIBBY

I'm offended! Seriously though, look after yourself, OK? That's an order.

SOPHIE

Thanks Lib. I will.

LIBBY

I have to ask… is he there? Tom I mean. Like you said.

SOPHIE

Yes.

LIBBY

Oh, Soph. Look, I'm not going to judge you. I know how much you miss him. But just be careful, OK?

SOPHIE

I'm fine, honestly. I know what I'm doing. It's OK. I know how to cross the road safely, look both ways.

LIBBY

Very funny. Well, look. Call me – day or night – if you need.

SOPHIE

Thanks.

Sophie lay for a moment, flicking through social media. Will hadn't posted anything, which was far from surprising. Libby had posted one of the non-smiling selfies she'd favoured since discovering her newly etched crows' feet and deciding her skin was smoother when she kept her expression neutral. Otherwise, nothing.

This wasn't doing her any good, she decided, forcing herself to get up and move. Straightening the bed, she stood, checked her reflection in the mirror, grabbed her bag and took the shuddering lift down to the foyer. Tom would just have to catch up.

Montmartre was just as it had been all those years ago. Perhaps there was a little more graffiti outside the metro, a few shops boarded up, their windows whitened from the inside; maybe it was a bit busier. But essentially, it hadn't changed. Probably in fifty, a hundred years' time some other tourist would walk down these same streets and wonder the same thing. Perhaps even—

'Hey, no fair! Why didn't you wait for me?'

The voice made her jump and she whirled around, almost knocking her bag into a passing woman who stepped back, alarmed, then continued on her way, muttering at the strange young lady spinning around in the street for no discernible reason. But it didn't matter.

'I wasn't sure when you'd be back... so...'

They moved to the edge of the street, against the cool stone of a building, where they'd no longer be in anyone's way.

'Yes, but what I if I hadn't found you?'

She was going to say something about his being needy, but stopped herself. She wasn't sure how this was going to play out; wasn't sure of the rules any more than he was. 'Sorry,' she said instead.

He was silent for a moment. 'It's OK. It's not your fault I'm like this.'

'No, but I should have thought...'

He smiled, leaning for a moment against the stone, his eyes closed. 'No, let's not.'

'Not what?'

'Talk about it. It's fine. I found you.'

'What made you choose Montmartre?' she asked as they fell into step together again.

'No idea. Just sort of found myself here,' he admitted. 'I thought, where would Sophie go?'

'Nice to know I'm so predictable,' she said, smiling.

'You and all the other tourists.'

They joined the throng of people making their way up the cobbled streets. The sun warmed Sophie's back between the straps of her dress; she inwardly scolded herself for forgetting sun cream. Something about the back of her neck, her upper shoulders and back seemed to absorb the sun's rays, as if those parts of her body were determined to get burnt one way or the other.

They stood silently on the edge of the square, looking at the familiar artists – none of whom they recognised individually, but who made up the centre of the cobbled area, filling it with easels, paper, small stools, chairs for subjects.

'I told Libby I was coming to see you,' she said.

'You did?' He looked surprised. 'What did she say?'

'She told me to be careful,' she admitted.

'That's it?'

Sophie shook her head. 'Pretty sure she thinks I'm borderline insane.'

Tom laughed. She'd forgotten how much she loved the sound of it. 'Exactly how I like my women,' he said. 'Just crazy enough.'

'Thanks very much,' she grinned.

'And she's not going to tell Will? Don't want him sending the cavalry out to rescue you.'

'The cavalry being...?' she smiled.

He grinned. 'No idea. His parents? Yours? Libby?'

She giggled at the idea of it. 'No, I think she knows me well enough to know that I'm going to keep myself safe. Good old sensible Sophie.' She felt her mouth quiver, giving away the emotions that bubbled underneath.

'This is hard for you, isn't it?' he said.

She shook her head, lying. 'It's good. I want this.'

They moved off, meandering around the different artists, peering over shoulders at easels, remarking over paintings they liked, more subtly grimacing at ones that were perhaps not quite at the artistic level of Vincent Van Gogh.

'Painting, madame?' a voice asked.

It was a woman, dressed in black, long hair glossy against her shoulders, paint on her sleeve.

'Oh, I don't think...'

'Go on,' Tom nodded. 'For old times' sake!'

'I thought you were anti-nostalgia?'

'Only when it suits me.'

They smiled at each other, the years between before and now falling away.

The woman was standing patiently waiting when Sophie broke her gaze. 'Sorry,' Sophie said. 'Go on then. Yes, please.'

She sat on the small bench and lightly patted the seat next to her. But Tom shook his head.

Sometimes she forgot. Just for a moment. It was understandable, she told herself. It wasn't that she'd forgotten Will or why she was here; and it certainly didn't mean that she loved Will any less. But in this timeless place, with so many memories of Tom, it was understandable that she forgot that not everyone could see things the way she did.

She nodded. 'OK,' she said.

The woman looked up. 'Ready?'

And she lifted her paintbrush and began running it lightly over the canvas.

16

THE THIRD SUMMER – 2013

The voices woke her and she opened her eyes in the dark bedroom.

'She'll be fine, love' – her father's voice.

'I know, but...' – her mum replying.

'She's all grown-up. You can't make the mistakes for her.'

Her ears pricked; she crept out of bed, careful not to wake Tom, and made her way down the moonlit corridor. She stopped in the doorway of the bathroom, just opposite her parents' bedroom. If anyone got up, she could dart into the bathroom as if that was where she'd meant to go all along.

'She's only twenty-three!'

'I'd met you by then!'

'I know but... she seems so young.'

There was a sigh and a shifting of pillows. Sophie made a half-dart towards the bathroom, sure that the bedroom door was about to open. But it was a false alarm. She leant against the white-painted wood of the door-frame, her heart hammering.

'I admit, I'm not thrilled,' her dad said now. 'But Sophie's a sensible girl. I don't think she'd do anything rash.'

There was a shifting of bodies. 'Do you think I should say something, you know, about...?' her mother asked.

'Not yet. Let them have their happiness. They're so young,' her father replied.

What was it her mum had wanted to say? Something about Tom? About it being too soon?

There was a creak and a rustling sound. Then silence. Sophie moved closer to the bedroom, hoping to hear any more whispered insight her parents might impart. Then there was an unmistakable moan of pleasure, and she recoiled as if stung and hastily made her way back to bed. Crawling in beside Tom, who sleepily lay out his arm for her to cuddle into him, her mind was racing.

They were right, weren't they? It was too soon. She loved Tom; they loved each other. But they were only twenty-three. When she'd realised what Tom was planning, through hints and suspicions, she'd been shocked. Surely Tom, of all people, wasn't someone who'd want to settle down yet? At least, not officially?

When they'd visited his parents to tell them the news, it was clear from his mother's delight that she was all for it. 'It's an old-fashioned thing,' Tom had confided on the way back. 'Some of their friends are a bit weird about living in sin and all that.'

She'd smiled and nodded and touched the diamond on her finger, wondering how much the proposal had been about them, and how much about his parents' friends. Since when was Tom someone who'd toe the line, anyway?

But then how well did they know each other?

Then he'd put his arm around her and she'd snuggled into his side, breathed the soapy, vanilla smell of him and felt herself relax. Because she might doubt the timeline, but she didn't doubt the destination; she knew she wanted to be with Tom.

They'd made the weekend trip from Cambridge to Bedfordshire to tell her parents in person, on Tom's insistence.

'Why haven't you told them yet?' he'd asked idly one night when they'd popped out to the bar for a white wine.

'Oh! I just think... it would be better in person. With both of us. And there's no rush...'

He'd slapped his forehead as if annoyed at himself. 'Of course. I'm so sorry! I didn't even think. And there's me rushing to *my* parents,' he said. 'We'll go this weekend.'

And here they were, the journey passing more quickly than ever. 'Will they mind, your parents?' Tom had asked her. 'I should really have asked your dad for your hand.'

'I'm bloody glad you didn't!' Sophie had said. 'I'm actually a fully grown person.' She hated the traditional permission-asking, as if she were anyone's possession to give away.

'I know that. It's just your dad might have liked it.'

It was true, he might have.

She'd managed to avoid answering the other question, afraid of the answer herself.

Still, they'd said all the right things when they'd taken them to the pub for dinner and made the announcement. Sophie had slipped on her ring, and they'd both exclaimed over how pretty it was – even Dad!

Mum had kissed her, Dad had shaken Tom's hand forcefully and slapped him on the back. She'd felt, at the time, that she was in a TV drama – people doing all the clichéd things they're meant to do when this kind of news is announced.

Had it been fake? Had they been acting? She tried to close her eyes, settle into sleep; knew that things would seem different in the morning. But her racing thoughts wouldn't let her settle. Her parents had never said anything negative about Tom – they'd actually seemed to get on pretty well the few times they'd met. It was just the rush of it all; and perhaps they sensed her own reluctance.

She'd held back the other news. That Tom's mum and dad seemed to have taken the baton and were already talking venues; that her idea of a long engagement had been pushed aside. 'We'll pay for it all, of course,' his father had said. 'Now, I know that traditionally it's the bride's family, but we never had a daughter and I know this one' – he'd nodded at his wife – 'has been longing to plan a wedding almost since Tom was born.'

Tom's mum had laughed and lightly slapped her husband's arm, but hadn't contradicted him.

'Oh,' Sophie had responded at last. 'Well, that's very generous. We were actually thinking of a long engagement...'

'Well, now you don't need to!' Tom's father had responded, as if offering her the gift of a lifetime.

Tom's dad, it seemed, was used to getting his own way. Not because he was forceful, but because for some reason, nobody seemed to challenge him. Perhaps nobody wanted to. So Sophie had pushed her own misgivings down and smiled. 'Thank you,' she'd said. 'Honestly, that's so kind.'

Now, in the darkness of her childhood bedroom, with its unfamiliar double bed and the surprise of finding a man at her side in this space, she lay awake, unable to settle.

Tom, seeming to sense her restlessness, turned on his side and wrapped her in both of his arms, pulling her into a spooning position. His body was warm against hers, his breathing regular. Her Tom. It would be OK. They would be OK.

She steadied herself, trying to match Tom's calm – assured breaths until at last her eyelids felt heavy, she lost consciousness and finally fell into a deep sleep.

17

TWO WEEKS AGO

The day was simply going too fast. Sophie thought back to all the days she'd spent in school – the slow, mocking tick of a classroom clock; the fact that the hands never seemed to shift. And now here she was in Paris and time was slipping through her fingers like liquid.

She'd bought a baguette for dinner, filled with thick slices of freshly cut ham, and munched it on a bench with Tom at her side, the picture – that had turned out quite realistic and more expensive than she'd expected – next to her.

Then they'd stood and she'd brushed the crumbs from her front decisively. 'Right,' she said.

'Want to go and take a look at Notre Dame – or what's left of it?' he offered.

They were both surprised when she shook her head. 'Do you mind if we don't?' she asked. 'I think maybe it would be better just to be somewhere we could talk.'

'That sounds ominous.'

She laughed then. 'Tom, I don't think that after everything that happened, there can be any more bad news, do you?' she said. 'If what you said about luck being in a balance, you must have loads of great things to come.'

They were silent then, remembering.

'Do you forget?' she asked. 'Sometimes?'

'Forget that...?' He indicated his body.

She nodded.

'Sometimes,' he said. 'Sometimes it doesn't feel that different. Then I remember and...'

She felt a stab of grief. 'Oh, Tom.'

He shrugged. 'It is what it is, not much we can do about it now. And better not to dwell on all the bad stuff that happened.'

'You're telling me!'

They smiled sadly at each other. An old man with a dog sat on the end of the bench, leaving space between them, and began to fill an enormous pipe with tobacco.

'Do you ever visit your parents?' Sophie asked, more quietly now.

The man looked at her, his brow furrowed. '*Désolé,*' he said. '*Je ne comprends pas.* I don't understand.'

'Oh. No,' she said. 'I'm not talking to... Sorry.'

He turned back, impatient at her lack of French. Labelling her, no doubt, as another mad tourist. Sophie looked at Tom, who was shaking with laughter.

'What?' she mouthed.

'You, chatting up an old guy. Come on, Soph. What would Will say?'

She got to her feet. 'Think perhaps we'd better...'

The old man looked up again, impatiently, before shaking his head – apparently having given up on her.

'This is hard,' she said to Tom as they walked. 'I mean, all of it's hard, obviously. Seeing you. The... the goodbye bit. But just being here together. Forgetting.'

He wrapped an arm around her shoulders and she felt the tingle of it. 'I know,' he said.

They walked in silence for a while, both noticing how the light was fading; neither commenting.

'Have you seen anyone else since...?' she asked. 'Your parents?'

He shook his head. 'Just you.'

'That's sad.'

'Not sure anyone else wants to see me, to be honest,' he said. 'They've kind of moved on.'

'And I haven't?'

'You're trying to, and it's good. A new start. And you know, maybe things will work out this time. Maybe you'll even... well, you know. Babies. Motherhood.'

Her cheeks were hot. 'Maybe,' she said, and only he could understand the enormous pressure of hope and despair behind that word. 'Maybe not. I'm trying...' she took an enormous, shuddering breath. 'I guess I'm trying to take one day at a time this time. Not... push things too much. Not make it all about that. Trying just to... well, to live. Sorry.'

'No sorrys, remember?' he said. 'And it's great.'

'But how I was... with you. I ruined it, didn't I? I was so impatient for time to pass month after month. And it felt like we had so much of it. I didn't realise...' Tears pricked her eyes. 'I just wish I hadn't taken so much away,' she said simply.

He stopped and turned to look at her. 'No,' he said. 'You didn't. It was us. *Our* thing. I felt it just as much as you. And neither of us were to know. Plus, how do you think I feel? Becoming that mess of a person I was afterwards. That fucking wheelchair.'

She laughed through her tears. 'Come on, you looked hot and you know it.'

He smiled back. 'That's more like it,' he said. 'Come on, Soph. No regrets.'

They were halted by the sound of a clock chime ringing out, marking a quarter past eleven. Both froze.

'Bridge?' he said, his voice wavering a little.

She nodded. Just once.

18

AUTUMN 2013

Mum was crying.

Sophie went over and removed the glass of champagne from her hand, setting it on a nearby table. 'Mum!' she said. 'It's OK.'

Mum shook her head. 'Ignore me,' she said. 'You just look...'

Sophie looked down at herself, unrecognisable in a cloud of lace and taffeta. 'Like a swan?' she suggested, making her mum hiccup out a laugh through her tears.

'You're just all grown-up, is all,' she said.

'Well, yeah,' Sophie said. 'But at the end of the day, it's only a dress.'

Sam put an arm around the back of their mum. 'Plus, she looks a bit like candyfloss,' she said. 'I don't think it's the right one, unless you want any kids there trying to take a bite out of your train.'

Then they were all laughing, watched by the rather serious assistant who was standing patiently with a cream satin gown over her arm.

'Sorry,' Sophie said, looking at her. 'Another one.'

'Yes.' The assistant was all pasted-on smile. 'I think this one could be fabulous on you.'

'I'm sorry,' her mum said as they walked out, deposit paid, into the market day furore. 'I should be paying for it really. Me and Dad.'

Sophie shook her head. She'd been embarrassed to hand over her debit card – topped up generously by Tom's father for the purpose – over to the shop assistant in front of Mum. Knew how it might make her feel. 'Mum, Tom's parents have pots of money,' she said. 'His dad's a lawyer. They don't mind. Insisted, in fact.'

Mum nodded. 'Yes, I know,' she said, opening her mouth afterwards as if to say more, but closing it again.

Sophie reached out and squeezed her mother's hand. She knew it was humiliating for her mum and dad to feel they couldn't pay for their eldest's wedding. But she'd never been a stickler for tradition – who could be, in this day and age – and it seemed sensible to accept the offer from Tom's parents. Always well off, Tom's dad had recently floated his company on the stock exchange and received, as a thank you, 'money for absolutely nothing' as he'd put it himself.

She didn't begrudge Tom's family their wealth. But it did sometimes irk her when they were so blasé about restaurants and new cars and handing over credit cards for this and that. Because it just wasn't her experience. Throughout her childhood they'd had to be careful. Money hadn't been too tight, but it had always been an issue. She imagined what it would be like to break free from those bounds, to be fairly confident you could spend a great deal of money spontaneously without it having much effect.

And she hated how it seemed to make her parents feel. She hadn't brought up the conversation they'd had three months ago when the engagement had been announced. She'd wanted to say something, to gently dissuade them from their reservations, explained they weren't going to rush. But then Tom had told her his dad had found 'just the venue' and there was a cancellation, and suddenly she was speeding towards a wedding date that she'd hoped to kick to the kerb just for a little while.

But it would be OK, she told herself. She knew Tom well enough. Loved him completely. They were both settled in their new jobs, their flat. Not much would change if they got married. And she couldn't exactly back out now in any case. She'd just hoped that she'd have time to persuade her parents of all Tom's good points before the big day. Now it looked as if there might not be time.

'You do like Tom, don't you?' she said now, aloud.

'What kind of paranoid question is *that*?' Sam snorted, her still teenage brain clearly shocked at the simple openness of it. 'Of course they do, and even if they don't, who cares?' She looked at their mum. 'Sorry, Mum,' she added as an afterthought.

'Sam! It's important,' Sophie admonished.

'Well of course we do,' her mum said, grabbing her hand and squeezing it as they walked. 'He's a lovely boy.'

'But?' Sophie prompted.

Her mum shook her head. But nothing.

Later, she snuggled against Tom on the sofa as they watched *Britain's Got Talent*, laughing, cringing and exclaiming over the contestants in what had become a bit of a Saturday night ritual for them, and thought about the dress, its expensive satin length, the fact that the deposit alone would have more or less paid for a whole year's rent when she was at university. The assistant had been right: she'd looked good in it. Even Sophie could admit that. But she wasn't quite sure if she'd looked like herself. She shuffled against Tom and he adjusted his arm. 'Everything OK?' he asked.

'Yeah, just thinking.'

'Careful, might be dangerous.'

She laughed, mock-slapped him. 'Very funny.'

'Mum like the dress?' he asked.

'Yeah.'

'Good.'

It would be better to be like Tom about it, she decided. He didn't particularly care what colour his tie was, or whether the best man would prefer a grey or blue suit. He was letting the whole wedding thing wash over him, relying on Sophie and his mother to direct him and simply electing to turn up and make his vows. Tom, in her situation, wouldn't be worried whether the dress reflected his personality or not. He'd just shove it on.

The thought of Tom in her wedding dress made her snort.

'What?' he said, looking at the screen, then down at her.

'Nothing. Just thinking,' she said again.

He kissed the top of her head. 'My little weirdo,' he said affectionately, and she smiled.

'Yep! That's me!' Then, 'Tom, do your parents like me?'

'What sort of question is that?'

'Humour me.'

He shifted, looked at her. 'Of course they do. Why wouldn't they? Hang on, don't your parents like *me*?'

She coloured. 'Of course they do,' she parroted.

And she remembered Sam. Of course, it didn't matter anyway.

19

TWO WEEKS AGO

It was as if time were bearing down on them. And she wasn't ready to say goodbye. It was dark now, the shops had closed and the streets had changed – people passed them dressed-up, moving in groups, clouds of perfume and cigarettes. Restaurants and bars were packed, their windows clouding with condensation.

Libby's name flashed up on her phone screen.

Sophie's initial reaction was to bin the call, but she found herself answering, miming a 'sorry' to Tom.

'Hi Soph,' came the familiar voice.

'Hi yourself.'

'So, how's Paris? Spent all your honeymoon savings on high fashion? Fallen in love with a penniless French artist?'

'Lib, it's not a good time.'

There was a pause. 'Sorry, chick.'

'It's OK.'

'But... well, have you done it? Drawn a line in the sand or the... I don't know, the sediment of the Seine?'

A flash of anger. 'Libby!'

'Sorry. I didn't mean to sound flippant. I'm just... it's hard knowing you're there on your own. I'll feel a lot better when it's done.'

'I'm just waiting for midnight.'

'I know. And I get all the symbolism and everything of waiting until midnight, but this isn't a Richard Curtis movie, hon, it's real life.'

'I know that!'

'It's dangerous. Out there on your own.'

'I'll be careful.'

There was a long pause. 'Just make sure you are,' Libby said firmly.

'Always.'

'And no leaving glass slippers behind.'

'What?'

'You know. Cinderella? Midnight? Prince Charming chasing her down with her size sixes?'

Sophie laughed. 'No chance of that,' she said, looking at her scuffed trainers.

'Well good. And listen, call me when you've done it.'

'At midnight?'

'Eleven o'clock here. But promise you will? I won't be asleep, believe me.'

'OK.'

She ended the call and fell into step next to Tom, their aimless meandering past brightly lit shops offering too much choice at too high a price, their doors closed fast to customers until tomorrow. The Champs-Élysées had never been her favourite part of Paris. She preferred the back streets, the Latin quarter, the bits that felt hidden and special. 'Are you OK?' she asked him.

'Yeah.' But something about him had changed. His feet

dragged a little and she was reminded a bit of a teenager being forced to the shops. Somehow so much younger than her.

'Did you hear Libby?' she asked.

He shook his head. 'Got the gist though.'

She nodded, not making eye contact. 'Sorry.'

'Are you?'

She stopped, looked up at him. He stepped closer, looking down at her. 'Fuck it, Sophie,' he said. 'I'm scared.'

The feeling of helplessness she'd lived with for the last of their years rose then. A kind of sick terror, an impotent rage that this was happening. 'I know,' she said. 'I mean, we could...'

'Could what?'

'Delay it?' she said, her hand on the silver locket, as if reassuring herself she still had it. 'Do something different? Wait?'

He shook his head sadly. 'I don't think it would help. Once you walk away from me... Well, my life as I know it will be over.'

'I'm sure there'll be something,' she lied. 'A better thing, maybe.'

He laughed quietly to himself. 'I hope so.'

It was five to twelve when they reached the bridge. It was almost eerily empty compared with the day. A few people walked on the shadowed pavement, meandering or pacing, walking in groups, pairs or alone. They broke away and stood at the water's edge, looking over the wall to its churning mass reflecting the clear sky, the stars, the glow of nearby windows and the street lights. It looked alive.

'You're sure?' she asked him, trying to keep the tremor from her voice.

He nodded.

'But where will you go?' she asked him.

He looked at her. 'What do you mean?'

'Where will I be able to find you?'

'Sophie, you won't,' he said sadly, reaching as if to brush some hair from her eyes.

'But...' Could she really bear for this to be the last time? A real goodbye? It was the right thing to do. It made sense for both of them. But when she imagined flinging the last of their connection away, she couldn't bear it.

He shook his head, his face fond, amused, sad. 'Soph,' he said. 'You won't find me. I'll be gone.'

'But you're...'

'I'm already gone, Soph.'

'You're right here!' she said.

'But you know I'm not really here, don't you?' he said, his eyes crinkling with sympathy. 'I'm not here any more, Soph.'

'You're...'

But suddenly she was staring at nothing. At a memory projected into the present. And it hit her hard in the centre of her stomach that he was truly gone. That he wasn't coming back. That Tom had never really been here at all.

Stifling a sob, she pulled the locket from her neck and, kissing it, threw it into the Seine. It glittered on the surface of the water for a moment, then was pulled under, taken by the current, and even though she strained her eyes, she couldn't see it any more.

20

THE FOURTH SUMMER – 2014

She hadn't said anything but she'd been a little disappointed when she'd realised Tom had booked a plane to Paris rather than the train for their honeymoon. 'I just wanted it to be a bit different,' he'd said. 'Travel in style.' He'd kissed her then, the tickets discarded on the side in their immaculate kitchen. 'Only the best for Mrs Gardner-to-be.'

'But still the same destination?' she said, teasing. 'So not that different, really.'

'Well, it's tradition now, isn't it? Seemed like the right place.'

She laughed, agreeing. 'Our place.'

'Maldives next time, though.'

'So you keep saying.'

Later, Libby laughed at her when she told her they were going to Paris yet again, this time for their honeymoon. 'You guys know there are other places, right?'

But Sophie was pleased. Not only because Paris had become their place – and although they'd been there a lot, they had barely touched the surface of what they could do and see – but because it was familiar, and after the upheaval and nervousness that came with getting married, she was looking forward to being somewhere that felt reassuringly known.

That day, months ago, when he'd tossed the tickets on the table, their August wedding had still seemed like a distant dream. Something indistinct she didn't have to worry about too much. But the summer term at school had raced by and she'd found herself two nights ago trying on the dress for the last time, slipping her feet into satin sandals. Telling a reluctant Sam that pink really *was* her colour and that – besides – bridesmaids ought to do what they're told.

'Can I at least wear my Doc Martens with it?' Sam had asked, looking at herself in the mirror, aghast.

Sophie hadn't known whether or not her sister was joking. 'Sorry,' she'd said. 'Satin slippers only, I'm afraid.'

'Never thought you'd make me wear pink.'

It had been a joke, but Sophie had felt it keenly. The pink hadn't actually been her choice: Julie, Tom's mum, had suggested the dress and she hadn't felt able to say no. That inability seemed to sum up the whole wedding somehow – people who had fixed ideas about what a wedding should be trampling over her uncertainty until she barely recognised any of it.

Then suddenly it was the day itself. She was made-up, styled, fitted into a dress that made her look like someone else entirely. She'd linked her arm with her father's – his steady presence an anchor somehow – and they'd looked at each other in the church vestibule, eyebrows raised.

'Sure you want this, kid?' he'd said softly.

She'd nodded. She wasn't sure about any of the decor and colour choices, the hair or make-up or shoes or flowers or the three-tier fruit cake festooned with elaborate royal icing, but she was sure about Tom. And when it came down to it, that was all that mattered.

He'd squeezed her arm and then she'd found herself stepping into the role of 'bride' for the day – the only thing that hadn't felt surreal had been Tom's look when he'd turned in the church and seen her for the first time. He'd smiled, their eyes had locked, and she'd almost got the giggles. It was all so ridiculous. But at least it was them.

The day itself had passed in a blur. She'd been a chattel, pulled in this direction or that. Not her own person. One moment standing, holding hands in front of the registrar, the next, racing back down the confetti-scattered aisle. Then the photos, the endless photos when she'd wished she could be making real memories.

The wedding breakfast – although it seemed an odd word for it, given it was served at 3 p.m. and consisted mainly of chicken – was the first time she'd sat down all day. Three glasses of champagne and it was all that she could do not to nod off into her cake as the speeches passed over her – her father joking about his little girl, Tom telling everyone how lucky he was. Then best man Will was there, standing up in his grey morning suit, looking completely out of place somehow. He'd done everything the other men had done but he still looked like a rugby player playing dress-up.

Will had made the usual jokes about Tom's past, his reputation at uni, how when Sophie had first met him he'd been wearing a dress (cue: laughter and hilarity). Then he'd raised a glass to them both and caught her eye. She'd smiled sleepily and raised her glass in return, grateful that Tom had such a loyal friend, and that he had – as asked – kept mostly off the subject of Tom's exes: not naming any, not telling the story about the girl who used to follow him to the bus stop, keeping it all vague and non-specific as she'd hoped.

She'd thought she'd want the day to last forever, but in reality she was glad when it was over, the last loitering guests finally bid farewell and she and Tom could stumble back to their room, sink into bed and sigh with pleasure at the soft mattress, feather duvet, deep, soft pillows.

There had been no sex, just a tiredly whispered: 'Goodnight, Mrs Gardner' and an arm curling around her, pulling her to him. Which had been absolutely perfect.

Now, as the plane taxied along the runway at Charles de Gaulle, she couldn't help comparing the tarmacked newness of the airport with the more traditional building of the station. On the train, she'd felt as if she'd threaded right into the heart of Paris from the off; the plane instead took them to somewhere both familiar and generic; was functional rather than romantic.

Still, with Tom on her arm, a wedding band on her finger and a glass of champagne fizzing in her stomach, she had to admit she was looking forward to the break.

Her first year of proper teaching had been challenging and she'd ached with exhaustion by the time the end of the academic year arrived. Tom had been working long hours too, getting back at their flat at eight or sometimes later, despite the fact his office was a stone's throw away. Gone were the lazy student afternoons in her house or his college room, watching *Countdown* or reruns of property programmes and feeling gloriously and luxuriously bored. Instead, they had snatched time together and made promises that it wouldn't always be this way.

The hotel his father had chosen, Hotel Le Marianne, was just off the Champs-Élysées and made last year's smart hotel look shabby in comparison. He'd booked out the hotel's biggest suite and he'd had the room filled with bottles of champagne and chocolates and decadent products for the bath and shower. The bed was enormous – soft and feather-padded – and if they'd wanted, they needn't have left it at all: room service was exquisite and everything was covered by his father's credit card.

She'd felt slightly sick when she'd seen the price of the rooms – it seemed an awful lot to spend on an experience rather than something tangible. Not much of an investment. But she'd tried to push her thoughts down – after all, this would be her one and only honeymoon and the last thing she wanted to do was ruin it. It was so generous of Tom's father, too.

As soon as they were left alone, Tom had turned to her, grinning, and taken her in his arms. 'We ought to make up for lost time, don't you think?' he'd said playfully into her ear. 'Don't want the marriage to be annulled because it hasn't been consummated, after all.' She'd laughed and held him around the back of the neck as he kissed her and slowly drew down the straps on her shoulders, sliding her dress off.

But later, after they'd showered and dressed, she felt a familiar restlessness, the call of everything that was out there waiting to be seen. Clipping her earrings on, she'd noticed him watching her in the mirror from his place on the bed.

'Don't tell me,' he'd smiled. 'You want to go to the fucking Louvre.'

'Tom!' she'd said, half insulted, half amused.

'I'm kidding. Anywhere you want to go is fine by me.'

'Well, if you must know, I just fancy going for a walk,' she'd admitted. 'Getting some fresh air.'

'Or inhaling some traffic fumes?'

'OK, I'm hoping to inhale some pollution and wondered if you'd like to join me,' she said, turning with a smile. 'I don't know. I feel kind of restless. Just want to walk, look at the sights. Maybe get a bite to eat somewhere?'

'Sounds good,' he said, lazily getting up and doing up the top button he'd unfastened on his black jeans. 'Will I do?'

She looked at him, amused. She'd carefully selected an outfit – a green silk dress with sandals – and taken the time to curl her hair under as she'd dried it. He'd pulled on the same jeans he'd worn for the flight, albeit with clean underwear. Yet in his lazy, half-arsed way, he looked just as ready for the night as she did.

'You'll do.'

She liked it that the evening had started to fall, and that the lights in the shop windows gave out a comforting glow. It was only 9 p.m., but August was on the cusp of giving way to September and beyond it, the autumn and winter. She could see people inside the bars – a riot of colour against polished wood – and the people she passed on the street looked smart and purposeful. Every now and then the words 'I'm married!' would pop into her head, and she could hardly believe that she'd tied the knot with this man who'd turned in a few short years from a serial dater to a one-woman man. She looked at him.

'What?' he asked.

'Just thinking,' she said. 'Never had you down as the marrying kind.'

'Me neither.' He looked at her. 'Yet here we are.'

'Here we are indeed.'

Later, after a simple meal in a tiny brasserie, they began to meander the streets, winding their way back to the hotel, hand in hand, letting the noise of the Parisian evening settle over them. People passed, showering them with snippets of conversations – words in French, English, other languages rained down on them piecemeal, meaningless. The rumble of occasional traffic on the road, even at this hour, the odd horn being honked, all fading into the background of their walk. The sound of their own shoes hitting the pavement, the occasional clink of her earrings as she moved, their own breathing and heartbeat – everything together and separate at once. This was it, she thought. The perfect evening. The perfect moment. Newly married, honeymooners, young and with life simply stretching in front of them. She wanted to grab it, hold the moment to her, preserve it before it slipped away.

He looked at his watch pointedly as they began to cross the bridge. Almost midnight – he'd clearly planned it. Smiling, she stopped momentarily, leaning on the balustrade to admire the view. He wrapped his arms around her. 'I just feel,' he said, 'as if no one and nothing can touch us.'

She nodded. She knew exactly what he meant.

He brought his hand out in front of her so she could see he was holding a necklace – a small silver locket which caught the light. 'For you, Mrs Gardner,' he said.

'Oh, Tom, it's lovely.' She let him fasten it around her neck and felt her hand travel to it as they stared into the endless night sky, on their bridge, in *their* place, at the start of a whole life full of adventures.

21

TWO WEEKS AGO

The urge to get home was almost overwhelming. As she watched the locket disappear into the water, she felt a terrible lurch of loneliness. What was she doing here? Why had she decided it was best to come alone? And Tom. Had he really been here? Had it all been in her head?

Before Tom died, she hadn't thought much about whether or not there was an afterlife. There was a vague sense of 'heaven' or 'somewhere better' that she'd imagined when her grandparents had died, but all of that stuff hadn't seemed to apply to her, in her twenties and only just at the start of things.

Then after Tom had died, she'd felt for a long time as if he was still with her. She'd spoken to him, believed she'd seen signs – a white feather outside her front door, a book falling open on a certain page. All the things she'd seen other people do when they were in grief had become her things.

That wishful thinking had disappeared over the dark months that followed and it was only recently she'd begun to see him again. Something both welcome and terrifying at once. Stress, her GP had said. But how could it be? She'd convinced herself it was her fault – that she hadn't scattered his ashes as she'd promised. And could only think of one way to end it, to say goodbye. Here, in the place that had come to mean everything.

Feeling hot, she raced along the streets, upsetting one or two meandering tourists as she pushed past them in her haste. Reaching into her pocket, she pulled out her phone and called Will. But her call went to voicemail.

'Stupid, stupid,' she muttered to herself as she turned the final corner and saw the cheap façade of her hotel. She shouldn't have come alone, should have accepted Sam's offer, or Libby's. She'd been afraid of their judgement, and had wanted – she realised now – to indulge her fantasy of Tom appearing by her side. Had she been mad? Had he been there? She shook her head; now wasn't the time.

She scrolled her numbers and walked into the foyer of the Cler, phone clamped to her ear. Thankfully, Libby answered after two rings.

'Hi, sweetheart.'

'Libby,' Sophie coughed out the name in a dry sob.

'OK, OK, calm down, Soph,' her friend's voice switched to serious. 'I take it you've... done the deed?'

She nodded, but of course Libby couldn't see her. 'Mm,' she managed.

'OK. Well, well done. It was never going to be easy, was it, that final goodbye.'

'I know.' Her voice was almost a whisper. She pressed the button to call the lift, squeezing her eyes with her thumb and middle finger, making coloured shapes dance in her vision.

'So. You've just got to concentrate on coming home now. Are you all packed for tomorrow?'

'I think I'm going to come tonight. I can't stay. I know it's late but...'

Libby, in the practical way that she always did, took this news on board. 'Right, no problem,' she said. 'Let me sort the ticket. You just get yourself ready.'

'Thank you.'

'And...' Libby paused, as if thinking about whether to go on. 'Tom isn't *there* any more?'

'He's gone,' she said, her words coming out surprisingly loudly as she exited the lift. A woman putting her card into the reader on her room's door looked up at her briefly, then vanished into her room.

'Well, good. That's good.' Libby said, soothing.

Sophie let herself into her room, phone still at her ear. The room looked empty, stark, devoid of any personality. Her bag, her trainers, the keys on the bedside table were the only evidence it had ever been inhabited. She sat on the bed and slipped off her sandals, feeling a sense of relief as her hot feet touched the soft carpet. 'Is it?' she said.

'Now, come on.'

'I know.' Sophie wiped a tear from her eye. 'I'm just all over the place. I thought I'd be fine. I should be fine by now, right?'

Libby was silent for a moment. 'I don't think there's any *should* about these things,' she said. 'I still miss my nan. And I know it's not the same, because you kind of grow up knowing that you're going to lose your grandparents, don't you? But it was still a shock somehow. And some days I don't think about her at all. Other days...'

'You can't stop?' suggested Sophie.

'Exactly. So call this what it is – a bad day. A day of grief. And maybe it was inevitable. You were saying goodbye to... well, a lot. Him, of course. Part of your life, too.'

'A shit part,' she said, half laughing.

'No,' Libby said. 'I mean, I'm not saying that *none* of that time was shit. Finding out about Tom was… well, it was right down there. And the baby stuff. Really tough. But you had some good times, too. Maybe think about those.'

'Yes,' Sophie sniffed and wiped her nose on the back of her hand. 'You're right.'

'Damn straight, I'm right!' her best friend said, sounding more invigorated somehow. 'Come on, Soph. Get yourself sorted, get yourself home and then you can have a good cry on my shoulder or Will's, or both if you like.'

'OK,' Sophie said, obediently. 'I will. And Libby?'

'Yes?'

'Thanks. You know. For being there.'

'Pfft, what am I for, if not to pick you up and set you back on the tracks. You'd do the same for me.'

It was hard to imagine Libby ever needing that sort of reset – she was practical, successful in her role as a curator in an art gallery and seemed completely unbreakable. But she was right: Sophie would do the same for her if there were ever a need.

She ended the call and was about to start clearing her debris from around the room when her phone flashed again. Will.

'Hi,' she said, her voice steadier than when she'd tried to call him earlier.

'Hi, you,' he said, his voice warm and so welcome in her ear. 'All OK?'

'Yes. All OK. Just… emotional.'

'Of course you are.'

'I'm coming home tonight. I can't stay. Libby is sorting it.'

'Very sensible,' he said. Then, 'Does this mean I have to hoover?'

She smiled. 'Damn right it does. I expect everything ship-shape when I get home!'

'Righto, Captain!' he joked. 'But look,' his voice settled into a more serious tone. 'Just be careful, OK? Get yourself home. I'm proud of you.'

'Proud?'

'Can't have been easy, what you've done. Lots of people would have... I don't know, taken a shortcut. But you did our Tom proud.'

'Thank you. And you know... I'm sorry I didn't ask you to come with me. It seemed like something that was better alone...'

'I get it, don't worry.'

'I know, but you loved him too, I know that.'

'But I love you more,' Will said simply.

She leant her head against the wall, steadying her breathing. 'You too,' she said. 'I love you too.'

22

THE FIFTH SUMMER – 2015

She'd been looking forward to the trip all year. Every time she'd had a difficult class, or a mountain of homework to mark. At each commute on a rainy, winter's day and every time she'd woken up to realise it was Monday morning, she'd tried to think of Paris, the trip they'd booked during her six-week summer break where they'd be able to relax and discover each other again.

Now, stuffing items into her suitcase, all she could think of was her conversation with her mum. Innocuous at first, then potentially life-altering. Told over a cup of tea as if it were just another conversational titbit.

Sophie had popped over to her parents' two Saturdays ago, on her own this time, giving Tom the chance to catch up on a bit of admin and (she hoped) finally clean his side of the bedroom. It had been pleasant, driving along in the July air, knowing that all that stood between her and her summer was a week of activities – sports day, a theatre trip, presentations, and barely a meeting in sight.

'Come over for tea,' Mum had said on the phone. 'It'd be nice to see you.'

And Sophie had thought nothing of it. Why should she have?

It was a bit odd, granted, that Dad had to pop out so soon after she'd arrived, but the prospect of sitting and having a chat with Mum was a pleasant one. Only when Mum had set the porcelain mug in front of her on the pine table and sat opposite her, her face had looked different.

Instantly, Sophie had been on her guard. 'Everything OK?' she'd asked, trying to keep her tone light.

'Oh, yes,' Mum had smiled. 'Yes, all good here!' She'd given a little high laugh, different from her ordinary one, and taken a sip of tea, gasping slightly at its heat. Then she had set the mug down and looked at Sophie with a small, kind smile. 'Just thought we could have a little chat.'

Having a little chat was Mum-speak for a serious conversation.

'Oh, God. What is it, Mum? Are you sick? Is Dad sick? Is Sam OK?'

Mum had laughed. 'Sorry love. We're all fine. I didn't mean to alarm you. We're all fine. Don't worry.' She'd reached over the table and covered Sophie's hand with hers. 'I just wanted to see how things are going with Tom?'

'Oh!' Sophie had frowned. 'Well, yeah, we're good.'

'Good. Good.' Another pat of the hand. 'Any... plans?'

'Well, other than Paris, no. We thought we'd just take it easy this year. Tom's only got a couple of weeks booked because his work is—'

'No, I mean *plans.*' Mum had looked at her meaningfully.

'Sorry... I?'

'Oh, for goodness' sake, Sophie! You've been married for a

year!' Mum had shaken her head as if Sophie was being completely ridiculous. 'I'm talking about babies!'

Mum had never seemed particularly comfortable discussing what she called 'ladies' things.' Periods, ovulation, contraception, conception, babies. She'd always preferred to smother them in euphemisms so vague that sometimes Sophie wasn't 100 per cent sure what they were talking about. This was a case in point.

'Oh!' Sophie had said, and laughed. 'No. Not for a good few years, I think.' She looked at her stomach. She had put on a little weight over the term – too many generous staff members bringing in biscuits – but surely she didn't look pregnant?

'Well, you might want to get on with it a little more quickly than that.' Mum's tone was suddenly serious and something in Sophie's stomach dropped.

'What do you mean?'

Mum had explained, in a meandering way, how conceiving Sophie and Sam had been a little difficult. 'We waited almost two years for you to come along, then it was a bit easier with Sam. But then, well...' and her expression had darkened as she'd told Sophie about the brother she'd almost had, the miscarriage and the early menopause that had followed.

It must have taken a lot out of Mum to be so open with things she'd kept close to her chest all Sophie's life. It would have been worse if she hadn't told her at all, if she'd left her to find out the hard way, Sophie had tried to console herself as she drove home, her shoulders rigid with stress. But it was still a bombshell. Still, something she might have been grateful to know earlier.

'Well, when you said you were getting married so young, I thought I might not have to tell you,' Mum had said when she'd raised it. 'And if you planned to have a baby right away, well.

Perhaps you'd never have needed to know. You've got a few years yet, I'm sure.'

But did she? Mum had gone through menopause in her midthirties, suffered odd symptoms for a few years beforehand which may have been why her wanted third child had never materialised. And she'd chosen now as the time to tell Sophie that if she didn't – as her Mum rather indelicately put it – *get on with it*, she might never be a mother.

Sophie stuffed another dress roughly into her case. She hadn't even known for sure if she wanted to be a mother. She'd assumed it was something that she'd eventually feel something about one way or the other. But not yet. Not in her twenties. It hadn't seemed to matter, particularly.

Now, knowing that she might be denied the chance at all – and with a freshly received private blood test result confirming her ovarian reserve was, as the doctor had put it, 'suboptimal', she felt a craving to bear life. Where had it come from? Was it ridiculous – a weird, childish 'wanting what I can't have' impulse? Or was it something deeper, biological? Something that she'd never had to consider fully before – this strange, desperate need to be a mother?

'Thanks a lot, Mum,' she said to nobody as she zipped the case closed. Gone was her hope of a relaxed holiday. Instead, this was the holiday she'd have to sit her husband down and tell him they had to decide whether they wanted a family or not – and if they did, that the odds were against them.

The worst thing was that, in her first year of marriage, the only complaint she'd had about Tom was that he sometimes seemed a bit immature. 'I feel like his mum,' she'd raged to Sam on the phone more than once when she'd found his clothes draped over the wash-basket, or discovered he'd neglected to pick up any milk on the way home. 'He's just so used to having these things done for him!'

Sam had laughed. 'I think that might just be "being a man",' she'd joked.

'Well, not on my watch.'

'It's fine. You can train him out of it.'

It was said in jest, but suddenly the doubts seemed to flood her brain. Tom was barely ready to look after himself, let alone a child. What if he said he didn't want children? What if he wasn't ready and didn't feel the same urgency?

What if he decided to cut and run when he found out that she had this enormous defect?

Sophie sat on the bed in the fading light and looked at her passport. That girl, so innocent; her, just a few years ago. Not knowing what was ahead.

She'd looked forward to connecting with Tom on this trip. To being together, to exploring the city, to spending long, lazy mornings in bed in their hotel.

Now, all she could think of was the conversation they had to have. And whether it would break them.

23

TWO WEEKS AGO

She sat on the train, feeling such a mixture of relief and grief as it began to pull out of the station that she had to turn her face away from the other passengers, didn't want them to see her face crumple.

Luckily, the carriage was quite empty – it was late: an extra few trains had been laid on for the summer season, but it appeared uptake was low. It meant she had a little arrangement of four seats to herself, and the only other passengers in her eyeline were a man in a creased suit, scrolling on his phone, and a woman with a book who eyed her occasionally but hadn't felt prompted to ask if she was OK.

She reminded herself of the facts. She'd said goodbye to Tom, just as she'd planned. She'd put an end to this stage of her grief; an end, she hoped, to the hallucinations. She'd done it alone. Yes, she was emotional, but that was to be expected. And she was going home to Will, a man she loved fiercely and who loved her back.

It was OK. It was OK.

The train entered the tunnel and the announcement came

on, first in French then in English – safety warnings, information, the driver then telling them what the weather would be like on arrival.

She tried to still her breathing, distract herself with her phone, to close her eyes and sleep. But all she could see was the silver locket falling, falling and being engulfed by the water. And she'd thought in that moment how much Tom had always hated the water, always preferred to be above it than on it. Had never agreed to take a boat trip with her on the Seine. And she'd thought of that part of him enclosed in the silver heart that would be battered and buffeted by the water, that would be nudged by fish or other river-dwelling creatures. How, if it wasn't swept too far, the boats he'd always avoided would travel over him every day.

And she'd felt a surge of regret. A feeling that she'd somehow missed, got something wrong.

But it was the bridge, she reminded herself. The bridge where he'd first been aware of his place in the universe, where he'd felt that sense of magic and love and eternity.

She didn't believe that Tom was in those scooped-up ashes in any case. Didn't believe, if she was honest, that he was anywhere. But if he was – if there were ghosts, if there was something else waiting for us on the other side, he would be there. Not in the bottom of the Seine but somewhere else, living in a way she couldn't imagine. Free from pain and part of the universe he'd glimpsed all that time ago.

It was this thought that, finally, enabled her to close her eyes and give in to the heaviness of sleep.

24

THE FIFTH SUMMER – 2015

Sophie had planned to speak to Tom on the last night of their trip. Partly because she hadn't wanted to spoil the holiday – although in all honesty, the anxiety she felt had spoiled it a little already – partly because if it didn't go well, they wouldn't have to pretend. They could go home, have some space, work out what to do next.

But the anxiety that had been steadily building since she'd packed her case had become almost unbearable. She'd been functioning – playing the part of the Sophie she usually was. But clearly, acting wasn't her forte.

'Are you OK?' Tom had asked her more than once. And, 'Have I done something wrong?'

And she'd lied and said she was fine and tried to smile and enjoy some of their usual haunts. But her mood had affected them both and rather than being upbeat and humorous, Tom had fallen silent by her side as they'd traipsed the Latin quarter, walked the Champs-Élysées.

Now, settled in a small restaurant for an early dinner, she

could feel her secret – the question she wished she didn't have to ask – build inside her. And she was pretty sure he could too.

'For fuck's sake, Sophie,' he said at last, after she'd drained her white wine at record speed. 'Just tell me what's wrong?'

She looked at him, at his worried face, and glanced away. The quickly ingested wine made her head swim. Turning back towards him, she realised that none of her plans made sense. She'd been delaying the inevitable. 'I've got something to tell you,' she said.

'That's obvious,' he almost snapped. 'You're killing me, Soph. Just – whatever it is – tell me? Are you sick? Has something... happened? Is there someone else?'

She laughed, not sure whether it was humour or hysteria driving her. 'Oh, Tom,' she said. 'Of course there's not someone else. Have you seen how knackered I am these days? There's barely enough energy for us, let alone...' but she trailed off. His face remained serious. Her fault. 'Sorry.' She took a deep breath, fiddled with the stem of her wine glass.

And she told him. Not in the confusing, euphemism-drenched way of her mother. But clearly, precisely, biologically. Using facts and setting out her position. Trying not to give in to the wave of emotion that made her want to beg him to do this with her, to take this journey earlier with her than they might have planned. Because he had to want to. That was the whole point.

'So, not ideal,' she said, shrugging. 'And I suppose I have to ask you – do you feel ready? I mean, do you think we can do this? Do you want to?'

'Sophie, I—'

'Because you *have* to want to, Tom. Otherwise, you can wait. Maybe start again with... Look, I don't have a choice. But you... well, you've got years and years.'

'Listen, Soph—'

'And I would have told you, if I'd known. Before we'd married. Before a lot of it, really. You have to believe me. I haven't kept—'

'Soph, will you shut the fuck up and actually let me speak?' The expletive made her look. Not the word itself, but the way it was delivered – with a smile. A little amusement. Had he not understood?

His eyes were on hers. 'Yes,' he said.

'Yes what?'

He shrugged. 'Let's have a family. Now.'

'But Tom, we're only... I mean we wanted to be together first, didn't we? We wanted to explore and live our twenties, have adventures and—'

He shrugged again. 'I can't think of a much greater adventure than creating a human or two, can you?'

'Well, no...'

'Besides,' he reached his hand and grabbed hers, waited until her eyes met his and looked directly at her, seriously. 'Soph, we have our whole lives ahead of us. So we have a baby early. There are advantages. They'll be off our hands by the time we're forty-five. We can live out all our adventures then!'

'At forty-five? Isn't that a bit... well, past it?'

'Forty-five is the new thirty-five,' he said, with another playful shrug. 'I'm sure I've read that somewhere.'

She felt herself begin to smile. 'You're serious?'

'Of course. Do I want to have lots of sex? Hell, yes. And do I want to make you happy? Hell, yes,' he said, grinning. 'And do I want to have a family with you?' He paused. 'I can't think of anything that would make me happier.'

She stood then, almost knocking the glass and leant over the table to kiss him. He put his hands on her shoulders and pushed her back slightly, laughing. 'When I said we could get on with it, I didn't mean we'd try right here in the restaurant!' he joked.

A couple seated near them clearly overheard and glanced at her, half amused, half alarmed.

But she was so happy she didn't care.

'Thank you, Tom,' she said, sinking back into her seat and feeling her body let go of the tension it had held for the last fortnight. And feeling something else come over her. An excitement, an urgency, the thrill of imagining a different sort of future – one full of possibilities, hope and life.

'No, thank YOU,' he said, taking a sip of his wine. The tension had left his face too; she should have told him from the start instead of putting him through the wringer.

'What for?'

'For loving me? For wanting to bear my hundreds of children—'

'Steady on!'

'And,' he said with a smile, 'for getting my mum off my back. She's been giving me grandmother hints for months!'

25

THE SIXTH SUMMER – 2016

She zipped up the canvas pouch and added it to her suitcase. Thermometer, ovulation sticks, a little piece of rose quartz that some magazine had highlighted for its fertility-enhancing properties – she didn't believe in all that, but there was nothing wrong with being thorough.

She didn't hear Tom come up behind her, so she jumped when he slipped his arms around her. 'Finished yet?' he said.

'Just packing the baby-making stuff,' she said. 'Don't want to leave anything behind.'

He snorted. 'I'm pretty sure I'm not going to leave my dick behind, if that's what you mean.'

'Tom!' she snapped. Then calmed herself. He was only trying to make her laugh. 'No, I mean the ovulation sticks. Don't want to miss our window.'

He turned her around and shook his head, looking into her eyes. 'Soph, we are not going to miss our window. I tell you what. We'll have sex every couple of hours – surely that ought to do it!' he grinned. 'And it's pretty much a win-win situation from where I'm standing.'

She reached and pushed back a random strand of his hair. Her Tom. Supremely confident that this – the next challenge of his life – would prove as easily surmountable as all the others that had come his way. Confident that all it would take would be their anniversary weekend at a posh hotel and bam! Baby on board. After almost twelve months of trying and failing. She'd love him to be right. But it was better to be sure – to give themselves the best chance.

'Ha ha,' she said. 'As if you'd have the stamina.' She smiled.

'Anything for you, m'lady.' He doffed an imaginary cap.

'But it's important, Tom,' she said, the unease that had settled over her ever since they'd agreed that they were definitely 'trying' for a baby, spiking again. 'People do all sorts of things, they take ages to get pregnant sometimes. I just think... well, this stuff exists, why not give us the best chance?'

He chuckled. 'That's what I love about you.'

'My endless paranoia?'

'Your preparedness.'

'Doesn't sound very sexy.'

He laughed again. 'Oh, believe me, I love an organised woman.'

She allowed him to envelop her in his arms and rested her head on his chest, hearing the reassuring thrum of his heartbeat. It had only been a year. Lots of couples took longer than that to conceive. And when he held her in his arms, she felt she took on a bit of his optimism. That it would work. That things would turn out OK.

'Not boring though?' she asked, her self-doubt returning the minute he released her.

'Never boring,' he confirmed.

'Even though we're going to Paris – again.'

'Even though. Paris is our place anyway, you said that. I reckon we should go for all our anniversaries.'

'Sounds like a plan.'

'Then on our seventieth anniversary when we're both – God – ninety-odd, we'll climb up the Eiffel Tower and sling ourselves off together. A sort of romantic, low-carbon emission Thelma and Louise moment.'

'That sounds... well, bloody awful.'

'It does, doesn't it.' He smiled, still somehow pleased with himself. 'It sounded better in my head.'

In actual fact, she'd worried he might have forgotten their anniversary. His work had become busy and, more often than not, in the evenings he'd fall asleep on the sofa. *Like an old man,* she'd tell him.

She was busy too, but settling more into her role and able to plan lessons more quickly than she had in the past, meaning she suddenly had more space in which to worry.

This time she'd been the one to book Paris, despite questioning whether it was too much to go yet again.

She'd laughed with surprise when he'd come home that evening and, dropping his work bag down the side of the sofa, had suggested, 'Shall we book Paris for our anniversary after all? I need something to look forward to after this bloody project is finished!'

'Already on it,' she'd said grinning, and he'd raised an eyebrow.

'Great.' He walked over to her, wrapped his arms around her waist. 'I've got a good feeling about this,' he said. 'I honestly feel like Paris is where it might happen. You know. The baby.'

'You do?' It meant nothing, really, but the words gave her a frisson of hope all the same.

'Why not? We can relax, do all the Paris things. And just

think. One day we'll be able to tell him or her that they were conceived in the most romantic city in the world.'

'That would probably give them the ick.'

'True.' He kissed her. 'But still. This is our time, Soph. I really feel that.'

'Don't jinx it!'

He laughed, easily, confidently. 'You, Sophie Gardner, have got to drop this paranoia. You're with me now. Nothing could go wrong.'

'Well now you've really done it,' she said, grimacing. 'Tempting fate.'

'Ah, fate, do your worst. You're no match for Tom Gardner.'

26

TWO WEEKS AGO

She looked for Will in the crowds of commuters waiting close to the platform as the train drew in to St Pancras, but couldn't see him. But the minute she trudged out of the train, wheeling her little suitcase through the barrier, he was there, taking it from her and slipping an arm around her back. She leant into him, feeling some deep part of her start to relax. Because she was home.

They didn't talk much on the way to the car. Reaching it, he opened the door for her and let her slide into her seat. As he closed the door, their eyes met through the window and he gave a small, worried smile. She smiled back – a tired, but hopefully reassuring one.

'Thanks for driving,' she said.

'Knew you'd be tired.'

It was disorientating, coming back to earth, to reality. The space at her throat where the locket had been. Her job done. Had she done enough, she wondered? Had she really let him go?

Her whole body felt heavy against the car seat which she

adjusted, feeling herself sink gratefully into a more restful pose. 'Do you mind if I close my eyes for a bit?' she asked Will.

'Of course,' he said. 'It's more than an hour 'til we get home.'

She drifted into a half-sleep, lulled by the car's movement, and allowed herself to let go of full consciousness – half-dreaming, half-awake. She disappeared for a moment but came to abruptly when the car stopped at a traffic light.

She looked and saw Will watching her. 'Are you OK?' he asked.

'Yeah. Tired,' she said. She studied the side of his face as he drove, his expression fixed, his eyes looking steadfastly ahead. What had it been like for him when she was away? Had he been able to relax and have a restful weekend despite everything? Or had he worried about her, how she'd feel in Paris on her own?

'I'm glad to be back though,' she said, touching his hand where it rested on the gear stick. 'Obviously.'

His expression seemed to lighten. 'Glad to hear it!' he quipped, but she sensed that he genuinely was. She wondered what it felt like for him – trying to support her when she was mourning another man. A man she might well still be with, if things had turned out differently.

'I love you, you know.'

'I know,' he said.

It was pitch-black. The street lights burned orange into the night and although there was a lot of traffic, it wasn't enough to impede them. They moved forward at pace, and she lay her head back against the seat and watched the lights blur and merge in her vision as they streamed past. 'Sorry,' she said out of nowhere.

'What for?'

She shrugged. 'Everything.'

He put his hand briefly on her leg. 'Idiot,' he said.

She felt herself smile. 'Yup,' she agreed.

As more familiar sights and sounds came her way, she began to feel farther and farther away from her weekend in Paris. As if on some level it had been a dream. This time yesterday, she'd been sitting on a bench with Tom. Now she was on her way home, with her fiancé at her side. Two different worlds. Two different lives.

They didn't need to say anything else. To discuss the reason behind her words and his forgiveness. And she was glad. She shifted slightly and found her eyelids getting heavy. This time she didn't wake up until they were home. He opened the car door for her as if she were an invalid. They walked to the front door and he let them both in. 'Drink?' he asked.

'Straight to bed, I think.'

'OK. You go up, I'll be there in a minute,' he said, setting her suitcase down in the hallway and making his way to the kitchen. Moments later she could hear the sound of running water, the clinking of cups being put away from the dishwasher.

Back in her bedroom, she didn't bother to wash her face or even clean her teeth. She simply peeled her clothes off and pulled her familiar T-shirt over her head. Climbing under the covers, she sighed. It was time to let go now. To move forward with Will. She'd finally said goodbye.

27

NOW

She woke late the following morning to find a note from Will on her pillow.

At the office, call me if you need to.

She lay back, her head flooded with Paris and Tom; how depleted he'd been when they'd returned from Paris that last time. And how quickly things had happened afterwards.

* * *

It had been a wonderful funeral. At least according to the people who'd enthusiastically shaken her hand or moved in for a hug as she stood outside the church afterwards, stiffly taking her place next to Tom's parents and feeling a sense of unreality.

There were some traditional readings – that one about only being in the next room, and reassurances from the vicar that Tom would be in a better place. She wanted to stand and scream at the banality of it all. To ask the vicar how he *knew?* Wanted to say that it was all nonsense – that there was no better place for Tom than at her side. But she held it together, somehow, sitting primly in the black shift dress she bought for the occasion, Libby on one side of her, Sam on the other, both clutching hands and squeezing her reassuringly during the worst parts.

Sophie took to the pulpit herself, trying to stumble out some words about Tom. But she felt herself break down and in the end, her mum came and helped her back to her seat. She saw the eyes of Tom's family and friends on her as she moved, some sympathetic, others curious. They were strangers to her, and now they always would be.

Later, when they were back from the wake that followed the service and it was all over, she felt stiff, numb, emotionless.

'You're sure you're OK?' her mum asked for the zillionth time.

She turned, slightly distracted, from where she was standing in the kitchen, gazing at a kettle which had boiled two minutes previously. 'Huh?' she said.

Her mum walked over, put a hand on Sophie's shoulder. 'Me and your dad. We can stay if you want?'

She shook her head. 'I've got to... sort of get on with things,' she said, trying to sound capable and upbeat, despite the fact her voice sounded wobbly even to her. 'It's what Tom would have wanted.'

In fact, she had absolutely no idea what Tom would have wanted. But it was something you said, wasn't it? A way to give yourself permission to continue when everything in you just wanted you to lie down and give up.

Her mum nodded, brow still furrowed. 'Well, if you're sure.'

'I'm sure, Mum. Thank you.'

Mum saved some of the leftover food, packing it neatly into plastic boxes and stacking them in Sophie's near-empty fridge.

She'd helped arrange everything when even Tom's parents had seemed to take a back seat, too wracked with grief to be of any use. Dad was there too, a prop for Mum more than anything. Not sure what to do or say, but with a ready arm to wrap around her mother's back.

Sophie loved them. But she needed them to leave. The effort of holding herself together for them was becoming almost unbearable. She needed to be alone to scream and wail and throw things across the room – to release her grief, but also the anger she felt at how cruel and unfair life had been for Tom, in the end. Her privileged, unlucky boy.

The minute she waved them off, her face sporting a fixed smile, she went to the cupboard and pulled out a large black bag. Going to the fridge, she began to load the plastic boxes of food into it. Sausage rolls and mini quiches, slightly dry triangles of bread filled with smoked salmon and cheese and ham; she could barely eat as it was, she wasn't going to eat this death food. The bag soon filled up and it took another before the fridge was empty.

She felt hot, sweaty, animated. Pulling her hair into a scruffy ponytail, she looked around the room for anything else she could get rid of. Mum had tactfully disposed of the leftover wine – the one thing that might have actually been helpful – and stacked the empty bottles into the recycling. There was the service sheet from the funeral – as if his parting were part of a show and this was their souvenir. She stuffed that into the bag too. Why would she want to keep something so devastating?

Suddenly she wanted it all gone. All of it.

She grabbed another bin bag and made her way to the living room. Tom's unfinished box of soft tissues, the book he'd been reading, a stray hoodie left draped uselessly over a chair – all of them went in. Her eyes glanced at the wall – the pictures of their trips abroad: Paris, Mexico, Milan. They were too much. She pulled them from their hooks and threw them into the bag too.

By now, her hands were shaking. But she couldn't stop. She moved to the fireplace and swept every photo and condolence card into the depths of the plastic bag. Removed every trace of him from the room. Any trace of *them*. Of what they'd meant to each other.

The flat was on the second floor and taking anything to the main bins meant negotiating the stairs. She took the food bags first, letting them bump noisily down the steps after her as she descended, not caring whether she upset the neighbours.

Her shoulders were screaming, her arms ached as she went up for the final bag. The bag of Tom's things, their things, their life together. Because what was it actually for? She held in a sob as she pulled the heavy bag, some splits already appearing in the plastic where corners of frames and photos and glass shards pushed back against their confinement. She dragged it to the top of the communal, tiled steps that led to the bins at the back of the property and stepping ahead, gave it a tug. The crash of it descending three steps at once reverberated in the room. She pulled again, angry; three more steps. Then the bag began to give in to gravity. It continued down, bumping and crashing and she staggered after it, still holding the top – slightly uselessly – as it half pulled her down with it.

For a moment, she wanted to let it. Let the bag drag her down the stairs, feel the impact of each tile, each hard, cold surface as she went. Make the pain inside her real, visible; expressed in bruises and cuts on her body. But almost as soon as she had the thought, she let go of the bag, shocked at herself, and watched it make its way down to the flat space at the bottom on its own, shedding debris as it did. Then she followed it, sank down next to it, pulled to her the framed picture of Tom that was half exiting the sack.

The energy, the anger, the indignation she felt ebbed away and she clung to the picture, feeling sobs heave up through her body. She'd cut her hand, the blood wet against her palm, but it didn't matter. Because Tom was gone. Tom was gone. Tom was gone.

She hardly heard the noise of someone being buzzed into the building. Hardly felt the hands reach down for her and help her up. Didn't acknowledge the arm around her as he led her back upstairs. He dressed her cut as she lay on the bed, then returned to the stairwell and rescued all the things she'd wanted to say goodbye to but would have regretted later.

After a while, the noises stopped and her bedroom door opened. He stood there, holding a cup of tea. 'It seems stupid,' Will said, 'but I thought I'd make you tea. It's what people do, isn't it?'

She turned to him, her eyes swollen and red. 'Thank you,' she managed.

He came, sat on the edge of the mattress. Let his hand hover over her back before he pulled it away, clearly deciding against it.

She shuffled to sitting and took the tea which was far too milky, but welcome all the same. 'Sorry,' she said.

'What for?'

She shrugged. 'I don't know. Losing it, I suppose?'

'Hey,' he said. 'You're entitled to lose it. I'd be more worried if you *weren't* losing it!'

'Seriously?' it was the first time she'd come close to smiling since... well, for a long time anyway.

He coughed out a short laugh. 'Well, no. But I'd wonder

whether you were kind of losing it inside, or something,' he said. 'I mean, I'm losing it and I wasn't even married to the guy.'

'You are?'

He shrugged. 'Pretty much,' he said, clearing his throat. 'I mean, it sucks doesn't it, what happened. And he's my best mate. *Was* my best mate. I'm just glad I popped by. I wanted to check, you know. And you shouldn't be alone. Not now.'

The simple correction of tense almost set her off again.

'And I promised him I'd look out for you,' he said, roughly wiping a hand across his eyes.

'What?'

'Yeah, sorry. I don't think I was meant to tell you. But Tom made me promise. Last month – God, it's *insane* to think he was here last month – he said I'd better keep an eye on you or I'd be subject to some serious haunting.'

She snorted then, out of the blue. 'That is *very* Tom,' she said.

'Yup.'

They were both silent.

'You don't have to, you know,' she said. 'Look after me, I mean. I'm OK. I'll be OK.'

'I know,' he said. 'But...'

'But you promised.'

He nodded. 'And I guess... it would be nice to speak to someone sometimes who gets it. Who Tom was and why he was... you know.'

'Maybe. I'm just so sick of talking though, Will. Because it doesn't do anything, does it? He's gone. And no amount of talking is going to change that.' She turned her face into her pillow and shifted so that her back was to him.

Moments later he stood and left the room quietly, pulling the door into place with a small click.

28

THE SIXTH SUMMER – 2016

She watched, drying her hands at the small bathroom sink, as the tiny plastic window flooded with moisture, sending a stream of pink across the paper inside. Holding her breath, she watched the line form – the first one strong and definite, the second only a possibility, a ghost, merging from white to a splash of pink; then as soon as she thought she'd seen it, it seemed to disappear, and once the two minutes were up, she was left – as she always seemed to be – with a negative test.

Was she even ovulating? Strange, when she'd paid no attention to her period, her cycle before, it had seemed to be a reliable, predictable thing. But now she was starting to question whether everything was working and – if it was – whether it was working well; it seemed her body was refusing to play ball.

'Come back to bed!' Tom groaned from the other side of the wall.

'Just a minute!' she said, trying to keep her tone upbeat as she slipped the test into the bin and covered it with loo roll, somehow ashamed of having him know about her body's failure.

She opened the door and stiffly climbed beneath the covers, feeling his relaxed warmth against her pale skin.

He kissed the back of her neck. 'I love it when you're all cold,' he said, wrapping his legs around her.

She tried to laugh. 'Yeah,' she managed.

She could feel the heat of him, the hardness of him against her and felt her body respond. As they made love, she tried to get into the moment, but her mind kept travelling back to the wrapped test in the bin – and when, afterwards, he made a joke about 'making babies' she felt a flicker of anger and had to swallow it down. It had been a year. Surely the time to joke was over?

Just relax, she told herself. Relaxing was important too.

It was late morning by the time they left the hotel room, holding hands along the Champs-Élysées, as they had last year and the one before that. The sun beamed down, its heat radiating from the pavements; everything felt sticky and uncomfortable. But she breathed it all in, tried to lose herself in Paris as she'd always been able to.

It worked, after a fashion. She stood for a photograph at La Défense, using the enormous archway as a frame and flinging out her arms to strike a pose, then shared it on Facebook with some cheery comment about the holiday.

They sat afterwards at a cafe, sipping overpriced but deliciously cool white wine.

'Just think,' he said then. 'Next year, we could be here with a little baby carrier. Or an enormous bump.' He looked at her, his face bright.

'Stop it, Tom,' she found herself snapping.

He set his glass down then. 'Come on, Soph, why shouldn't it happen for us? The doctors said you were still fertile.'

'I know,' she admitted, her hands worrying at the stem of her wine glass. 'It's just... you read stories, don't you? About infertility.'

'Correction,' he said, sitting forward, '*you* read stories. And you're always going to find those worst-case scenarios if you look for them. Yes, it's really shitty for some people when they start on this road, but it doesn't mean it has to be for us.'

She nodded. 'It's just terrifying.'

'But it doesn't have to be,' he said, squeezing her hand.

She nodded.

'Want to talk about something else?' he suggested.

She smiled then. 'You read my mind.'

* * *

It was still dark when she woke in their bed, feeling sticky and warm and desperate for a wee. She crept again into the en suite and, feeling vaguely ridiculous, pulled another ovulation stick out of its packet, knowing exactly what Tom would say if he knew what she was doing and at what time of the morning. Only the instructions said it should be the first pee of the day – she was just trying to be thorough.

Sitting there, holding the little white stick, watching again the tiny window flood with pink-tinged moisture, she felt exhausted. She set it down on the edge of the vanity unit, flushed the loo, then stood looking at herself in the mirror as she washed her hands. Twenty-six had come from nowhere and while she knew her parents would laugh at the idea, she'd begun to feel suddenly old. People were talking about 'quarter-life crises' on YouTube and she wondered whether that was what she was feeling.

Teaching, while rewarding, had taken its toll on her health, although she'd never admit as much to Tom. She knew, if she did, he'd insist she give up work and tell her that he could support her. Which he could, she knew. But she also knew that she'd probably take him up on the offer – and then what? Who would she be then?

She'd always associated the sense of dissatisfaction with which she'd grown up with the fact that her family hadn't had money. That everything was always hard-won. That she had to strive for more to get what she wanted. That restless energy had always been channelled into her studies, then her work; now, she supposed, glancing at the stick, she was probably transferring the feeling again to the fact she wanted a baby.

Tom, conversely, always seemed happy with what he had. Never really looking forward, but able to do what she never could: stay in the moment and make the best of now. Did that come from his upbringing too, she wondered? He'd never known to yearn for things, so had never developed that sense of wanting something just out of reach all the time. Or were they just different – different needs, wants, desires?

Then her eye caught the stick and her heart pounded. There were two lines. She had to remind herself, for a moment, that this wasn't a pregnancy test, but an ovulation test. It wasn't any guarantee of a baby.

But it was a sign her body was working as it should, and that they had as good a chance as anyone of becoming parents.

Slipping the test into the bin, she left the en suite and climbed into bed, nudging Tom to wake him, then kissing him deeply. His arms wrapped around her, first lazily, then hungrily. And she felt her mood shift as she allowed herself to be gathered up with it.

But later, as he slept and she lay on the cusp of sleep, her mind buzzed with it all – replaying worries she'd had time and time again. Stories she'd read about other women. What if she couldn't have children at all? Would Tom feel the same way about her? What if she got pregnant then miscarried? What if they had to wait through months – maybe years – of uncertainty without any clear answers? She wished in some way she could fast-forward this year, move the time on so that she at least had some sort of certainty – knew whether she'd end up being a mum or being someone who never quite got there.

She was a fixer. In the past, when she'd come up against a problem, she'd dealt with it in a practical way. When she was short of money, she'd taken on extra pub shifts. When she'd worried about exams, she'd simply studied harder, completed past papers until she was sure she could succeed.

But there was no practical solution to this. No way of knowing whether they'd be the lucky ones to whom it all came easily, or whether she'd still be waiting this time next year.

Beside her, Tom snuffled in his sleep and she looked at him. Half jealous of his deep rest, half resentful. Because he never seemed to worry about anything, but that meant in some ways, she did the worrying for both of them.

29

NOW

Turning over in bed, Sophie looked at the sun through the gap in the curtains. Outside, she knew, people were carrying on with their lives; going to work, the supermarket, getting some petrol, cleaning. But she wasn't ready, yet, to join them.

Her mind kept flashing back to the bridge. To the words that Tom (her mind?) had spoken.

She wished she'd kept more of him, more mementoes. But when she'd been clearing the flat after the sale, she'd somehow wanted rid of it all – everything had been too painful back then.

* * *

Will came to help her clear; methodically encouraging her to sort Tom's things and stopping her from flinging it all away.

'What do you want to do with this?' he asked, holding up Tom's rugby shirt.

'Keep,' she said, nodding towards a rather overflowing cardboard box. Then, 'No, get rid of it.'

'You sure?'

'Yeah,' she sighed. 'I mean, it's not him, is it?' She felt herself get tearful again but choked her emotions back. They only had today to finish the job before the cleaners she'd booked arrived, and she didn't have time to break down. 'Thanks for helping me with this, by the way. I would have been hopeless.'

'It's OK,' he said. 'Any time.'

She nodded. 'You too, you know,' she said. 'If you ever need help.'

He smiled. 'Thanks. Although I don't think you'd want to help me clean out my flat. It's not the tidiest of places. And, well, it's hardly the standard of living you've been used to.'

She gave a small laugh. 'I'm sure it's great.'

He smiled. Tom had often joked about Will's flat, although she'd never been. 'Going back to your Harry Potter room, mate?' he'd ask. Or he'd make jokes about the possibility of Will letting out some of his space. 'You'll rattle around in that enormous place on your own!'

Will, she knew, came from a similar situation to her. 'Ordinary', as she would call it. 'Impoverished', maybe, through Tom's eyes. Yes, he'd made it to Cambridge, made friends with people like Tom, but had worked harder, taken less for granted. Now he had some high-tech, software-related job that she had no idea about, but still refused to move out of his tiny flat where the rent was affordable. 'I'm saving up for a deposit,' he'd often tell them. 'Have to save as much as I can.'

'I'm hardly used to the high life,' she told him now. 'You know I grew up in a Victorian terrace in Biggleswade? Tom used to joke he could fit my entire living space into one of their bathrooms.' She smiled sadly, the ache inside her intensifying as the memories came to the fore again.

'So you're a normal person?'

'Yes, or from Tom's point of view, "impoverished",' she said, putting on a posh accent for the last word. Will laughed, but she suddenly felt wretched. Tom wasn't here to defend himself; it didn't seem right. 'Sorry,' she added, to nobody.

They were silent for a moment. 'You know, I think it's OK. To joke about him,' Will ventured. 'I was going to say *it would be what he'd want* but that sounds really pathetic. But you know what I mean? Tom was a real person and he liked a joke. I like to think he'd be laughing along with us.'

She nodded. 'It's going to take time, I think, to remember him like that.'

'I know.'

'It's hard to know how to *be*,' she said.

'I get it, completely. I mean, I don't want to forget him, but talking about him is... it feels weird.'

'Yeah,' she said sadly, clearing the last of Tom's desk drawers.

'What will you do?' he asked then.

'What do you mean?'

'Well, I know you're going, like, home to your parents' for a bit. But after? Have you thought about it?'

She shook her head. Because it had been hard enough to imagine a future when she'd had Tom – optimistic, resilient, unlucky Tom – by her side. And when she looked into the future now, she saw nothing at all.

* * *

Sophie forced herself to fling back the duvet, step out onto the soft pile carpet and make her way to the shower. It was a time for new beginnings.

30

THE SIXTH SUMMER – 2016

'Come on,' he said. 'Just a sip.' He held out the glass, bubbles running up the golden liquid inside. Her mouth watered and for a moment she was tempted. Then she felt anger course through her veins, feeling a little like she'd been transported back to her teens, when friends had tried to ply her with cheap cider at the park. 'Tom! No!'

'It's not like you're actually pregnant!' he said, holding out a glass.

She gave him a look that clearly communicated how that particular reassurance had made her feel. 'Thanks for reminding me,' she said coldly. 'It's not like I'm thinking about that fact every single day.'

'I'm sorry,' he said, so deflated that she felt guilty. 'I didn't mean...'

'You never do,' she said snappily.

'Oh, come on. We're on holiday. I'm just trying to lighten the mood.' He sat back in his chair, arms crossed.

'Yes, well, maybe some of us find it harder to switch off from real life than others! I read that article, didn't I, saying it's better to avoid drink altogether. And I'm doing everything I can to make this work for us. I just don't feel as if we're on the same page.'

'Of course we are!' he said, his cheeks reddening slightly. 'How can you say that, Soph? You know I want a baby just as much as you do.'

A man sitting at the next table lifted his eyes from his bowl of mussels and looked at them for a moment.

'I *do*,' Tom insisted more quietly, shifting forward. 'I just don't think we should put our lives on hold for it, that's all. And you know, maybe if we stop thinking about it all the time, we'll be more likely to...'

'I can't stop thinking about it. That's the problem.'

'Would it really hurt to have a sip of wine? Take a break from it? Look, we could forget about it all this month if you like. It's not like we're anywhere near biological clock territory, even with the menopause thing. What's one month?'

He just didn't get it. She opened her mouth to say something sharp, but then took in his earnest expression. 'I know.' She reached for his hand then. 'I just... I don't want to do anything to jeopardise...'

'I just think, you know... You could relax a bit more about it.'

She stiffened, grabbing back her hand. 'Seriously? You're telling me to relax?'

He almost shrank from her. 'Sorry, sorry.' He held both his palms up in a gesture of defeat. 'I just meant, we're on holiday and...'

'Well, I can't relax! Never could. So I suppose now you're going to tell me it's all my own fault that I'm fucking barren.'

He glanced over at the man, whose head was now pointedly

turned towards the window, then back at Sophie. 'Come on, Soph. You know I don't think that.'

She felt herself soften a little, leant forward and touched his arm lightly. 'I know,' she said gently. 'I know what you're trying to say. I really do. And I get it. I'm sorry that I'm such a...'

'Bitch?' he suggested.

'Mess.'

'Sorry.'

She smiled then. Sighing deeply, she let her shoulders sink against the back of her chair. 'No, I'm sorry,' she said. 'I just don't seem to be able to switch off from it all.'

'I know.'

'I just wish... I wanted us to...' she trailed off. He knew all of it already, of course.

He reached for her hand and squeezed it. 'Want to know what I think?'

'Yes,' she said, rather cautiously, 'as long as you don't say something about relaxing more.'

'Noted,' he grinned. He looked at her, his expression loving. 'I think, Sophie Gardner, that you've had to work hard for everything you've got...'

'I can't help—'

'No! No, it's a good thing. Well, not good. Admirable though,' he said hastily. 'But you've kind of equated succeeding – getting what you want – with hard work.'

She nodded, sensing where this was going.

'But this shouldn't be hard work,' he said sadly. 'There's no reason why it should be. It should be... joyful.'

'Joyful? Seriously?' she cocked an eyebrow.

'Well, natural then.'

This was also a bad choice of word. 'If someone tells me one more time that it's natural, that we have to be patient, or to frickin' RELAX, I am going to smash something!' she'd told him a couple of months ago after going out with friends.

She sighed deeply, deciding not to pick him up on it this time. 'I get it,' she said. 'But at the same time, I don't want to do anything that might... well, hinder our chances.'

'Even drinking a couple of sips of champers?'

She shrugged. 'Well, yeah.'

He looked at her, then something seemed to change in his eyes. 'OK,' he said, setting his own glass down. 'OK, then I won't either.'

Finally, she felt herself smile. 'Thank you,' she said. 'It'll be worth it in the end. And look, for what it's worth, I *will* try to relax.'

'Good,' he told her. 'Because seriously, Sophie, we have all the time in the world.'

And in that moment, it really felt true. But then the worries flooded back, pushing her good humour aside. The stories and stories and stories online of women who'd never made it, others who'd fallen pregnant at the drop of a hat. The fact that it all seemed out of their hands. The helplessness she felt; the fear.

She tried as hard as she could to keep it inside, this rising anger that seemed to engulf her, that stopped her feeling like herself. That made her resent Tom for not being miserable enough, when she was clearly miserable enough for the both of them.

They left the restaurant and began the walk back and she wished for a moment that she'd had the champagne. That she'd grabbed the flute and chugged the whole lot, and allowed herself to escape on a wave of bubbles and alcohol. Then they'd be stumbling back, laughing; instead, they were more or less silent, watching happy couples stream past them as if they were the only ones swimming, defeatedly, downstream against a tide of joy.

Then, 'Bridge?' he said, glancing at his watch.

'What?'

'It's nearly midnight,' he flashed his watch at her as if for proof. 'I thought we could...'

'Seriously?'

He looked hurt. 'Why not?'

'Tom, I'm exhausted. I'm meant to be looking after myself. I need to get to bed.'

'OK.' His tone was flat.

But she couldn't leave it. 'What?'

'What do you mean?'

'Oh, come on. You're sulking. Does it really mean so much to you? A fucking bridge?'

'Yes. It does, actually,' he said. 'And I thought it meant something to you too.'

Something turned over inside her. 'It did once.'

'But not any more?' He stopped, looked at her. A man in a black hat walking too close stumbled and nearly crashed into them, then carried on, muttering under his breath.

'Tom. Seriously? Magic? Possibility? You can't tell me that you still believe all that crap,' she said. Hating herself, but feeling unable to stop.

He dropped her hand. 'It's not crap. Well, maybe it is. But I thought...'

'If the last few months have taught me anything, it's that there's no magic, no possibility. There's fucking science and a bit of luck and that's about it.'

'Right.' His tone was final, cutting her off. 'Let's go to the hotel then.'

'Oh look, Tom, ignore me. I...'

'It's fine.'

She'd said nasty things to him sometimes, in arguments. She'd been mean, and petty, and done all the things that couples do when they bicker. She'd even, once, smashed his favourite mug during a blazing row. Things she felt ashamed about.

But this, she realised, hurrying by his side, was the first time she'd ever really hurt him.

31

NOW

She felt better after the shower. Cleansed of Paris; properly back in her own life again. Slipping on a bathrobe, she made her way to the kitchen and put on the kettle. The flat was tidy – Will had clearly gone to quite a bit of effort to make things nice when she'd been away. She was reminded of the moment after they'd finished the flat clearance; how it had been devastating but cleansing all at once.

* * *

'It looks so... empty,' she told him.

'Well, that was kind of the idea,' he pointed out.

She smiled, 'I know, but still...'

'I know.'

'He's properly gone.'

Will nodded. He opened his mouth then closed it again and Sophie was glad. There was nothing he could have said to make it better – meaningless words about Tom still being there in their hearts – the kind of thing people said at funerals or on TV.

Tom's parents had turned up to fill the car with some of his old possessions. While they hadn't been unkind to Sophie in any way, they'd been cold, purposeful. Sophie had seen Will's face crease with sympathy as she'd helped them carry boxes to the car.

'They hated me selling the flat,' she told him later. 'I think they felt like it was theirs, because they'd invested the deposit. But I tried to offer it back to them. They didn't want it, said Tom would have wanted me to have it.'

'No accounting for people,' Will said. 'You'd think they'd be grateful to you.'

She nodded, although she didn't need their gratefulness. What she didn't understand was how two people with so little apparent warmth had produced someone as open and loving as Tom had been. They'd been there for him throughout, of course, but in a monetary way – the best doctors, the best care, the best team. 'It's how they show their love,' Tom had said. But it had been Sophie who'd held his hand, who'd tried to give him hope when his was failing. Who'd tried to help him live in the face of it all.

The minute Tom had died, she'd felt as if she'd been expelled from his family. They'd seemed resentful that he'd left the flat to her – and that she was selling it. But it was too much to keep on her own. Besides, she hadn't wanted to; it was imbued with both happy and painful memories, both of which were almost too much to bear.

Her own parents had been different. Supportive. Had come over with food and hugs and words designed to help her heal. But she'd felt herself pushing them away. 'You never wanted me to marry him, anyway!' she'd snapped to her mum one day through her grief, and had watched her mother's face fall.

'Of course we did,' her mum had said.

It was easier to be angry, she realised, than sad. More powerful. Less diminishing. She knew she'd hurt her parents by pulling away, but she'd felt almost frightened of being comforted, at first; if she'd surrendered fully to grief she might never have resurfaced.

It was different with Will. Maybe because he was the one person whom she felt shared her grief, a little at least. He'd lost Tom too – his best friend through university and beyond. And because Tom had charged him with looking after her, helping her with the flat. And so, in accepting his friendship, she felt as if she was at least doing what Tom would have wanted.

She was staying in the flat for the last time tonight, before a brief sojourn at her parents' place, after which she wasn't quite sure what she'd do. The flat would sell; the estate agent had barely been able to contain his excitement when she'd listed it – close to the city centre, in good nick, and she wasn't fussed about price – but she wasn't sure what her next steps would be. In the five months since Tom had died, people had tried to reassure her: 'You're young! You've got time to make a completely new start.' They meant well, of course they did. But she couldn't feel it – not now; maybe not ever.

'Want to grab a bite?' Will asked her, after they'd stood in silence looking at the flat as the light had faded slightly and shadows had begun to form.

She nodded and they pulled the door closed behind them. 'Bye, Tom,' she said softly, as she often did these days when stepping out. Will patted her back briefly. 'Bye, mate,' he said too, as they made their way down the stairs and into the well-lit street.

* * *

The kettle clicked off and Sophie spooned a heap of instant coffee grounds into her mug, watching as they melted to rich black liquid once she covered them in boiling water. The aroma brought her back to the present; here she was. Back home. And somehow finally ready to move forward.

32

THE SEVENTH SUMMER – 2017

'This is lovely,' Tom said, sticking his fork into his coq au vin and smiling. 'What's yours like?'

She pushed her salmon around a little with her fork. 'It's OK.'

They ate in silence for a minute, the chatter of the restaurant seeming to highlight their own lack of communication. Then Tom laid his fork against his plate. 'Have I upset you or something?' he said, a hint of annoyance in his voice.

'No,' she said. 'Sorry. I'm just...'

'Just what? We're in Paris! Come on – I even endured the queues for Notre-Dame with you – and you know how I hate queuing.'

She smiled a little, thinking of the times he'd tried to persuade her not to join the crowds trying to make their way into the enormous cathedral with its gothic buttresses and leering gargoyles. She'd managed to make him visit it properly for the first time a couple of years ago – and he'd sulked in the queue like a child. Other times, she'd sent him on his way – told him to get a beer and that she'd catch up with him. And she'd spent hours wondering at the stonework, the art, the enormity and beauty of the centuries-old building.

Today he'd suggested Notre-Dame himself, to her surprise. And stood next to her in the queue with barely a whimper.

She felt a stab of guilt – he was working so hard to make her happy. But her mind seemed fixed on herself; her body, the baby she should be pregnant with by now. It didn't seem fair that she should carry the weight of their failure on her own, when he seemed lighter, freer.

'I'm sorry, it's all this baby stuff,' she admitted. 'I thought I'd got a handle on it. It's just... when we're here it makes me realise how long it's been.'

'I know it is.' He reached for her hand. 'But I guess as they say... It'll happen when it happens.'

She felt a spike of annoyance, snatching her hand way. 'But that's just it! What if it never happens? What if we just can't?' Tears pooled hotly in her eyes.

He shrugged, sighed. 'It will. I'm sure it will. And look, we've got years. We should be making the most of...'

'How can I make the most of anything? I just feel like I'm in this... this horrible waiting room and that other people keep jumping the queue. Do you know Sarah from work's pregnant now?'

'Yes. And I'm very happy for her, but it doesn't make any difference to us. It's not a race, Soph.'

'I get that it's not a race,' she said. A couple at the next table looked over and she lowered her voice. 'But it's been ages, Tom. Aren't you worried?'

He shook his head, reaching for her hand. She moved hers away. 'I'm not worried,' he said. 'Come on, Sophie. This is us! We'll be OK.'

She looked at him.

He sighed. 'OK, I'm a little worried. Sometimes. But we can't let it break us.'

She softened then. 'I know. And I know I've been unbearable recently. I just don't seem to be able to think of anything else again, suddenly.'

'I do understand.' This time when he reached his hand over the table, she let him hold hers.

'And I'm tired. I'm so tired, Tom.'

He nodded. 'Me too,' he admitted. 'I just feel... exhausted all the time. Do you think it's just getting older or something?'

She smiled then. 'Ha. Maybe. More likely stress. We've both been working so hard. And all this baby stuff.' She squeezed his hand lightly. 'I'm sorry. It's probably my fault.'

'Soph, not everything is your fault,' he said, taking a sip of wine. 'You're probably right. It's probably stress.'

They sat in silence for a minute. Then he picked up his fork. 'You just wait,' he said. 'This time next year, maybe everything will have changed. We'll be on the up. This is a blip.'

She nodded. 'Yeah, I hope so.'

They smiled at each other. She wondered, suddenly, what she was doing. Here she was, in Paris. With Tom. 'Pass me your glass,' she said.

'What?'

'Just give it.'

He gave it to her, cautiously, as if wondering whether it would soon be thrown in his face. Instead, she lifted it to her lips and drank the contents in three greedy gulps, smacking her lips.

Tom laughed. 'Well, that was unexpected.'

'But much needed.' She wiped her mouth. 'Oh, God. That felt good.'

'Shall I get another?' he looked at her, eyebrow cocked – and there he was again. Her Tom.

'You know what,' she said. 'Why the fuck not?'

They had planned to go to a show. But instead, two hours later, tickets forgotten and laughing as if they were students again and comparatively carefree, they fell into a taxi. 'My tolerance must be nothing these days,' she said. 'Two glasses and I can barely walk!'

'She isn't going to vomit is she, monsieur?' asked the driver cautiously.

'No. She's OK,' Tom smiled. 'Hotel?' he said turning to her.

'You know what?' she said, sitting up and feeling more energised than she had in an age. 'Let's go to the bridge.'

And there it was again, the easy smile she hadn't known she was missing.

'Great idea,' he said. 'And perfect timing,' he added, as somewhere in the Parisian streets a church bell began its midnight chime.

33

NOW

Sophie took her hot coffee to the table and set it down, slipping into one of their cushioned chairs and pulling Will's discarded newspaper towards her. Trying to keep hold of the feeling of release she'd experienced just now.

When she'd moved into her own place after Tom's death, she'd hoped that would help to free her. And it had in so many ways. But perhaps recent events – the hallucinations, Tom's ghost – had shown her she should have taken more time to grieve back then, instead of running away.

* * *

After the move, she fell into a dull routine. Her alarm woke her each morning and she reached out a hand to grab her phone and turn it off. Sitting up in bed, she sighed with tiredness before flinging off the covers and standing up, stretching her aching body. Somewhere, someone else was already up, playing music at 6.30 a.m.; her flat's thin walls were not effective at blocking out noise.

She tiredly took herself through her routine. Showering, dressing, eating a light breakfast, checking her lesson plans for the day. She took a moment to scroll through her messages too – one from Libby: a gif of a kitten with the words 'Not Monday!' emblazoned on the front. She liked the message and sent a gif back in response.

It was her second term at South Hill Academy and she was still finding her feet. It was easier now she'd found the flat, on the outskirts of the city but close enough that she still had a Cambridge postcode. Commuting from her parents' had been difficult, and she'd begun to feel a little odd living with them. When the flat she'd shared with Tom had sold, she'd begun to look for rentals and found this small, modern bedsit – worlds away from the flat she'd shared with Tom – and signed up for it almost immediately.

'It's time to get things back on track,' she'd told her mum, who'd nodded.

'Just... go easy on yourself,' Mum had said, pushing a strand of hair back behind Sophie's ear. 'It's early days, love.'

She'd smiled and enveloped her mum in a hug. If the situation were reversed, she wasn't sure she'd have had the patience that her parents had had. She'd fallen apart once she'd moved back home, staying in bed for days. Then she'd started going out, getting drunk, falling out of taxis and losing her key at 2 a.m. She'd argued, railed, blamed them, and they'd taken it with as much grace and love as possible. And eventually, the storm had blown itself out. The grief had settled in her stomach, a bowling ball of sadness and regret she managed to live around. Gradually, slowly, she'd come back to life.

Sam had been there too, sporadically. Her own life was just starting – she was out enjoying herself, she had a new boyfriend. Things were looking good. And Sophie was genuinely happy for her sister. But she struggled to spend proper time with her, her sister's carefree happiness contrasting so much with her grief that it meant both of them struggled to find common ground.

Libby had helped her move her few boxes of possessions into her new space. 'It's nice!' she'd said, her tone full of false positivity.

'I know it's a bit... well, bland.'

'But that's OK! Bland is good. A blank canvas for you to inject your personality into.'

'Maybe.' Sophie hadn't said, but she liked the simplicity of it. Didn't need anything beyond the essentials.

'And look, it doesn't have to be forever. If you want something more... central?'

'Just keeping things simple. Don't want to stretch the budget too much.'

'Didn't you literally just sell a flat?'

'A mortgaged flat.'

'I know, but you inherited the equity, didn't you? Don't you have about £200k stashed away somewhere?'

She'd nodded.

'And you're not using it because...'

'It's Tom's,' she'd said.

'You want to save it for something... permanent?'

She'd shrugged. 'I guess.'

Libby had looked at her, worry etched on her face. 'You know Tom would have wanted you to use the money, right? I mean, he loved you so... I have to say, if it were me, I'd be living like a queen!' Libby had grinned and stretched her arms expansively as if to indicate the extent of her largesse. Then, noting Sophie's expression, brought them down slowly. 'Sorry.'

'Don't be!' Sophie had said. 'I probably should. Tom definitely would want me to. But a lot of it's the life insurance. It just seems... weird.'

'OK.'

'And I want to give some of it back. To his parents. The deposit they gave him. I'm just not sure how...'

'Would they even want it?'

Sophie had shrugged. 'Maybe not. But it feels like the right thing. It's just easier to put it away for now... try not to think about it.'

'You, my friend, are a unique individual, you know that?'

'So I'm told.'

'Guess that's why we all love you so much.'

'That and my wealth,' Sophie had joked weakly.

'Well, yes. Of course. Most of us are hoping for a handout at some point.'

Sophie had found herself laughing. 'Thank you,' she'd said.

'What?'

'For being an idiot. Everyone's so gloomy around me. And I know, I get that I'm hardly the best company right now. But thanks for ignoring all that and being yourself. It's... nice. Kind of reminds me that there's a world out there.'

'Even if that world is filled with wise-cracking idiots?'

'Precisely.'

* * *

Sophie sipped the last of her coffee and set down her cup. Back then she'd wondered if she'd ever move past the grief. But here she was, doing the impossible. Moving on.

34

THE EIGHTH SUMMER – 2018

A fortnight before they were due to go to Paris, she woke in the night to find herself alone. Tom's side of the bed was cold; he'd clearly not been there for a while. Then she heard a noise from the living room – a brief, strange cry of pain.

Brow furrowed, she slipped out from under the covers and made her way to where Tom lay on the sofa, his arms wrapped around his middle. The TV was on, quietly flickering in the corner – an old film she recognised from years ago.

'What's up?' she asked.

'It's nothing,' he said. 'Go back to bed.'

'It doesn't look like nothing.'

'Just one of my stomach aches. It'll pass. Probably ate too much at dinner.'

She thought back to their simple meal of mild curry and rice. He'd barely touched it, she remembered.

'Are they getting worse?'

He shrugged. 'Hard to say.'

He'd mentioned the stomach aches before. Had been taking antacids after meals for a while to stave off indigestion. The GP had mentioned stress when he'd finally made an appointment. And it made sense – he'd been working doubly hard on a new project at work, and she knew her own stress about their inability to conceive had made things more difficult between them.

'Well, you need to go back to the doctor,' she said decisively. 'If this goes on, we'll book something when we get back from Paris.'

She saw something change in his face – a flicker of embarrassment running across it. 'Actually,' he said, 'I've got an appointment tomorrow. I was going to tell you.'

'Oh good,' she said.

'It's with a specialist. Mum booked it up.'

'A specialist?'

He shrugged. 'It's just Mum overreacting as normal. You know what she's like. Bypass the GP and go straight to the top.'

She sat on the edge of the sofa, rubbed a hand across his back. 'You don't think there's anything *really* wrong, do you?' It was the first time it had occurred to her. He'd started having the pains a few months ago, sometimes in his stomach, other times in his back. Had been a little tired.

When the GP had said it was stress, she'd felt guilty, and then angry because of the guilt. It was hardly her fault that he was picking up on the stress she felt at their possible infertility. How did he think *she* felt when it was her body refusing to comply?

He'd gone silent on the matter afterwards, popping chalky tablets into his mouth but never talking about pain. She'd assumed it was clearing up.

'I don't know,' he said now. 'Maybe. I've been googling.'

'Oh, come on, Tom. Dr Google always paints the worst-case scenario.'

'I know. But I think it might be gallstones, or something.'

'Not even sure what they are.'

He glanced at her, amused despite his pain. 'You and me both. At least until I started research. Now I'm quite the expert! Anyway, the long and short of it is, if the doc agrees, I might need to have surgery.'

'Before the holiday?' She felt instantly selfish to have said it out loud.

'Not necessarily.' He grimaced as another spasm ran through him. 'I'm guessing he might give me some seriously heavy painkillers though.'

'Sorry, the holiday – it doesn't matter, really. I don't know why I said it.'

'It's OK. We need it after the year we've had, I get it.'

She rubbed his back a little, feeling her eyelids get heavy. 'Do you want me to get you anything?' she asked. 'Paracetamol? Hot water bottle?'

'Nah. I'm fine. It'll be gone in a minute probably.'

'OK.'

'Look, go back to bed, Soph. It's OK. And you need your sleep.'

'If you're sure?'

'Course,' he said with a slightly pained smile. 'Go on. I'll be fine.'

35

NOW

It had been Sam who'd finally forced her to see that what she'd been doing wasn't living, but existing. To start to accept that she deserved more again. Sophie pushed the newspaper aside and went to the sink with her coffee cup, leaning on the counter to take in the view of their small garden, remembering.

* * *

Two months into her tenancy, one Sunday morning she heard the buzz of the intercom. Her first instinct was to ignore it – it would only be someone trying to sell something, or a delivery she'd forgotten she'd arranged. They could leave whatever it was downstairs.

But then someone – perhaps a disgruntled neighbour – buzzed the person in and whoever it was knocked directly on her front door.

Sophie looked at the clock. It was only 9 a.m. on a Saturday. Probably a delivery, she thought, pulling on her dressing gown and staggering to the door. Opening it into the fresh spring morning she found, rather than a delivery person clutching something from an online retailer, her sister standing there, under-eyes smudged with mascara, wearing a dress that looked like something you'd wear to a nightclub. Which she almost certainly had.

'Sam!' she said, surprised, wrapping her robe more tightly around her.

'Sorry – did I wake you up?'

'Not really. I was just being lazy. Come in.'

She led her sister to the sofa and Sam collapsed onto it gratefully. 'I'm bloody knackered,' she declared.

'Coffee?'

'You know it.'

Sophie switched on the kettle in the kitchen then made it back to the living room as it boiled. 'So?' she said.

'What?'

'What are you doing here? Not that you're unwelcome. It's great to see you. But I get the sneaking suspicion this isn't a planned visit,' she said, looking pointedly at her sister's attire.

'Whatever gives you that impression?'

Sophie shook her head. 'Just a hunch.'

The two sisters grinned at each other then. 'Ah, yeah. You got me,' Sam said. 'I was at a thing last night.'

'In Cambridge?'

'In London. And I met someone – before I knew it, I was on the train to Cambridge – it only takes an hour, you know? He lives here. Ian. The bloke, I mean.'

'So let me get this straight,' Sophie said, standing up as she heard the kettle switch itself off. 'You've run out of men in London so now you're moving on to the next city?'

'Sophie!' Sam lunged at her, ostensibly to give her a slap.

She laughed, running to the kitchen before Sam could reach her.

Coming back with coffee, she sat down opposite the baby sister who was no longer a baby but a fully-fledged woman in her twenties with a proper job and her own bedsit in London. 'So,' she said. 'Tell me about him.'

Later, once Sam had showered and borrowed some clothes more appropriate for daywear, they walked out in the early spring sunshine, making their way to The Anchor for a pub lunch. 'I can't believe you still go there,' Sam said. 'Doesn't it feel weird, after you worked there for all that time during uni?'

Sophie shook her head. 'No one recognises me; think most of the staff have changed. Besides, they do the best meals.'

An hour later, they were stuffed. Sitting opposite each other at a mahogany table, sipping after-lunch coffee and laughing about something their mum had said about their dad. 'Honestly, every time she rings now, she's relaying this stuff about his health,' Sam said. 'Last week we had a twenty-minute conversation about piles and I'm not kidding, I could not sleep for about two nights!'

'Gross!' Sophie laughed. 'She tends to talk to me about other stuff, luckily.'

'I think she shies away from health topics where you're concerned.'

This brought them both back down to earth. 'Sorry,' Sam said.

'Don't be silly. It is what it is,' Sophie said, acknowledging the awkward sadness that had muffled them both. 'It gets easier, apparently.'

'Didn't mean to put my foot in it.'

'Or Dad's arse?'

'Ha. Yeah, the ultimate conversation stopper.'

Sam wiped her eyes, still giggling a little. 'But seriously, Soph. How are you getting on?'

'Yeah, not bad. Work's going OK and the flat is... well, it's fine for now.'

'Yes, but,' Sam leant forward on the table, her face suddenly serious, 'how's it *really* going? Are you doing anything, outside work? Are you getting out?'

'Now you do sound like Mum,' Sophie deflected.

'Come on, if you can't talk to me, who can you talk to? I know it's hard on the phone, but I thought...'

'Hang on, is this an intervention?'

Sam laughed. 'No. I'm just worried...'

'Are you telling me you slept with a guy who lived in Cambridge just so you could come over and interrogate me?'

'Ha. He should be so lucky. No, but I thought while I was here I could just... ask.'

'I'm OK,' Sophie said firmly. 'Now do you want another coffee?'

'But you're not really... going out or doing anything besides work?'

'It's a difficult job,' she said. 'It takes up so much of my time.'

'Sophieeee,' Sam wheedled.

'What? It does. And I'm OK. I'm OK doing it and living in my flat. Everything's fine.'

'Sophieeee.'

'What?' she said again, feeling herself get hot.

'I guess I just want you to be more than fine, you know? Like, you're still young. You're right at the start of things. I just hope... you know. Don't forget to live, is all.'

'I am living.'

Sam looked at her, a sidelong glance that penetrated through all the bullshit.

'OK. OK. I get it. I have no social life. I've locked myself away in a shitty flat like... like...'

'Miss Havisham?'

'Sam! No. She's a complete recluse. I can't see her delivering the GCSE curriculum to a bunch of Year 11s.'

'Fair point. OK, so Boo Radley.'

'Boo Radley?'

'The Grinch?' Sam suggested. 'Look, I'm not like you. I don't know many literary characters. But I do know that I'm worried about you, sis, that's all.'

Sophie looked at her sister, the genuine concern etched on her face, and softened. 'OK,' she said. 'OK, you got me. I'm a recluse, sort of. I don't do anything.'

Sam grimaced sympathetically.

'I just... I'm just sad, Sam,' she said, her mouth wobbling. 'I know people think it's easy to move on. That I'm young, that what happened is just a tiny part of my story. But I don't know how to move on and I'm not sure I want to.'

'Oh, Soph.'

'It's OK. I'm happy. Well, not happy. But I'm fine. I'm getting up, I'm doing the things. I'm functioning. And I suppose it just has to be enough.'

'Enough for now?' Sam suggested.

'Maybe enough forever,' she admitted. 'I can't see...' Tears pooled in her eyes and she wiped them away angrily. 'I can't see a way forward beyond this. I... it doesn't feel like there's anything else for me. But it's OK. You don't need to worry. I'm not... desperate. I'm OK doing what I'm doing and just getting on with it.'

'But you deserve so much more...'

'Do I though? Maybe I had my luck already. Maybe that was the good bit, and the rest of my life is going to be, well, just OK.'

'No.' Sam said firmly. 'I'm not going to let it.'

'You don't understand! You...'

'Yes, I do.'

'How can you, I...'

'Look.' Sam grabbed her hand, more firmly than before, and Sophie looked down at it, silenced suddenly. 'When you were going through all that with Tom. All the treatment, all the worry. Something happened to me. I never told you because – well, you had enough going on. But it changed me, you know.'

'What?'

'I can't...' Sam suddenly looked different, vulnerable. 'Look, I was going out a lot. Partying. Making the most of my freedom after moving out. You know? And one night, well, someone I thought was a friend... he... well, he walked me home and he...' She looked at her sister, imploring her to not force her to say it.

'He raped you?'

Sam's tears spilled hotly down her cheeks. She nodded. Once. 'And I've dealt with it. I reported it. Had counselling. I don't want to talk about it any more. Not now, anyway.'

'But, Sam...'

'Please, Soph. I'm just telling you that afterwards, I was changed... I didn't want to go anywhere, do anything. But my therapist, and Katy – you know, the girl I lived with in third year – they kind of helped me to take my life back. Because I couldn't let him steal that. My future. My chances. And it's not always easy, but look at me! I'm here. I'm doing it. Dating. Going out. And it's better. It's better than when I shut myself away and wanted to protect myself from it all.'

'Oh, darling.' Sophie put another hand over her sister's, almost as if they were playing a game. 'I'm so sorry.'

Sam shook her head. 'Thanks. But look. Let's stop. It's better to keep it in the past.' She took a big, shuddering breath. 'I'm just trying to tell you that you can do it. If I can do it, you can. And that you think you don't need people, but you do. We all do.'

Sophie nodded, not sure what to say.

'Soph,' Sam looked at her earnestly, 'you just can't hide from it – life. It happens anyway. Whether you're locked in a flat or out there trying your best to find something that makes you happy. It goes by and it happens. And you can't protect yourself from it. Not really.'

'OK,' she said softly.

'So I want you to promise me that you'll try. Just... the next time a chance comes your way to do something – go out, meet friends, anything... just try? For me.'

Sophie nodded. 'OK.'

'Now,' Sam said, taking her hands back and wiping her eyes. 'Didn't you just offer me another coffee?'

* * *

On instinct, Sophie picked up her phone and sent her sister a message.

SOPHIE

> Thanks. For everything. You've always been there for me, sis.

The reply came almost instantly.

SAM

> Don't be silly. What are sisters for?

36

THE EIGHTH SUMMER – 2018

'I still don't know why we couldn't just get the results over the phone,' Tom complained as they sat in the comfortable leather chairs of his private consultant.

'Because it's important,' she said. 'What if there's something wrong?'

He laughed. 'If I do have gallstones, it's hardly an emergency,' he winced slightly, his hand hovering near his abdomen. 'I'd still want to have the holiday before they whip out my gallbladder or whatever.'

She grimaced, imagining the surgery. 'Don't do that,' she said.

'What?'

'Joke about it. I don't like the thought of it.'

'Still, it could have waited until we'd got back.'

'It's fine. We can go a day late. It's only Paris. It's not going anywhere.'

'Nor are we, by the looks of things.'

It had been Tom's parents who'd insisted they go private, rather than wait. 'Poor boy!' Tom had said, mimicking his mum after taking her call. 'What's the point of suffering if you don't need to?' He'd thrown himself down on the sofa next to Sophie and rolled his eyes. 'I knew it would be better not to tell them anything. They always overreact.'

'Still, it might be for the best,' she'd said gently. In truth, she was glad Tom's parents had forced his hand on this. Nobody should be consuming the amount of antacids he'd admitted he was now taking, and the referral from his doctor would take months. At least this way they could get things sorted.

In all honesty, his chronic indigestion was much more likely to do with stress. She'd been ringing IVF clinics in the past few weeks and her enquiries into fertility treatment had correlated almost exactly with the worsening of his stomach pain. She hoped Tom would get instructions to slow down, eat more healthily, give up drink for a bit – all things she'd tried to convince him to do anyway to aid their chances of conception, but which he seemed to think were pointless. 'I had my sperm checked, there's nothing wrong with it,' he'd say. 'What harm can it do to have a few biscuits or a drink in the evening?'

She hadn't been able to tell him. Shifting slightly in her seat and eyeing the only other patient in the room – a man of about sixty years old reading the *Daily Mail* – she admitted to herself, perhaps for the first time, that she'd been annoyed with him for not changing his lifestyle at all, because it felt that she had to bear all the suffering that came with infertility. And although it was pointless perhaps, it wouldn't hurt him to join her in it a little, just for solidarity if nothing else. He'd said he'd cut down more than once, but his promises proved empty time and time again.

Nature was cruel to females – she'd known that since her first terrible bout of period pain. And now, this inability to create life in the very womb she'd had to service all these years seemed almost personal. She'd wanted Tom to suffer, just a little. Just a fraction of what she had to. Because it wasn't fair. If the stomach pains did turn out to be stress, perhaps that would go some way to proving that he was more affected by this than he let on.

She wasn't proud of feeling this way, knew that if she stepped back from it all and looked at it rationally, that it wasn't fair. But not being proud of something doesn't make it disappear. She wondered what dark thoughts Tom had, and whether he ever resented her in the way she'd started to resent him every time her irregular cycle – which teased her periodically by switching from four to six weeks – disappointed her again.

She—

'Tom Gardner?' The consultant stood in his doorway, as a woman made her way out and back to the reception area. He was reading Tom's name from a file, as if there were twenty patients in the room rather than just two. It was pretty obvious who Tom was.

They both stood obediently. 'Do you want me to come in with you?' Sophie asked.

'Why not?' he said, taking her hand for a squeeze. 'Don't want you to miss any of the fun.'

They walked in, feeling a little like renegade pupils being taken before the Head. The consultant sat at his desk and, without talking to them, tapped on his keyboard and looked at the screen for a moment before turning to them and clasping his hands together in front of himself like a character in a TV drama.

'If you could just wait a moment, our consultant, Mr Sullivan, is going to join us for this one,' he said.

It was then that something changed inside Sophie. Something icy clenched in her chest. 'Why?' she asked.

'Just protocol,' he said, smiling authoritatively at her and failing to answer her question at all.

She looked at Tom, staring straight ahead, and suddenly noticed his cheekbone jutting out in a way she hadn't acknowledged before. He'd lost more weight than she'd realised. And suddenly something sank deep inside her.

Tom grinned at her and raised an eyebrow, seemingly unaware.

But she sensed at that moment – deep down – that what they'd treated as a joke, as something trivial and annoying at worst, was something else entirely.

37

NOW

Another text flashed on her phone.

WILL

All OK?

SOPHIE

Getting there *grimace emoji*. Love you.

And she really did, she thought. In so many ways, she didn't deserve the loyal, dependable Will. Especially after she'd cut him out of her life so brutally. But he'd kept reappearing – through chance, or design – until she'd finally been able to see the truth that was right in front of her all along.

* * *

It was her promise to Sam that had prompted her to go to the party. She'd accepted an invitation to the pub after work, and her colleague Rachel had taken the chance to persuade her on another night out. Two glasses of wine down and more at one with the world than she'd been for some time, Sophie had found herself accepting the invite.

'There'll be some fit blokes there too,' Rachel – who had no idea about Sophie's past and so couldn't be blamed for being tactless – said. 'I'll introduce you to some of them.'

'Thanks, but no thanks.'

'Oh, live a little. Think of those rowers' arms!' Rachel had said, flexing a rather pathetic bicep and grinning.

Rachel's brother, Ted, was a rower, and trained with the professional club. The party was to be held at the clubhouse – an annual event to mark the summer and the tail end of the regatta season. Apparently, it was 'the more the merrier,' especially when it came to women. 'There are like 75 per cent men at the club,' Rachel had told her. 'Ted is relying on me to even up the numbers.'

'Oh, OK,' she'd said, draining her glass and looking at her watch. 'If you insist.'

Which is why she found herself the following Saturday night wearing a dress that hadn't left her closet for years, and standing awkwardly near the bar of the clubhouse as people conversed loudly around her. The air was filled with the kind of posh, raucous laughter that only seemed to come from privileged people; for a moment she was brought back to the summer ball all those years ago – when everything had seemed so awful; before she'd known what awful really meant.

'Sophie!' cried a voice, and Rachel made her way past groups of chatting men, grabbed her and kissed her on each cheek. 'You came!'

'Yep!' she said, trying to smile. 'Look, I'm not sure I'll be able to stay long. I'm—'

'Sure, sure,' said Rachel, clearly already a few glasses down. 'But look, let me introduce you to some of the gang.' She grabbed Sophie's hand and led her through the mingling groups to a table at the back of the room were several people sat and chatted.

'Guys!' she said loudly, making Sophie blush. 'This is Sophie from school. I mean, she's a teacher, obviously, not a pupil,' she tittered. 'Sophie, this is the gang. Ted, Archie, Simon, Flick and Will.'

Sophie smiled as the seated group turned to look at her. And then she gave an unexpected gasp.

'I think we already know each other,' Will said, standing up and giving her a brief hug. His arms were strong and warm inside his polo shirt, his smile open and friendly. She embraced him too, awkwardly, aware that it was she who'd dropped contact and eventually unfriended him on social media. It hadn't been personal, it had been survival. The only way she could keep going had been to push Tom and everything associated with him to the back of her mind.

'Hi, Will!' she said, trying to sound upbeat. 'Long time no see!'

'Yes.' He smiled and moved away from the table, touching her upper back lightly, then found a space for them on the crowded floor. 'It's good to see you. Seriously.'

'You too.' And she realised it was true. Because somehow, over the months apart, he'd become 'just Will' again. 'Sorry for being crap,' she added.

He laughed. 'If we're going to apologise for all the times we've been crap, we could be here forever.'

She smiled. 'Still. I unfriended you on Facebook.'

'You did?' He looked genuinely surprised. 'I don't actually go on there much these days.'

She laughed. She'd been worried when she'd done it that

she might upset him. 'Oh,' she said. 'Well, in that case, forget I said anything.'

He smiled at her. 'Want to get out of here for a bit? Get some air?'

She nodded. 'If you do.'

It was a relief to step out of the noisy clubhouse and into the warm evening air. The Cam sparkled and caught the sunlight, reflected the blue endless sky. She breathed deeply, feeling the air fill her lungs, and then she let it out in an enormous sigh.

'You OK?' Will said, grinning at the noise.

She grimaced. 'Sorry. I'm not a big fan of gatherings like that. These days, at least.'

They acknowledged Tom's loss quietly between them. 'Yeah, I know what you mean,' Will said. 'Nicer to be able to actually talk.'

She nodded, wondering if he really meant it. They continued to walk, up onto the pavement and along, past open grounds and parks, old buildings, heading towards the town centre, but aimlessly. She glanced at his face from time to time and saw a smile spread across it. 'What?' she asked.

'Just remembering how we met. That evening, you know, after the play,' he said. 'Seems a long time ago.'

'Yeah, maybe just a bit,' she said, thinking back to how she and Libby had stumbled into the halls without a thought. Carefree.

'I always kicked myself for not coming over sooner, introducing myself, before Tom monopolised everything,' he admitted.

'Yeah?'

He nodded. 'I think I was a bit in awe of you and Libby at first. You seemed so... kind of free. Different from the girls who were at our college.'

'Poorer?'

He laughed. 'More fun. Anyway, we're not all rich toffs, you know. I'm boringly ordinary, for instance.'

'True.' Will had spoken to her briefly in the past about what it was like to go to Cambridge simply on academic merit, rather than the sense of historic entitlement some of his peers had seemed to feel. He'd felt on the outskirts of everything at first, only being granted access to the inner circle due to his rugby and rowing skills.

'And you're still rowing now?' she said, thinking of the club they'd just left.

'Now and then. Not competitively. Just... exercise, I guess. And I love it.'

'That's good.'

'Yeah. You know, you should come with me sometime,' he said, suddenly animated.

She laughed properly at this. 'Seriously?' she said. 'I'm about as coordinated as...' She wracked her brain for an example, but failed to come up with anything. 'I mean, I can't... And I'm pathetically weak,' she said, showing him her arm as evidence.

'Don't flex that enormous bicep at me!' he joked. 'You'll make me feel inadequate!'

She laughed again. It was surprisingly easy this evening. Nice to see Will again.

'Anyway, no excuse at all, I'm afraid. Everyone has to start somewhere.'

'I just...' she said, beginning to refuse again. Then she thought, why not? 'OK, then,' she said. 'If you promise you'll do the lion's share of the actual rowing.'

'That's a given,' he said. 'Just wait until you get out there on the water. 5 a.m. Everything's kind of magical...'

'5 a.m.?' Admittedly, she was often up at that hour, restless, sitting at her kitchen table with a cup of tea. But the thought of venturing out into the cool morning air when it was barely light was far from appealing.

'Best time of the day,' he said, looking at her. 'What? I'm serious!'

'Yeah, you're all right,' she said. 'I think I'll stick to my warm bed at that time.'

He turned to her, serious now. 'Tell you what,' he said. 'You come and try with me one morning and if you don't love it, I won't ever ask you again.'

His seriousness floored her. 'You're that sure I'm going to like it?'

He nodded. 'There's nothing like it, Soph. It really helped me, too, after... you know. And maybe...' he shrugged awkwardly, his meaning clear. That it might help her to forget about Tom for a little while.

She wondered whether he thought about his friend as often as she did. Being a widow, half of a couple without Tom, gave her the biggest claim on mourning, she supposed, but losing a best friend must be tough too. 'Do you...' she began, then cut herself short, not knowing how to finish the sentence.

'Still miss him? Of course.'

She nodded. 'OK.'

'OK, what?'

'OK. I'll join you at 5 a.m. But it had better be worth it.'

* * *

She smiled now, remembering how torn she'd been about the early hour, the intense exercise. How she'd almost not made it at all. And how forcing herself up and out of the flat that morning had changed her life.

38

THE EIGHTH SUMMER – 2018

'Well, the good news is you're young,' said the doctor, as if he was telling them something they didn't already know.

'That's the good news!' Sophie found herself saying. Tom put a calming hand on her leg.

'OK, so what's the plan?' he asked, so calmly that Sophie wondered whether he'd heard the same diagnosis as she had.

The two doctors glanced at each other. 'Well,' said the younger of the pair, 'well, with stage 4, we tend not to be able to operate.'

Sophie stood up then. 'NOT operate?' she cried. She felt hot, white rage coursing around her body. 'You *have* to operate. You have to give him a chance. You can't just give up on him!'

The two doctors regarded her impassively. This, clearly, was just part of an ordinary workday for them. But they didn't understand! This wasn't some ordinary patient. This was Tom! And he was absolutely, completely essential to her life.

'I'm afraid it wouldn't do any good,' Dr Sullivan said, his face grave. 'The cancer has spread.' He pointed to the CT scan on screen with his biro. 'We can see traces here in the liver and there's a possibility it's migrated elsewhere too.'

'Then operate there too!' she said.

She wondered, suddenly, why Tom wasn't standing up next to her, demanding to be heard. This was the expensive private healthcare his parents raved about – surely they should be able to do anything?

'Sit down, Sophie.' Tom didn't look up at her. His gaze was fixed on his hands, folded neatly on his lap.

'But Tom... I...'

'Sit down.'

She sank back into her chair obediently.

Tom looked up then, making eye contact with the doctors. One looked away, the other held his gaze. 'So, what's the plan?' he asked again.

It struck Sophie later that his choice of words were exactly the same as he might have chosen if he were talking about what to watch on Netflix, or planning a holiday itinerary. Innocuous, simple.

The doctors nodded, exchanged infuriating eye contact again, then Dr Sullivan opened a beige folder. 'So,' he said, pointing to a printed text with his biro, 'in these cases where the cancer has been caught quite late and, ahem, spread'– his eyes remained fixed on the paper, he didn't seem able to look up at Tom – 'what we aim for is to drive the cancer into remission with chemotherapy.'

Sophie felt something lift. So there was hope! She'd assumed no surgery meant no options.

Tom took a deep breath next to her. She reached over and grabbed his hand, squeezing it firmly.

They sat silently as the doctors mapped out the next twelve weeks of their lives. Appointments and scans and check-ups and chemo sessions and recovery time. Side effects and risks and outcomes and schedules and support. They nodded; two schoolkids being assigned a new timetable with very little say in what would happen and when. Sophie felt Tom's hand – hot, slightly sweaty. She gave it a squeeze.

The worst of it was that she'd been impatient with him. His tiredness, his nausea. In recent weeks, he hadn't always wanted sex, even when she'd been ovulating and explained to him the small window they had in which to conceive. She'd noticed that he looked a bit paler than usual, a bit run-down – but had reasoned that she probably looked similar. Teaching was a full-on, full-time job and the constant fact of infertility was weighing heavily on her at all times.

Now this. The feeling that if she'd taken him more seriously more quickly, they might have caught the cancer before it became inoperable. Her rational mind overruled this emotional leap – he was a grown man, quite able to go to the doctor's any time he saw fit. But she also knew that he would have gone if she'd encouraged him.

Then a thought: 'What about fertility?' she found herself blurting out, interrupting Dr Sullivan's explanation of cold caps and hair loss.

He looked at her. 'We do recommend that men freeze a quantity of sperm before treatment begins, to make parenthood a possibility in the future,' he said. 'At your age, it's definitely something we'd recommend.'

Tom nodded. 'So I'll be infertile, after?'

'Not necessarily, but treatment can and often does decrease sperm production.'

'Right, OK.' Tom looked at her worriedly and she felt a stab of guilt that this was the first time he'd raised his head to look her way. As if he was more worried about this than any other aspect of what they'd just been told. She squeezed his hand again, hoping he'd be reassured. It didn't matter. Nothing mattered. She just wished she'd realised that before they were on this journey.

The doctor finished his talk and sat looking at them expectantly. 'If that's all OK, we could get your first treatment booked in for later this week,' he said, as if he was a hairdresser fitting them in for a cut and colour. What were they supposed to say – 'Brilliant news!' or 'Wow, thanks – really appreciate it!'?

'What's the prognosis?' Tom asked, his voice seeming loud in the tiny room.

Sophie stiffened.

The two doctors glanced at each other again. She wanted to stand, reach over and bang their heads together. But she managed to stay seated.

'Well, it's always hard to say,' Dr Fieldman said, his voice seeming far too young and light for the situation. 'Obviously, as Dr Sullivan says, you have youth on your side. You're very young to have any sort of cancer, and pancreatic in particular is much more prevalent in the over-fifties.'

'Right?' Tom prompted. Sophie wondered how he was managing to remain so calm.

'There have been cases – admittedly rare – in which the patients have lived for ten years or more, with regular treatment and monitoring.'

'OK, and what about the less rare cases?'

Another glance. 'Well, on average, people at this stage have six months, perhaps a little more. But again, you're young. It could be up to a year, perhaps more,' Dr Sullivan said, as if this were good news.

'Six months!' Sophie's voice sounded shrill, unlike her own.

'But of course, there are exceptions, and I think in someone so young—'

'He's only twenty-eight!' Sophie cried, outraged, as if the doctors themselves were responsible for choosing cancer's next victim.

'Yes, we realise that. I know this must be very distressing for you, Miss... Miss...'

'It's MRS,' she said coldly. 'Mrs Gardner.'

Tom was looking at her intensely as they walked out twenty minutes later, still hand in hand.

'You were formidable in there,' he said, shaking his head, a slight smile on his face.

'Tom!' she said. 'Is that all you can say after... all that?'

His head dropped a little and she was immediately sorry that she'd spoken.

'What should I say?' he asked her, his face impassive. 'Obviously it's a shit diagnosis. Possibly the shittiest. But it just means I have to be the unicorn.'

'You... what?'

'You think I'm going to quit, leave all this?' he said. 'No. I'll be the ten-year survivor they tell people about during their appointments. Why not?'

She looked at him, incredulous at his optimism. 'Yes,' she said, buoyed, 'yes, you have to be.'

'And before all of it, Paris?' he said to her.

'Are you crazy?'

'Why not? It'll get our mind off things. And after all, it is a tradition now.'

39

NOW

Back in their bedroom, Sophie slipped into jeans and a T-shirt, the clean, soft clothes feeling good against her freshly showered skin. Her body felt strong, supple; fitter than it had in her twenties since she'd taken up rowing three years ago and had amazed herself by falling in love with it.

* * *

That first morning, she was surprised at the temperature on leaving the house. The days had been cool recently and she'd expected to feel chilly, but the early morning air was surprisingly pleasant. It was 4.45 a.m., a time she'd never willingly seen before, and she had a whole day of teaching scheduled in for after the row. She was already regretting it.

Will's Audi was waiting in the street behind her apartment block, its lights on although barely necessary; the sun had already half-risen and the sky was white and bright and luminous. She took a breath, then walked to the car, pulling open the door and sliding herself in. 'Morning,' she said.

'Morning yourself. I didn't think you'd come.'

'Oh. Well, a promise is a promise,' she said, trying to keep her tone light.

'It is at that,' he said, starting the engine, 'and you are not going to regret this.'

'So you keep saying,' she told him, and was rewarded with one of his easy, relaxed smiles.

They set off through the city streets, passing early morning cyclists, and late night revellers returning home to bed. Market traders were making their way to the centre, and one or two insomniacs walked their dogs. Will parked in a precariously small space between a van and a motorbike then turned to her. 'We have to walk the rest, I'm afraid. Parking's a bitch.'

She'd been worried that she'd have to join the club or have a lesson or something equally painful before taking Will up on his challenge, but he'd explained that the club was pretty relaxed about things like that. 'As long as you're with a member, it'll be fine,' he'd said.

'I suppose this is where you take all the girls,' she quipped then stopped, embarrassed.

But he laughed. 'Only the ones that will agree to it,' he said, 'so you're pretty much the first.'

They arrived and he left her standing on the bank for a moment as he disappeared into the clubhouse. He returned shortly with a smile. 'OK, we're good to go!' He pointed at the white rowing boats lined up at the edge of the water. 'Your carriage awaits, m'lady.' He flung his backpack into the vessel, then used the rope to pull it up against the shore, making it safe for her to stumble across without falling.

Feeling her heart rate increase, she stepped into the boat, which wobbled precariously as she lowered herself onto the seat. Will watched her, amused, before climbing in himself, setting the vessel off again. 'Don't worry,' he said, turning to her where she sat behind him. 'You'll get your sea legs soon enough!'

'Sea legs? Isn't this a river?'

'See! You're already an expert.'

He handed her an oar, which was heavier and more unwieldy than she'd imagined, and pushed off with his own oar, paddling one side to straighten the boat. 'OK,' he said, 'just follow my lead.'

She dipped one end of the oar into the water and pulled, hearing the gentle sound of the river lapping against the boat.

'Keep it steady,' Will advised. 'Try to stay in sync with me. That's it.'

And suddenly, she found a wobbly, but distinct rhythm in her movement. Her attention focused in on the rowing, the sounds of wildlife and birds and the distant sound of traffic as the day came into itself. The sun sparkled on the river's surface and the water foamed as she pulled it again and again and again, driving the boat forward. Although it was hard work, the feeling of gliding on the transparent liquid – her heart pumping, her skin prickled with moisture – was pleasant and she found herself driving harder and picking up speed.

In the seat in front, Will laughed. 'You're a natural!' he said, glancing over his shoulder at her with an enormous grin.

And it was their undoing. The boat rocked violently at his sudden movement, the sides lurching wildly as they struggled to regain control. And suddenly Sophie found herself submerged in the cold water of the Cam, water in her ears and eyes, and the oar pulled out of her hands in the process. She emerged, coughing and spluttering, to find Will by her side, next to their overturned boat. His worried expression smoothed as he saw she was OK. 'Come on,' he said, swimming towards the bank, tugging the boat behind him. She followed and they clambered up, water streaming from their clothing.

And although the whole experience had been shocking, and although she felt freezing and weighed down and utterly disgusting, when Sophie looked at Will and saw the barely disguised amusement in his eyes, she found laughter bubbling up inside her.

He caught the mood and suddenly together they were shaking with half-suppressed giggles, her leaning towards him, him towards her. 'I can't believe we...' she gasped.

'Told you it was relaxing,' he replied, before letting out another bark of laughter.

Once the humour had subsided and the cold had fully seeped in, Will stood up. 'I'd give you my jumper, but...' He gestured to the damp wool as it clung to his chest. 'Oh, but hang on!' He rummaged in his backpack. 'Yes!' He held up a fleece, as triumphant as an angler hooking an enormous fish. 'It's still dry.'

'Oh, God. No. You have it,' she said as he offered it to her.

'Come on, Soph. I have an extra layer of fat to keep me warm.'

The cold had reached her bones now and it was impossible to refuse. 'OK, thank you.'

He turned his back as she pulled her top and T-shirt over her head, holding the fleece out behind him for her to grab. She slipped it over her head, feeling an instant shiver of grateful warmth.

'Thanks.'

He turned. 'Suits you!' he said, noting how swamped she was in the man-size garment.

'Thanks. You know you should take yours off.'

He raised an eyebrow.

'Your jumper. I know you don't have anything to replace it with, it's just... it'll make you colder, I think.'

He nodded and slipped the jumper over his head, revealing a little glimpse of belly button that made him somehow seem boyish. His T-shirt clung to his chest underneath and she could see the pink of his flesh through the material. She hoped he wouldn't freeze to death before they got back.

'What now?'

'Well, we'll have to row back,' he said with a grimace.

'You think I'm getting back in that thing?'

'It's that or walk back to the club – no one's letting you in a taxi in that state.'

She looked down at herself. It was true. Nobody was going to let her soak their upholstery. 'Bugger,' she said. Suddenly it didn't seem quite so funny.

'It'll be fine.' Will kneeled on the bank and reached into the boat with his oar, pulling the vessel towards them.

'I don't even have an oar!'

'It's just there,' he said, pointing to where her oar had floated and was caught on the branches of an overhanging shrub.

She felt a sudden exhaustion. It was half past five, she was soaked through. The morning, although it looked promising, was still not warm enough to counter the deep ache of cold that had reached her bones. And now she had to row. She stood up with a guttural sigh.

'Ah, come on. We'll make a rower out of you yet,' Will said, grinning.

But she couldn't return his good humour. 'Let's just get this over with,' she said, stepping cautiously into the boat as he held it as still as he could.

After a few attempts, she was able to lift her oar back onto the boat as Will held it steady. Then, careful not to look around, he told her again to get into the rhythm, to start rowing. She did – doggedly, determined to get to the club as soon as possible and put all this behind her.

But as she rowed, and as her body began to warm despite its sodden covering, she fell into the rhythm again, and began to feel that sense of peace she'd experienced shortly before they'd capsized.

By the time they reached the clubhouse and Will had carefully secured the boat, she was feeling, if not positive, then certainly not as negative as she had. And that was really saying something.

Standing on the bank now, Will reached out his hand to help her from the boat and she took it gratefully, feeling strange when she stood again on solid ground, her body still expecting it to lurch and buck beneath her. She looked at Will who was studying her face, his brow furrowed.

'What?' she said.

'Not quite sure what to say. I mean, I guess it wasn't the pleasant experience I was hoping for.'

'No. Not really.'

'Sorry,' he said. 'I really thought you'd enjoy it. And you know, I think you would have if I hadn't been stupid enough to—'

She looked at him. 'No, I did. I did enjoy it.'

'You did?' He looked incredulous.

'Yeah. I mean, not *all* of it,' she said, wringing some water out of her hair pointedly.

'Well, no.'

'But it was good. I get what you mean. It's hard work, but sort of soothing at the same time.'

He nodded. 'That's how I've always found it. I kind of feel different on the water – I mean, I know I'm still in Cambridge and everyone is still around, and all the things that exist in the world are still, well, there. But you kind of feel separate too, don't you? Like you've escaped it all for a bit.'

'Yeah,' she agreed. 'I get that.'

'So you think you might be a convert?'

She smiled. 'I wouldn't go that far. But you know... I might try it again sometime.'

'Good,' Will said. 'That's really good.'

As they walked back to his car, wondering how she was going to protect his upholstery from her soggy back and bottom, she thought of Tom for the first time. Always in her mind, or deep in her gut where her sadness seemed to lie, he had disappeared for a moment. And although she missed him with every fibre of her being, she realised that having a break from her grief had made her feel more able to carry it once more.

* * *

Had it been then? She wondered now. Had those been the moments when she first started to fall in love with him?

40

THE EIGHTH SUMMER – 2018

'I don't know, Libby, it feels like a farce going to Paris when he's so ill. I mean, even if they can't start treatment yet, he should be resting, surely?' she said, tucking the phone under her chin as she spoke and zipping up her half-heartedly packed suitcase.

'But it's what he wants,' Libby pointed out.

Sophie sighed, turning to sit on the bed. 'I know,' she said, feeling depleted. 'He kind of wants a short break before he starts treatment. And it's only two nights. And they weren't going to be able to start much before then anyway...'

'So why not go! Enjoy yourselves!'

Sophie shook her head. 'But how can we?'

Libby was silent for a moment, then 'But what's the alternative? Sit around in the flat and wait for his treatment? Maybe if you can put it to the back of your minds just for one last break.'

Tears pooled, hot and insistent, in Sophie's eyes. 'How can I, though?'

'Well, maybe you can't. But perhaps Tom can. Maybe he needs to...'

'So I'm just meant to pretend?'

'I'm really sorry, but I think you have to. If that's what he wants.'

Sophie had got used to the misery of infertility, carrying her disappointment with her almost constantly over the past year. But now, this, Tom's – well, what? Terminal illness? Neither of them were calling it that, but what else was 'incurable cancer'? It seemed too much to bear. Yet this time, she wasn't the one carrying the majority of the pain. He was. His feelings had to come first.

'Oh God, Libby, what am I going to do?'

'You,' said Libby, 'are going to try to make the best of things.'

'Yeah.' She picked a thread from the eiderdown, idly watching as it snaked away from her across the embroidered satin. 'I'm not so good at that.'

Libby gave a small snort of laughter. 'Understatement of the century.'

Sophie smiled weakly. 'But how do you do it?'

'What?'

'Well, you always seem to be so... upbeat. In the moment. And I know it hasn't always been... easy.'

Libby's father had been diagnosed with Alzheimer's two years ago, and was now in a home. At just sixty-two, it was unbelievably cruel. They spoke about it sometimes, and Libby was both grieving and stressed about the situation. But what amazed Sophie was her capacity to rise above it. To throw herself fully into a night out, or immerse herself in a book. To talk about trivial things in the face of such monstrous bad luck.

Libby sighed. 'Ah, chick. It's not easy,' she admitted. 'But I figured, what's the alternative?'

'What do you mean?'

'Well, if I sit and think about Dad and all the things that have happened so far, and what's going to happen next, I could probably reduce myself to a blubbering wreck on a daily basis,' she said. 'And I did, for a while. Remember when he was diagnosed?'

Sophie nodded. 'Yeah.'

'Well, I couldn't understand why Mum didn't seem as affected. I mean, she was sad, worried. But not floored. Not devastated. And I asked her. You know, "How come you're not frightened?" And she told me that she was, of course. But that she'd learned that life was about seeing all this stuff – whether it's your own illness or pain, or grief, or worry – and living anyway. Or else what was the point?'

'But... how?'

'That's what I asked,' Libby told her. 'And she said you just have to kind of keep doing the things... you know. Get up, have a shower, wear something nice, eat, work, go through the motions. And that eventually your mind catches up. Realises you are living anyway. Kind of demotes the worry.'

'I just don't think I could...'

'But you have to,' Libby said. 'For Tom. He needs you to do that. To be strong in the face of it all. And you know, he's here right now. He's relatively OK. And who knows what might happen in the future. Good things, maybe. But if not, then this time is even more precious.'

Sophie fiddled with the zip on the suitcase. 'Yeah, I get that,' she said.

'I know. It's not easy. But like Mum says, a lot of the time, you or someone you love, or even other people, farther away, are going through something awful. If you let it floor you each time, you'd never get up at all.'

'She's pretty wise, your mum.'

'I know.'

'Mine just told me to make sure we were eating properly.'

'Oh, Soph. But you know, it's kind of the same thing. Keeping on, in spite of it.'

'If you say so.'

'And I suppose Tom's parents have thrown money at the problem.'

'Just a bit.'

'Well, I mean. That can't hurt, I suppose.'

The door to the flat opened, signalling Tom's return. 'I'd better go,' Sophie said. 'But thanks. You've really helped.'

By the time Tom entered the room, she was standing next to the packed suitcase, her phone squirrelled away. 'OK?' she asked him.

'Not too bad. Apart from the late-stage cancer, that is.' He grinned and she tried to mirror him.

'Ha. Well, yes. There is that.' She walked up to him and wrapped her arms around his neck, leaning in to kiss him deeply.

'What's that for?' he asked.

'Just love you,' she said simply. 'Now come on, let's get your case packed too.'

'You're sure you're OK with going?'

'Pretty much. And you know, it'll be good for us. To get away for a couple of nights.'

He nuzzled into her. 'Thank you.'

She blinked rapidly to ward off threatened tears. 'You're welcome. Let's go have the holiday of a lifetime.'

41

NOW

It had been a few weeks later when she'd first noticed how much fitter she'd become, Sophie remembered as she wandered through to the living room and curled up on the sofa, enjoying the silence; the chance to process.

* * *

She'd noticed as she got changed after the shower that she actually had a bicep muscle. She'd flexed it in the bathroom mirror, feeling weirdly pleased with herself. She'd never craved a muscular frame, but it was nice to see that rowing was making a difference to her body.

Twice a week now, she made her way to the club where she'd join Will for a morning row. They worked together in unison, often silently, pushing away the water and the thoughts and everything except that moment in time. Once or twice she'd even been out by herself.

Now, parking in her usual spot, she exited the car and realised that although she had a physical activity ahead, she felt primed and ready for it. This must be what being fit feels like, she thought to herself with a small smile.

Sam and Libby had both written her off as mad. Had suggested that an hour or so extra in bed would do much more for her than rowing, but she'd caught the bug somehow. Rowing was slowly becoming part of her. A thing she did whatever the weather and the circumstances.

This morning, a light rain threatened and the weather had begun to turn autumnal, as if nature were practising for the change in season that was just around the corner. The sun had not yet bothered trying to clamber into the sky, and it remained a dark, charcoal grey in the half-light. A new term at school had brought new challenges, as well as a reminder that time was moving on whether she liked it or not. She loved the sense of renewal a change in season brought, but hated the fact that yet another landmark had passed without Tom there to witness it.

She zipped up her waterproof coat and walked towards the clubhouse where she knew Will would be waiting. Always there, and always with a smile of welcome.

'Lovely morning for it!' he said as she approached.

'Isn't it just!'

'Nice coat; new?'

'Yeah, thought I'd better invest in some proper kit if I'm going to be doing this through the winter.'

He raised an eyebrow. 'Really? Serious stuff then.'

She shrugged. 'Someone once told me it was good for body and mind,' she said with a small grin. 'So thought I'd try to stick it out through the colder months.'

'Well, good,' he said, turning and walking towards the riverbank. 'Because you know, you keep me going.'

'I do? I thought you'd been doing this for years.'

He shrugged. 'Yeah. And I'm not saying I'd quit if you did.'

He paused. 'It's just... it's a lot more fun with you there,' he admitted.

'Not many people have accused me of being fun before.'

'Well, my threshold is very low.'

She snorted and he turned at her and grinned.

'What was that?' he asked.

'What? A laugh?'

'Sounded more like a sneeze.'

She smiled. 'I've always laughed like that. Tom used to... Tom used to call me Miss Piggy.'

'Oh. I've just never noticed it before, I guess,' he said.

People had commented on Sophie's laugh ever since school – sometimes mocking, sometimes roaring with laughter alongside her. She'd been embarrassed about it for years, holding it back sometimes, self-consciously. But when she'd laughed in front of Tom, he'd told her it was adorable, made her feel able to be herself.

She hadn't snorted since Tom's diagnosis. Gentle laughter, sometimes forced, had been all she'd been able to manage.

Maybe this was the first time she'd completely abandoned herself to something funny, since Tom. She fell silent as they walked.

'OK?' he said. 'I didn't mean to offend you, you know.'

'I know. You haven't.'

He held the boat steady as she clambered into it, more confidently than she'd used to, surer of what she was doing. And then sat and watched him get into his habitual place. They set off, in companionable silence, both together and separate as they fell into their thoughts.

People talked about acceptance. About moving on, moving past grief. Tom was always with her, in the back or forefront of her mind. But was this what letting go felt like? She felt a pang of grief. She didn't want to let go of him, not yet. It was too soon, too raw. She didn't want to feel the awful pain of grief, but if it went away, it would be letting go of Tom, giving up on him somehow.

She thought of his ashes, still squirreled away in her apartment, sitting and waiting for the time when she would feel ready to scatter them. It wasn't yet. She wasn't ready yet. Even if holding on to him meant holding onto grief.

The rain intensified, sprinkling her anorak with moisture; the sky was white with a smudge of grey cloud here and there. All was dull. She looked at Will's back, his muscular shoulders, the ease of movement as he plunged the oar into the water. Then she forced herself to concentrate on the movement, the rhythm, the sights and smells and sensations of gliding on the water, propelling herself on and on and on.

* * *

The rowing had fallen away again recently, what with the wedding plans and her sudden need to scatter Tom's ashes. But they'd start again, Sophie thought now. They'd get back on the river tomorrow.

42

THE EIGHTH SUMMER – 2018

'Can you stop?' Tom said suddenly as they sat opposite each other in the corner of the carriage, a small plastic table of food between them.

She looked up at him over her plate of coq au vin – usually her favourite; she'd been moving the chicken around her plate like a toddler reluctant to eat a meal. 'What?' she said, thinking for a moment he was about to chastise her for playing with her food the way her parents had used to.

'Looking at me like that.'

'I wasn't!'

'You were. Every couple of minutes you look at me and you look so... fucking sad,' he said leaning forward, half smiling, half annoyed. 'I'm not dead yet, you know?'

'Sorry,' she said, making a face.

'There you go again!'

'What?'

'There is no way the normal Sophie would have said sorry just then. You'd have told me I was being paranoid or narcissistic or something,' he said, folding his arms, point made.

He was right, actually. 'Well, you know, I think we've pretty much established you're both of those things over the past few years,' she said. 'Seemed cruel to point them out.' She smiled, hoping he'd meet her eyes and join her.

He did, almost. 'Good one,' he said and sat back a little. His plate was also barely touched.

'Sorry,' she said again. 'I know this is... I know you want a normal trip.'

He nodded. 'Hard to keep up the pretence, I guess,' he said. 'When you think about what's happening next.'

'Oh, Tom.' She felt her eyes well with tears but blinked them back. This was the opposite of what he needed. 'Look, nobody knows what's happening next. It could be fine. You could be fine...'

'Chemo is happening next,' he said simply.

'Oh. Yes.'

'You don't think it's going to work?' he asked, his tone a little sharp.

'Of course I do, of course I do,' she said, sitting forward, touching his leg. 'It's going to work, you'll go into remission. They said that some people live more than ten years.'

'What was it though, something like 1 per cent?'

The statistic silenced her. 'You're young,' she ventured.

He laughed. 'Yep. Young and carefree, so they say.'

She made a face. 'Come on, Tom,' she said.

He sighed – the action somehow seemed to make his whole body slump. 'I know. *I'm* doing it now, dwelling on it all when this is meant to be a break from... or before it all. But I can't help wondering somehow if... no, it's stupid.'

'What?' she prompted gently.

'Ever since I've known you, you've said I've had it easy, that things have just kind of come to me, because of my upbringing or my parents or whatever,' he said.

She nodded, feeling sick.

'Well, maybe you're right. Maybe I have been too lucky. Maybe everyone gets the same amount of luck and I've used mine all up without realising.'

'No,' she said. 'Don't think like that. I'm just a pessimist, is all – I have no idea what I'm talking about half the time.'

He was silent for a moment then reached out a hand. 'OK, enough,' he said as the familiar sights of the Paris suburbs began to flicker past the window like slides in an old movie. 'No cancer talk for two days.'

She nodded.

'No being miserable.'

She nodded.

'This is our holiday. Our time. And our place. And we're going to make the most of it.'

She looked at him, her sick, beautiful, dependable boy and she gave a final nod. 'Damn right we are,' she said.

An hour later, the train pulled into the Gare du Nord and they alighted, following the familiar route through the building and out onto the streets of Paris. There she tried to centre herself, live in the moment. Taking a deep breath of Parisian air, with its edge of fumes and cigarettes, she reminded herself that whatever came next, they were here; they were safe, and for the next two days at least, the future could wait.

43

NOW

Another text from Will startled her and Sophie realised she'd fallen asleep for a moment. Hardly surprising after being up almost all night. She hoped that he, at work despite it all, was coping. She checked her phone.

WILL
All OK?

SOPHIE
Yes.

She thought how often Will had shown up for her, just when she'd needed him to.

* * *

A few weeks after they'd started rowing together, she'd been alone in her flat when the doorbell rang, prompting her to think yet again about how she really ought to change the tune of it.

'Greensleeves' wasn't really her, after all. Placing her mug on the coffee table, she stood up and made her way to the door, opening it without a thought. It would no doubt be something boring she'd ordered. Once in a while she'd put something through online, then completely forget about it. The result would be a mystery package which she'd open excitedly only to find dishcloths or something equally dull inside.

'Oh,' she said, when she opened the door to Will who was carrying a bag from the local bakery.

'Hi,' he said. 'Look, I won't stop, I just wanted to drop these off. You said you were sick?' His voice took on an upward inflexion as he looked at her – patently *not* sick – standing in front of him.

She grimaced. 'Yeah,' she said. 'I'm feeling a bit better now. Just... couldn't face rowing this morning.'

He nodded. 'Sure,' he said.

'Sorry.'

'It's fine.' He paused, seeming to wrestle with something. 'You obviously don't ever *have* to come. I love you coming, but you know. If you're going off it, or it's getting too much...'

She shook her head vehemently. 'No, it's not that.'

He nodded. 'Good. Well, OK. See you in a couple of days then?'

She felt herself flood with guilt. 'Look, seeing as I'm not infectious or anything, do you have time to share these with me?' She peeped in the bag and saw two Chelsea buns – her favourites.

'You're sure?'

She nodded and stepped back to let him in. He made his way straight to the kitchen and began to boil the kettle. 'You sit. I know where everything is.'

They'd started having a drink together after weekend rows, sometimes at a coffee shop, sometimes at his place or hers, and he moved around her kitchen as if he lived there. 'No, I can do it,' she said.

'You're sick. Or tired or...'

'I'm actually fine,' she admitted.

He looked at her. 'Oh.'

'Yeah. Sorry. I'm not quite sure why I lied,' she said, ironically lying again. Because she *did* know why, really.

'It's OK.'

'Oh, shit,' she said, walking into the kitchen to stand near him. 'Sorry. I do know.'

'It's OK,' he repeated, smiling as the kettle shuddered to a boil. 'I'm not your boss. You don't owe me an explanation.'

'Thank you. Did you still go?'

He nodded. 'Bloody shoulder's killing me. I think I'm used to the extra help now.'

'Whoops. Sorry.'

'You and your sorrys,' he said.

A memory flickered. *Tom*. She nodded rather than let herself reply.

Minutes later, he handed her a cup as she sat on the sofa, and he sank into the chair opposite. 'Could probably do with a rest from it myself,' he admitted. 'It's just that I feel like if I miss it, I might never go back. So easy to get out of a routine.'

She blew the steam from the top of her mug. 'Yeah, I know what you mean.'

They were silent again, sipping their coffee. Will tore the edge from a Chelsea bun and popped it into his mouth.

'We're friends, aren't we?' she found herself saying.

He looked up, surprised. 'Well, yeah,' he said. 'I'd say so. Why?'

'No reason.'

He gave her a strange look but kept on chewing, washing down the last of the mouthful with a slug of coffee. 'Do you want me to go?' he asked. 'You seem...'

'Sorry. I mean... I know,' she corrected herself. Then, 'No. Don't go. Have your coffee. It's me, not you. I'm just a bit...'

He smiled weakly and took another sip. 'OK,' he said, clearly a bit bemused.

'It's just... Do you ever worry that you might be forgetting him?'

'Tom?' He shook his head. 'No. Not really.'

'Maybe forgetting's not the right word. It's just... the rowing. When I'm doing it, when I'm with you, things don't seem quite so bad. Not quite so raw. And sometimes, just for a bit, I forget to think about him, you know?'

He smiled softly, sympathetically. 'But isn't that a good thing?' he asked. 'I mean, it's natural to move on... well, a bit at least. And it's great that you're able to give yourself a break from it.'

The tears came then, surprising them both. 'I'm just scared I'm going to forget him, Will,' she said. 'He's been gone almost two years and I'm already...'

He was next to her then, arm around her back. 'No,' he said. 'Come on, Sophie. You're never going to forget Tom. He was your first love, you married him. Looked after him. He was a huge part of your life.'

She nodded, knowing his words made sense but unable to completely absorb them. Then, 'First love?' she said.

'Yeah. I mean he was, wasn't he?'

She shrugged. 'There wasn't really anyone before him.'

'Well then.'

'But I always thought of him as the love of my life, you know. "First love" makes him seem...'

'What?'

'Replaceable.'

He laughed, a short bark of humour. 'Replace Tom?' he said. 'I'd like to see someone try. He was... well, unique. A great mate. A good husband. A complete and utter idiot, with his heart in the right place.'

Will was the only person she knew who didn't seem afraid to talk about Tom. To joke about him in a way that made him still feel alive, relevant.

She smiled through her tears. 'I think that's fair,' she said.

'But it's also OK for you to move on. I don't mean find someone, get married, put the pics of Tom away – any of that,' he added hurriedly. 'But I mean, let yourself be happy – even if it's in a small way. Tom would want that.'

He was right. Even before he died, Tom had told her that he wanted her to be happy, to live her life. It was just she had no idea how or when that was supposed to happen.

'And I think,' Will added, 'I think you can be sad and happy at the same time, can't you? You'll always be a bit sad about Tom. But it doesn't mean you can't be happy about someone... something else, too.'

'Thank you,' she said, leaning into him, putting her arm around him reciprocally.

'What for?'

'Being so bloody wise.'

'That's not always seen as an asset,' he said, deflecting.

'Well, it is to me,' she said, and she straightened slightly and kissed him firmly on the cheek.

He turned to her, surprised, his hand moving to where her lips had touched his skin. 'Oh,' he said.

Then he leant towards her and gently brushed his lips on hers.

* * *

She closed her eyes now, thinking of the kiss. How utterly right it had felt. How utterly, utterly terrifying.

44

THE EIGHTH SUMMER – 2018

They'd booked into a familiar hotel, just off the Champs-Élysées. It was expensive and ordinarily she'd be aghast at what it cost, even though they could afford it. But in reality, she'd realised how little it all mattered. Money didn't do anything when it came to the important stuff. Tom's parents could probably buy the hospital where he was receiving his treatment – maybe several times over – but even the best protocol in the world might not be effective.

They arrived, tired and a little strung out from the journey, and flung their cases on the bed, sitting down next to them. 'God, I must be getting old!' Tom quipped. 'I feel knackered from that.'

Her silence highlighted what they were both thinking. 'Me too,' she added. 'Definitely.'

She wondered whether Tom had felt like this in the early years of their relationship, when she'd oohed and aahed over Parisian tourist traps and he'd felt a little jaded by it all; had seen it all before. It wasn't that she didn't love Paris, that she hadn't come to look forward to their yearly trips here. It was just that knowing that they had an enormous obstacle to overcome once home tarnished her enjoyment, yet she knew that Tom needed her to be upbeat, enthusiastic.

She stretched her mouth into a smile. 'So, where first?' she asked.

'How about the Centre Pompidou?'

'Brilliant.' In truth it wasn't one of her favourite Parisian destinations, the building – with its pipework on the outside, as if it were proudly showing off its underwear in public – didn't seem beautiful to her. But this wasn't about her, not at all.

'Or the Latin Quarter?'

'Yeah, you know what. I like the sound of that more,' she smiled, holding out her hand for his.

Ten minutes later, they emerged onto the street. August sun reflected heat back onto them. The air was sticky with it. There were others walking, some with parasols, others fanning themselves with papers or leaflets as they walked. Nobody looked happy to be out in the sunshine. 'Guess that's why all the locals leave in August,' said Tom. 'Too hot.'

'Yeah.'

They began the walk, one they'd done a few times before. Half an hour, then they usually stopped for a coffee or a beer in the sunshine, depending on time of day and weather, then meandered through the cobbles of the quarter, dropping into tiny boutiques, staring in the window of chocolatiers and patisseries longingly, sometimes succumbing.

Sophie breathed deeply, smelling the scent that felt unique to Paris. The fumes from the traffic, the waft of perfumes as expensive-looking women sashayed past, the fug of cigarettes from an outside table and under it all, something else. Something intangible – maybe the smell of cold stone, or worn pavements, or simply the mixture of all of it, familiar to her nose now as the smell of her parents' house, or the apartment she shared with Tom. Paris had become, in some ways, home to her. She laughed inwardly at the decadence of the idea – that Paris belonged to them, to her.

Then: 'Sophie,' he said. Then slightly more urgently, 'Sophie!'

She turned then, snapped out of her daydream and saw that his face was white, covered in a sheen of sweat.

'Oh, what is it?' she said, alarm in her voice.

'Nothing. Not really. Just... it's a bit hot. I wondered... should we sit? Maybe get a break. Um, you're looking a bit tired,' he said.

'Oh. Yes. I am a bit,' she lied. She pointed to a *tabac* outside which there were some fairly rudimentary metal chairs and tables, a couple of which were free. 'Shall we stop there? It looks... nice.'

Soon they were installed, and they ordered tall glasses of iced water, plus an espresso each, which came with a little gingery biscuit on the saucer. She bit into hers and watched him as he drank deeply from his glass.

'God, that's better,' he said smiling. But his smile was muted somehow.

'Tom, if you're feeling ill, we don't have to stay. We can...'

'I'm FINE.' The words came out sharply, loud enough to make a woman at the next table turn and look at him interestedly, over the top of her round sunglasses.

'You're clearly not.'

'Stop it!' he said.

'What?'

'Soph. Look, I realise you think I'm on my last legs or whatever—'

'I never said that!'

'But just let me... be. Can you? I don't want you to treat me like...'

'Like what? Someone who needs a little support right now? Someone who isn't very well?' she said, suddenly feeling reciprocal anger.

'Like someone who's weak,' he said, his eyes fixed on her.

She reached across, but he drew his hand away. 'Tom, what if... well, what if you *are* weak right now? Ill. Surely it's OK to look after you?'

His eyes softened and he looked down. 'Yeah, I guess. It's just, that's not who I wanted to be for you. I wanted to be... you know—'

'My strong man? My rock?' she said, teasing slightly, trying to lighten the mood.

'Well yeah, I guess.' He shrugged.

'Bit sexist?' she suggested, feeling the mood lift a little between them.

'Maybe a smidge.' He grinned and suddenly he was Tom again. 'Ah, jeez, sorry Soph. It's just... I hate all this.'

'Paris?' she said jokingly.

'No. Obviously. Just, well, that I can be just going through life, minding my own business. Maybe being a bit of a dick sometimes, a bit annoying. And yes, you're right, I've had a few helping hands along the way with work. But I've never asked for any of it. And I've never hurt anyone, you know.'

He turned his head abruptly but not before she saw the shimmer of tears.

'I know.'

'So it's hard to work out – why me? Why do I have this thing? Not even a, you know, *normal* cancer. Testicular. One that blokes my age have. Whip off one of my bollocks or whatever. I mean, I know it still sucks, but...' He met her eye. 'It said on the Internet that pancreatic, it's one of the worst. If not *the* worst. Because it gets caught late. When it's too late to, well – stop it.'

She nodded, feeling a lump form in her throat.

'Ah, listen to me,' he said, coughing slightly, clearing his throat. 'Bringing down the mood.'

'You are allowed to bring down the mood! Look, Tom, I've brought down the mood for – how long? – almost THREE YEARS with the infertility stuff. And it doesn't even matter, does it? It's not even important, not really. Not compared to this.'

'You haven't. And it is important.'

'Well, so is this. And you helped me. So let me. Give me a chance to help you.'

He looked at her, then, to her relief, raised a slightly humorous eyebrow. 'So you're saying that you need me to do this for you? That my being weak is fulfilling some dormant need in you to look after someone?'

She grinned. 'Well, yeah.'

'In that case, I'm all for it.'

And they were back.

'I know it's daft,' he said. 'But do you reckon we can make it to the bridge later? It's stupid, just...'

She nodded. She understood. 'Sure. Why not?' she said, trying to keep her tone light.

Because that's what it had come to, wasn't it? Dreams and wishes against the odds. He wanted that feeling of safety he'd felt as a child, when the universe had seemed benign and gracious, and his mother's love could protect him from harm.

She grabbed his hand. 'Midnight?' she suggested.

He smiled. 'Pathetic, eh.'

'Not at all,' she said. 'It'll be just what we need.'

She tried not to think over the course of the days that followed of the more sombre train ride back to the UK, back to reality – to tackling this enormous block in the road and seeing if they could actually be the lucky ones who made it through.

45

NOW

Sophie owed so many people a debt of gratitude for having got her through those first couple of years. Will, of course. Libby. And Sam – the baby sister who'd seemed suddenly so much older, more capable than Sophie herself.

When she'd met her in the pub that time, shortly after the kiss with Will, she'd looked entirely unlike herself. She'd changed her look; gone was the mousy shoulder-length do and instead, Sophie's sister had opted for a red bob which both suited her and made her seem young and vibrant. Which of course, at her age, she was, thought Sophie.

* * *

She smiled across the bar and gave a little wave before buying a glass of wine and walking over to join Sam at the sticky mahogany table in the little pub they met at whenever Sam was in town. Sam's career had taken off in recent years – she was a buyer for one of the major department stores – and she was always jetting off here and there. Or at least, it seemed that way.

Sophie put down her wine and then pulled out one of the chairs, sinking into it with a sigh.

'Rough week?' her sister said, taking a sip from a tall glass of orange juice.

'You could say that,' Sophie replied. The new term was now well underway but she was still adjusting to her new timetable and the children she'd been assigned this year. It was always difficult establishing yourself with new classes – they tested you constantly in the early weeks and you ended up completely drained by the weekend. 'Ah, it's OK,' she said, seeing a look of concern flit over her sister's face. 'Just the usual.'

'Brats?'

'Brats,' she said decisively, knowing that neither of them really meant it. She loved the children she taught – almost all of them. And she'd found over the years she'd been in the profession that even the most difficult child would have something loveable about them if you looked hard enough. Usually.

'So how's *your* work?' Sophie asked, taking a large gulp of wine and resisting the urge to emit a dramatic sigh of relief as it warmed her throat.

She was treated to a long story about a flight, a missing suitcase, a meeting in which Sam had taken the lead and got a great deal. It sounded so far removed from her own life that it was hard to imagine. Dressing in sharp, corporate wear, strutting into meetings with head held high. Not staggering into a classroom in the same creased skirt you had worn the day before, trying to balance your coffee on a pile of textbooks.

'Are you actually listening?' Sam asked her after a pause.

'Yes. Sorry. Yes, I am.'

Sam cocked an eyebrow. 'Sorry,' she said. 'I know I go on a bit.'

'Oh, God, it's not that. I was just thinking how... well, different our lives are,' Sophie admitted. 'I'm jealous really.'

'You could always make a career change.'

'Ah, not that. Although, yeah, sometimes I'd love to. More that you seem at the beginning of things – it's exciting. I'm happy for you. But it makes me feel kind of... washed up in comparison.'

'You?' Sam seemed incredulous.

'Yeah, you know. In my thirties. Widowed. It's hardly living the dream, is it.' She gave a wan smile and sipped her wine again, trying to deflect any sympathy.

'Sophie, is that how you see yourself?' Sam shook her head. 'You know how much in awe I am of you? You have this great career, and it's not one that everyone can do, is it? And yeah, you've had some hard times, but you've picked yourself up. You're doing OK. I mean, you are... aren't you?'

Sophie nodded. It didn't sound quite so desperate, described like that.

'Are you still rowing with Will?' her sister added, raising an inquisitive eyebrow. 'How's all that going?'

A flash of annoyance rose in her. 'It's not going at all,' she said. 'To be honest, I'm kind of distancing myself from him.'

'Oh. Sorry. Why? He seemed like a really nice guy.'

'He is.' She stopped, looking down at her almost empty glass and swirling the last of the wine around its base. 'I just... I'm not ready for anything, you know?'

'And he wants that?'

She shrugged. 'You know what, I think I wanted that too. Just for a moment. And it's been nice spending time with him, doing the rowing, that kind of thing. But it just feels...'

'How does it feel?' Sam asked softly.

'As if I'm cheating on Tom.'

Sam looked at her. 'Oh, Soph!'

'Well, yeah. I mean, moving on to anyone new would be... hard enough. But Will? They were friends for years!'

Sam nodded. 'Yeah, I see that. But I'm not sure... I don't know if I agree, if I'm honest.'

'What do you mean?'

'Well, firstly, Tom's been gone almost two years.'

'Nineteen months.'

'OK, well, nineteen months. It's a long time, Soph. In some ways at least. And if there's a chance to be happy, to have someone to love again, I don't think Tom would want you to pass that up.'

She shrugged. 'Maybe.'

'I mean, didn't you talk about this? Before he... died?'

'Yeah, a bit. He told me to go out and live my life.'

'Well then!'

'He didn't tell me to go and live it with his best friend!'

'Soph, you're being ridiculous. You know how hard it is to find someone you can really relate to?' Sam shook her head. 'It's impossible. But you've found that with Tom. And now maybe Will. Does it really matter that they were friends? Maybe Tom would have liked the idea of Will kind of being there for you. Rather than some stranger.'

She nodded. 'Maybe,' she said again.

'So, why not just see where it leads?'

Sophie thought about the kiss. How gentle it had been, how much feeling it had seemed to contain. The spark when their lips touched – a little bit of electricity. They'd pulled apart just seconds later, but something had shifted between them.

'Sorry,' Will had said.

'No,' she'd said. 'Don't be.'

'Thanks, Sam,' she said now.

'What for?'

'Making sense of it all. You're wise for a young'un.'

Sam grinned. 'Old head on young shoulders, that's me. But seriously, sis, if you think this thing with Will is the real deal, try not to question it too much. You deserve a bit of luck after everything that's happened.'

Sophie thought about Tom's conviction that he'd been 'too lucky' in the past. If there was a balance to be found, surely the scales tipped in favour of her having a good experience after what she'd been through.

'Maybe,' she said, then sat up. 'Anyway, tell me about you. Been seeing anyone?'

As Sam launched into a colourful anecdote about a restaurant booking and an undercooked steak, Sophie had sat, half listening, smiling at the sister who always seemed to know what to say.

She hoped that, moving forward, she could be the sort of sister to Sam that Sam had been to her. Someone less bogged down in her own struggles and open to the needs of others. Sitting there, Sophie found herself nodding 'yes', determined at least to try.

46

THE NINTH SUMMER – 2019

'This is the life!' Tom said, leaning back in his chair and tilting his bottle of beer slightly at Sophie. In front of them was the best meal they'd ever eaten on Eurostar – Business Premier tickets had been pricey, but the food was actually delicious, Sophie thought, looking at the pink salmon fillet, smelling the aroma of the white wine sauce and looking at the bubbles dancing up her champagne flute. She hadn't wanted to accept the tickets, booked by Tom's parents. Had thought it was all 'Too Much', but Tom had persuaded her. 'I know they're a bit difficult, but this is their way of showing love.'

'Really?'

'Yeah. They throw money at things rather than have real feelings,' he'd said. He'd smiled, but there had been an unease about it. 'We might as well benefit.'

She'd acquiesced, seeing that's what he really wanted to do. And after everything, surely that was the most important thing. She'd only had about half her champagne – she didn't want to end up blind drunk and incapable of organising herself at the other end, and wanted to give Tom the chance to kick back after a gruelling year of treatment after treatment after treatment.

Sophie had noticed a change in him since his most recent oncology appointment last month; something had lightened in him as he'd walked away from the hospital. He'd turned to her – still pale, still painfully thin, but suddenly in his eyes she could recognise *her* Tom, someone who'd been absent during the worst of the chemo, someone he'd tucked away beneath the pain and the indignity of it all.

'Fuck it,' he'd said. 'Let's go to Paris.'

'Really?'

'Yeah. Why not. It's a tradition and I'm damned if I'm letting cancer get in the way. Especially now there's no more chemo!'

'But last year...' she'd begun, knowing that their trip the year before had been far from ideal – his fear and hers creating a crackling tension between them.

'I know. It was shit. But it doesn't mean we can't kind of... rewrite that. In fact, that's what I hope to do. Rewrite it all. I want us to have only good memories of being there. And they mostly have been, haven't they?'

She'd looked at him and nodded. In reality, she'd have much rather gone on a trip somewhere warm, to lie in the sun and rest and let someone else do all the looking after and schedule planning. But she understood where he was coming from. 'Let's do it then,' she'd said.

It had been nice to see him enthusiastic about it too – he'd bought a Paris guidebook (not something he really needed, she'd thought) and had written them an itinerary. 'We'll need four days at least,' he'd told her seriously. 'To get to everything.'

'Everything being...?'

He'd looked at her. 'All the places. The bridge. The Centre

Pompidou, La Défense, the Louvre, the Latin Quarter. All of it. All our places.'

'Sure it won't be too much?'

He'd flicked a dismissive hand in the air. 'Stop worrying, woman!' he'd said jokingly. 'Can't a man plan a romantic trip for his wife without interference these days?'

She'd laughed, but hadn't been able to get the concern out of her tone entirely.

It was made worse when she'd answered the phone to Tom's mum a few days later. 'Are you sure it's a good idea, Sophie?' she'd said. 'I know you love Paris, but try to think about Tom. His needs.'

Before Tom's illness, she'd thought Julie's protectiveness over her son was sweet, and understandable given that he was her only child. But since the diagnosis, something had changed; there was a sense of challenge, of ownership. Sophie knew it was grief, knew that underneath her fear and devastation Julie was a nice person, a good mum. But it was hard to feel it at times like this when her voice snapped down the line.

She'd gripped the phone and tried to keep her calm. 'Julie, this is all Tom's idea,' she'd said. 'I'm trying to do what he wants.'

'But what he wants and what he *needs* are two very different things.'

She hadn't dignified that with a response. But she had made Tom promise that they'd get taxis everywhere instead of tackling the metro or trying to walk. He'd been more than happy to make that concession. 'I'll tell Mum,' he'd said.

'No, don't. We can get it.'

Tom had slipped an arm around her. 'It's not for us, Soph. It's for her. Mum, she always wants to fix things. Dad too. Most of the time, money's been able to achieve that. I don't think she knows how to handle this...' he had gestured vaguely at his body. 'It'll make her feel better to do this for us.'

Finishing her meal, Sophie sat back in her comfortable seat and watched the familiar view flash by. If someone had told her when she'd taken the train under the Channel for the first time that she'd be back every year for almost a decade, she wouldn't have believed them. She'd have scoffed at the idea that she and Tom would get married; that they'd be celebrating their fifth anniversary soon. Yet here she was.

You never know what life might throw at you, she thought, looking at her husband who'd fallen asleep, his champagne flute in his lap – thankfully drained. You have to be grateful for the moment you're in, because that's all you really have.

They'd just finished their coffee when the announcements started, first in French then in English, that they were approaching the Gare du Nord, that they ought to start preparing. She felt a surge of adrenaline as she braced herself for the job ahead – gathering together their rather excessive luggage, getting Tom into his chair, managing the chilled bag of medications. They'd alerted a porter at the start of the journey, but he was yet to turn up and assist.

She masked her worry with a smile. 'Right!' she said as breezily as she could. 'Let's get this show on the road.'

'Bonjour Paris!' he said, throwing his arms wide. 'Let's make this one count.'

'A holiday to remember,' she said, forcing a smile.

'A grand finale,' he added.

She wanted, suddenly, to shout at him. That it wasn't funny. That it was horrible, heart-wrenching, tragic, unfair, and terrifying. But she held it back. What was the alternative? she thought. Lie on the ground and kick and scream at the horror of it all?

They'd said he probably had four weeks; this is what he wanted. Nothing else mattered.

Instead, she nodded and grabbed the heavy, wheeled suitcase from the on-board storage. She took his arm, as if it were her rather than him who needed support, and they made their way clumsily to the exit. She set the case down, gave him a quick grin, as if this were a completely normal situation, and went back in for his wheelchair. Pulling it out of the rack, she felt a sob heave in her throat. But no. She wouldn't let it. They were going to have a wonderful time.

47

NOW

Will, Sam, and of course, Libby. The three of them had held her up in turn through those dark months. Libby, with her infectious optimism, had been the one who'd helped her to bring a little fun back, despite the pain. Booking those spa days, cinema, theatre tickets, and not taking no for an answer.

Late 2021, she'd found herself going to see *Les Misérables* in central London. Testament, once again, to her friend's persuasive skills.

* * *

Libby was waiting in the theatre foyer, looking at her watch, when Sophie rushed in. 'I'm so sorry!' she panted. 'I'm not used to the tube any more!'

Libby laughed. 'Hey, it's OK,' she said. 'As long as you don't stand me up.'

'As if.'

They linked arms and made their way to the bar, determined to get a glass of something in before the performance started. It was their fifth time watching *Les Misérables* and it was becoming something of a tradition.

'God, I love this show,' Sophie said.

'Even though it makes you sob your heart out?'

'Even so,' she smiled. It was true, the love story, the child getting shot, the misery and ecstasy of it all often left her with tears pouring down her face. But they were different tears. The kind of tears she'd shed over a book or a film. A caught-up-in-the-emotional-moment rather than the real sadness and misery she'd experienced with Tom.

'So, how are things with Will?' Libby asked as they took their glasses over to a standing table in the corner, giving others a chance to get to the bar before curtain up.

'What do you mean?'

'Come on. You two have been getting close.'

Sophie's hands felt hot. 'Not really. We're just friends!' She thought about the kiss. About how, when she was with Will, she felt different; lighter.

'Sure about that?' Libby's eyebrow rose in a teasing challenge.

'Seriously,' she said, her voice coming out more sharply than she expected it to. 'It's nothing.'

'Sorry,' Libby said, chastened.

'No, I'm sorry. I didn't mean to snap. It's just everyone seems to be sure we're getting together. And I like Will, I do. A lot. It's just... it doesn't seem right somehow.'

'In what way?'

'Come on, Libby. Tom's... well, it's only been two years. And they used to be best friends.'

'OK,' Libby said. Then, nodding at the barman, 'Plenty of options if you'd rather someone brand new,' she quipped. 'Do you want me to get his number for you?!'

'Libby!' she said, half infuriated, half laughing. 'No, thank you.'

Libby shrugged.

'Anyway, what about you?'

Libby put a hand on her chest, dramatically. She was wearing electric blue nail polish, Sophie noticed, set with little silver gems. 'Me?' she said.

'Yeah. Anyone on the horizon?'

A little shake of the head. 'Nobody worth talking about.'

'Are you sure?' Sophie wheedled.

Libby looked uncharacteristically serious. 'OK. Maybe,' she said. 'There's been someone. Recently.'

'Ooh!' Sophie leant forward, interested. 'Tell me everything!'

'Well, he's nice. It's just...' She picked up a beer mat and started to tear off the corner.

'What, skeletons in the closet? Weird job? Funny looking?' Sophie teased.

Libby shook her head. 'No, it's me.'

'Oh. Just not sure?'

Another shake. 'Fuck it. OK. Well, if you must know, I'm nervous. You know about... getting too serious.'

'Nervous? You?'

Libby's eyes were shining. 'Oh, I know. I put on a veneer. Loud Libby, jokey Libby. And I am, I guess. But... I do worry sometimes.'

'About getting hurt?'

'One way or another. I mean you had Tom. And...' she trailed off. 'Stupid of me.'

Sophie grabbed her hand. 'No! Not stupid. It's... it's normal to be a bit scared.'

'You think?'

'It means that you actually care about something, if you're frightened to lose it.'

Libby nodded. 'Maybe.'

'But Libby. You deserve it. Happiness. Or the possibility of it. What happened to me was... well, all sorts of horrible. But that's the lottery of life, I suppose. And you can't let it hold you back. Make you afraid. Maybe it's even more reason to seize happiness if you have a chance of it?'

'Maybe you're right.'

Sophie nodded. She wasn't quite sure where the words had come from; somewhere deep inside she'd thought had died alongside Tom. But she'd believed every word as they'd fallen from her lips. You shouldn't fear life, she thought. You just had to live it. If Tom's experience had taught them anything, it should be that.

They sipped their drinks silently.

'Nearly time,' Sophie said, looking at her phone.

'Cool. Shall we order some more drinks for the interval?'

'You know, what if I did start liking Will. I mean, what would you think of it?' Sophie found herself blurting.

'Well,' Libby said carefully, 'I'd think it was a good thing. Finding someone. And we've known Will for years – he's a good guy.'

'He is.'

Libby leant slightly against the table. 'You know there was a time, at first, when I thought you might end up with Will? Before it all took off properly with Tom.'

'No, you didn't! Did you?'

'Well, yeah. You two just seemed...'

'Seemed what?'

'Well, like a fit I suppose.' Libby shrugged as if the information she'd just imparted were no big deal.

'And you didn't think that about me and Tom?' Sophie felt an unexpected flash of anger.

'Well, no. Not at first. But then I thought, well, what do I know?' Libby shrugged. 'People are attracted to each other for all sorts of reasons. You and Tom were kind of like, well, chalk and cheese. You seemed really different from each other... but sometimes I think we're attracted to people for that reason, aren't we? You know, we fill in each other's gaps.' She smiled.

Ordinarily, Sophie would have had something to say about Libby's choice of words, but she was too – what? Incensed? Shocked? Interested? 'What, complete each other?'

'Well, yeah. If you're into romcom terminology. Yes.'

'So not chalk and cheese then?'

'OK, maybe not. Cheese and pickle?' Libby suggested.

Sophie's mouth turned up, involuntarily almost. It was impossible not to love Libby. 'Right,' she said. 'Thanks, I guess.'

There was a shuffle of people as the time for the performance to start grew closer. People began to return glasses, to make their way to their seats or to join the queue for the loos. Libby got up as if everything were ordinary. As if she hadn't said something that, to Sophie, seemed life-altering.

'But,' she said. 'Seriously. You didn't think Tom and I... well, would work out?'

'I didn't say that,' she said. 'Just at first you seemed different. But you proved me wrong, didn't you?'

Sophie was quiet. 'I guess we did.'

The melancholy that washed over them both whenever Tom was mentioned stilled them for a moment.

'Come on,' Libby said decisively, linking her arm through Sophie's. 'If we're going to be "*misérables*", we might as well make the most of it. It's starting soon.'

But Sophie wasn't ready. 'So you think that... I mean, Will

and me... That it's OK? That if I... we... saw each other a bit, it wouldn't be a betrayal of Tom?'

'Course not!'

'Even though Tom and I said we'd be together forever? I mean, I made a promise, Libby.'

'Yes, you did. But it included... you know... 'Til... well, 'til death do us part.' Libby grimaced at her own words. 'So, you know.'

'Yeah, maybe.'

'You deserve a bit of fun, at least. It doesn't matter whether Will's the second love of your life, or just someone nice to date. It's OK to move on.'

Sophie snatched her arm away, suddenly defensive. 'Two years isn't long, Libby!' she said.

'For God's sake.' Libby, usually the coolest of cucumbers, was beginning to sound impatient. 'Look, you've got to stop feeling so guilty about everything. What happened to Tom, it was awful. But you know, it happened to you too. You deserve happiness. And who's to say what would have happened if Tom hadn't got sick. I mean, things weren't... great with you guys before that, were they?'

'They were OK.'

There was a silence as the two women looked at each other. As if neither could quite believe Libby had said that.

'Sorry,' she added. 'Too much. No relationship is perfect, after all. I suppose I'm just saying... We don't know what life might have waiting around the corner. And maybe it's time to think about living again?'

Sophie's body filled with indignant adrenaline. She wanted to march out of the theatre, into a taxi and get home as soon as possible. She wanted to yell at her friend. She wanted to shake her to say, 'Tom and I – we weren't like that! We loved each other!'

But looking at Libby's face, she softened. People sometimes said the wrong thing for the right reasons. So many of the friends on the periphery of Sophie's life had melted away when she was bereaved. Had crossed the street to avoid an awkward conversation. Had not known what to say, so had said nothing at all. Libby had always been there. And while Sophie didn't always appreciate her interventions, didn't always agree with what she said, she was grateful that she was still at her side, still talking to her. Not worried, as others seemed to be, that bereavement might be catching. She felt a shiver of longing and frustration, sadness and residual anger run through her and wondered, not for the first time, how the simple five letters of grief could encompass such a range of emotions.

'Shit,' Libby said.

'What?'

'I've upset you, haven't I? I'm such an idiot.'

'You're not, you're not!' Sophie wiped her eyes, annoyed that they were betraying her. 'I mean, you aren't exactly tactful.'

Libby snorted.

'But you're here. You're saying something. And there isn't anything you can say that would be right. Most people run away from that.'

Libby nodded. 'Soph, you guys loved each other. Anyone could see that. Just, I love you too. And I want to help. I'm just not very good at it.'

'Not very good?'

'Shit. I am completely and utterly shit at it.'

Sophie felt the ghost of a smile flicker on her lips. 'That's more like it.' She slipped an arm around her friend. 'But thanks,' she said.

Libby's eyebrows raised. 'For what?'

'Ah, you know.' And she gave her friend a small smile, which was returned.

The pair walked into the theatre to lose themselves in other people's misery and heartache and redemption, and forget about their own traumas for a while.

* * *

She'd book tickets again, thought Sophie now. To another musical. Because Libby loved them. And it was time she started being a better friend.

48

THE NINTH SUMMER – 2019

People gave them a wide berth. The young girl, in her summer dress, hair shoulder-length and styled, make-up on, making the best of things. And the boy, thin, pale, in a wheelchair. A contrast between someone at the beginning of life and what they'd been told would soon be the end of life. Occasionally, Sophie would catch a glance of herself and Tom, in the reflection of a taxi as the driver removed the chair for her, or in a shop window as they passed. And she'd be surprised and horrified anew at what she saw.

But the rest of the time, it was just her and Tom, Tom and her. It was as if Tom had emerged from a cocoon: the worry, the treatment, the dread had been removed. There wasn't any point to any of it now. And beneath it all there he was, the boy she'd fallen in love with and the man he'd become.

'The Louvre?' he asked when they first exited the hotel, wheelchair at their side, ready in case he became exhausted.

'Seriously?'

He shrugged. 'Like it or not, it's one of *our* places. Maybe I've even come to like it a bit over the years.'

'Even the *Mona Lisa*?'

'Still think she looks like George Harrison, but you know. She's got something about her. Bit like an old friend.'

Sophie snorted. 'Well, she does always seem to smile at you.'

'Exactly.' He linked his arm through hers as the taxi drew up. 'Got to say goodbye to the old girl.'

Something like fear prickled through the bubble they were creating, and they were both silent as they got themselves into the taxi's back seat. But when he turned to her again, his thin face beaming, it was as if it had never happened.

'You sure?' she said.

He nodded. 'Onwards, James!' he said to the taxi driver who turned to them bemused.

'*Louvre, s'il vous plaît*,' Sophie said apologetically as they both giggled.

It was strange, but Tom had been right. Being in Paris made the rest of the year – all the trauma of it – kind of fall away. They were back in *their* place and just for a few days they could suspend it all: the past, the future. And just be Sophie and Tom. Tom and Sophie.

After they'd visited some of their favourite artworks and scooted past the remainder, Sophie suggested they go back to the hotel for a rest. 'It's been tiring,' she said.

'Only if *you're* tired,' he said, shrugging a shoulder. 'I'm OK, honestly.'

She looked at him, his open, honest eyes. 'You're sure?'

'Yeah. It's weird. It's like... I don't know. Maybe I just feel better than I did before. You know, during all the treatment. I mean, the painkillers are pretty heavy, but even so I'm kind of... it's like I feel better.'

They looked at each other for a moment then, both unable to express the tiny hope they both carried that, despite his diagnosis, something miraculous could yet happen. Because it did, sometimes, didn't it? People lived for a long time under the cloud of a terminal diagnosis. And doctors made mistakes all the time.

Sophie broke her gaze away and straightened up, hand in the small of her back where she'd been bending to push. 'OK,' she said. 'How about we go over the bridge?'

'The Pont du Carrousel?'

'Yeah. But maybe not midnight, this time? Maybe now would be better.'

He gave a single, decisive nod. 'Yeah. Think so,' he said softly.

It wasn't far, but they took a taxi anyway, both silently acknowledging that it was probably for the best. Soon they were standing and looking over the Seine, everything the same and yet different from the years before; the flick book of almost a decade where they'd stood here and wondered about the future playing through their minds.

'It's beautiful,' Tom said, standing next to her, a thin arm at her back.

'Yes,' she said. 'Want to take a boat ride?'

He shook his head. 'Happier just standing here for a bit, if that's OK?'

'Of course.' They'd always elected to watch the boats rather than travel on them. They'd both agreed that they'd rather be on the bridge watching the action than be on the boat looking up at staring tourists. But she sometimes watched the passengers with jealousy, wondering what it would be like to be on the boat rather than on the outside.

A silence fell over them as they stood, lost in thought. The sun was warm on their backs, the river glistened underneath them, and Sophie thought of all the people who had stood in this very spot over the centuries, looking at views very similar to that she saw now, and thought about their own pasts and futures and the fragility of life. We think we're in control of it all, she thought. But we're not. We're so temporary.

'Cheer up, love, it might never happen!' Tom said in her ear, just at the point when she felt close to tears, and instead, she felt laughter bubble up inside her.

'God, I'm going to miss you,' she said.

He was silent. 'Well, with any luck you won't have to,' he said. 'How do you fancy being haunted for eternity?'

She smiled sadly. 'Do you promise?'

And they kissed, his cold lips against her warm ones, the two of them together, balancing each other out as they always had.

49

NOW

Sophie felt embarrassed sometimes when she thought about how she'd treated Will back then. Grief did odd things to you, true. But it was no excuse for pushing him away the way she had. Looking out at the white, brightening sky outside the window, she thought back to that morning in November when she'd sent him away.

* * *

'Actually, I need to speak with you,' Sophie said as Will tied the boat to its mooring. He looked up at her, his forehead wrinkling, eyes wide.

'Yeah?'

She nodded, feeling slightly teary. She pulled her warm coat around her, her arms still aching from the morning's rowing. She was getting good at it; had begun to look forward to their sessions twice a week. It would be sad to leave it behind.

They walked back to the clubhouse. It was still only seven and they often went to get a coffee and warm up afterwards, before she disappeared home to shower and get ready for work, and he did the same. This time, the walk felt awkward, the silence between them growing as she struggled to find the right way to say it.

'Will, I don't think I can do this any more.'

He turned to her. 'But you're getting so good at it! Today, I mean, you were amazing. I was actually going to suggest...'

'No, Will. Not the rowing. This,' she said, waving her hand between them. 'You and me.'

'What do you mean?'

After the kiss, he'd pulled away; neither of them had mentioned it outright since. They'd continued as they always had, meeting at five, rowing, talking, laughing together. But with this unanswered question hanging between them. She'd sensed he'd been waiting for her to bring it up.

'Look, Will,' Sophie put her hand on his arm and they both stopped walking. 'I think you're amazing. A great friend, an above-average rower,' she grinned – but it was not returned. 'Just... I don't think I can carry on meeting up like this. It's just... it doesn't feel right.'

'Why not? I don't understand. Have I upset you? Was it... the other day?'

She shook her head. 'No. Well, yes, but not in the way you think.'

He looked at her, waiting for her to clarify.

'I wanted you to kiss me. The other day. I... I suppose I'd been waiting for it in a way. For something to happen between us. We've got close, we get on. And I'd begun to feel...' She shrugged, not quite sure how to say it.

'Well, me too.' He stepped towards her, but she took a small step back. He looked at her, incredulous.

'Will, I can't.'

'It's fine, we can just...'

'No, Will. I can't be with you like that. It's too much, too soon. And it feels – I'm so mixed up because of Tom and...' She trailed off.

'It's fine,' he said, running a hand through his hair. 'Look, Sophie. I get it. We're friends. And if you're never ready for anything else, well, friends is enough. It really is. Seriously.'

She shook her head. 'I can't, Will. I can't even be your friend right now.'

'But why not?' He put a hand on her arm. 'Rowing together doesn't mean anything. And it's been good for you – for me too. I can talk to you so easily. Please don't do this.'

'I just... I need space,' she said. 'Because I do want more. When you kissed me... But I can't, Will. You have to understand.'

And she picked up her pace and walked away from him. She heard his footsteps on the ground just behind her, but she didn't turn. Eventually, he stopped, let her go. When she got to her car and opened the door, she finally allowed herself to glance back. But by that time, he'd disappeared into the building and other than a few other rowers meandering along the Cam, she was completely alone.

* * *

Although she'd never been alone, not truly. She saw that now. She'd missed Tom so viscerally back then that it had been impossible to see clearly how many people she had holding her up.

50

THE NINTH SUMMER – 2019

The nights were always the worst. Tom found it impossible to lie flat, and needed propping and supporting with pillows before he could get to anything approaching comfortable. She'd asked for a couple of extra pillows from the hotel, but still had to call for another one to get him into his new position.

'Do you want a hot water bottle?' she suggested, once he was comfortable.

'What am I? A hundred years old?' he asked, half joking, half rattled.

'They said it might help, you know, with the pain.'

'It's too bloody hot.'

She nodded. He was right. August was not a good time to need the pain relief of heat.

'Well, I've got the... medicine, if you need it.'

He nodded. 'I'm already rattling, but I'll bear it in mind.'

'Or how about I turn up the air con, then the hot water bottle will...'

'Soph. Just stop. Please.'

It was impossible to know how much he was suffering. *Some*

people experience a lot of pain, others find it more tolerable, the specialist had told them. But knowing Tom as she did, she suspected he was struggling a lot more than he was willing to show.

He'd begun to grunt sometimes in his sleep, wake up suddenly with a cry. She didn't know whether it was his mind or body leading to these episodes and didn't know how to ask. During the day, other than seeming exhausted, needing to rest or sleep from time to time, he seemed more like his usual self. But at night, everything felt different.

She'd promised, five years before, standing in front of him in her wedding dress, that she'd care for him in sickness and in health. And she'd meant it. But with his prognosis so uncertain – weeks, maybe a little over a month – she'd begun to feel more and more afraid. How would she know if he was going to die? Might he just pass away? Each time she woke in the night, she'd put out a hand to touch his skin, unable to sleep until she discovered that it was still warm, that Tom was still with her.

This morning, she was relieved when the sun finally made itself known, bathing the tops of the buildings in light and starting to find its way through the gaps in the shutters and into their bedroom. He was sleeping, his face yellow-tinged in the half-light, his cheeks slightly sunken. Careful not to wake him, she climbed out of bed and made her way to the en suite. There, she ran some water and washed her face, inspecting herself in the mirror, noticing the grey shadows under her eyes that had formed over the past few weeks. Her body ached for sleep, but her mind was active, whirring already.

Today they'd booked to go to the Eiffel Tower, and while she loved it, it was the last place she wanted to be. What she wanted more than anything was to go home – close to other people who could help, even his family. His doctors. Proper care.

But there was no way she could let him see that. She stepped into the shower and turned up the heat, tried to lose herself in the rhythm of it, the ritual of washing her hair, then her body, of towelling herself off. Stepping out, she wiped the steam from the mirror and began to brush her hair. The show would go on, and she wasn't going to let him down.

Tom hated his wheelchair, hadn't wanted her to bring it. But she had, of course. It was lightweight, relatively easy to transport. Today she would insist that they brought it to the tower, to ensure that he could rest when needed.

They'd booked the lift and made sure they secured tickets for earlier in the day when it would hopefully be quieter; she'd contacted them directly to let them know the situation. As much as possible, she'd been upbeat and breezy in her conversations with Tom about it, as if it would all be straightforward.

When she exited the bathroom, he was awake; he looked at her and smiled. 'Come back to bed,' he said, patting the mattress next to him.

'Ah, maybe later,' she said, smiling. 'Got to get ready for the tower. Are you excited?'

He grinned, and there he was again, her Tom. 'Doesn't sound much like me.'

'Maybe not,' she admitted. 'Still, I'm looking forward to being up there again.'

Two hours later, they were climbing out of the taxi. Him, frail on her arm, but determinedly refusing to sit in the chair. The tower loomed in front of them and she was surprised, suddenly, that it looked exactly the same as it always had. It had been there for over a century before either of them was born, and would be there, too, after they'd both gone. She'd liked that at first – the history and timelessness of it – but today she felt only the impermanence of everything other than the tower. The people swarming up and down it, those taking pictures, herself here today and before across the years. Fragile, replaceable, weak.

She shook her head, tried to smile. 'Well, here we are!'

'Yes. Don't fancy the stairs today?'

'Tom! You know you couldn't...' but she looked at him: his mouth stretched wide in a smile. 'Oh, very funny!' she said, laughing too. It was nice to laugh, even when the subject matter was dark. 'Doubt I've got it in me myself,' she said, 'not as young as I used to be.'

He agreed to sit in the chair while they queued, but not without offering it to her from time to time. 'Come on,' he said. 'I don't want to hog it!'

She laughed but refused.

He was still Tom. Still trying to see the humour in things. Still refusing all but the essential help. An old man with a cane offered to let them pass, indicating through a mixture of broken English and mime that they could actually skip the queue altogether, but Tom had shaken his head. '*Non, merci*,' he'd insisted.

Then they were in the lift, both familiar and alien all at once, drawing up through the inside of the tower, past staircase after staircase. 'Can you believe that we walked up all those?' she said to Tom quietly, and he shook his head.

People around them chatted in various languages, took photos, exclaimed over the view; they were silent, Tom lost in thought and Sophie just trying to commit everything to memory. Every moment, every second of this trip.

They exited on the second floor and moved to the separate lift that would take them to the top. There were fewer people with them now. She put her hand on Tom's shoulder and he lifted his hand to hers, their fingers interlocking. She squeezed gently. There was no need for words. Every moment of this trip had been a goodbye, and this was no different. The place they'd come the first time, the place where they'd agreed to get married. The place where they'd argued about fertility – something that seemed so trivial in this moment – and the place they'd resolved that they'd find the strength to beat the cancer.

And this time. The goodbye to a tower that would hold their memories for them for as long as it stood, centuries into the future.

51

NOW

It had taken two years to lift herself back to life properly, she remembered, sitting on the couch, drifting with her thoughts. To move flats, get a new job, start building herself up again. She remembered the early days when she'd first moved, how she'd fallen into a routine. How she'd realised – perhaps for the first time – that some sort of life was still possible without him.

* * *

The alarm went off and she sat up in bed, keen to get rid of its annoying trill as quickly as possible. Drawing back the duvet, she climbed out of bed and went to the bathroom to take a shower. Waking up in her new flat was still a dream come true – it was modest, small – sure – but it was clean, in a better part of town, quiet and importantly, *hers*. She'd said goodbye to the frugality of the white bedsit and it felt good.

She'd finally made it through the threshold and was onto the upper pay scale in teaching and, after much persuading by Libby, Sam and her parents, had used the money from the sale of her and Tom's flat as a deposit on her own place. 'It doesn't mean you've moved on from Tom just because you're not living in a shithole any more,' Libby had told her approvingly, and she'd smiled.

Her classes were going well; she'd made some proper friends in the staffroom and they'd all pile down to the pub on a Friday night. And although she'd stopped rowing, she'd joined the gym down the road from her building, spending an hour each time she went on the rowing machine. It wasn't the same, but it was something.

Sophie saw more of Sam, too. Her sister was still seeing Ian so she spent most of her weekends in Cambridge, always squeezing in time to see Sophie.

It wasn't quite happiness. But it was enough.

An hour later, she closed the door behind her and walked down the stairs to the foyer, then out into the spring sunshine, not yet enough to warm the air but enough to brighten it. She felt her mood lift – things always felt better in the spring, more optimistic. With the promise of summer ahead. She tried not to think about Paris – so synonymous with the approaching summer.

She kept her mind in the present moment, as she'd learned to do over the past two years, and thought about the lessons ahead today and the meeting she had to attend after school. Teaching was a job that would take from you as much as you were willing to give, and although that had caused stress for her in the past, it was a comfort now – she let it fill all the spaces in her life and her head where thoughts of Tom had threatened to overwhelm her.

It was Friday – payday – and she'd go to the cemetery after school, as she often did, to sit in the memorial gardens close to where Tom's cremation had taken place. In that first, raw week when they'd arranged the funeral, Julie had asked her if they could invest in a plaque – somewhere 'to come and remember Tom'. Sophie had been ambivalent at the time, convinced it was pointless, but hadn't said so. And now she was grateful for it. The quiet ritual of visiting the place where they'd said goodbye gave her a strange sense of comfort. She didn't believe Tom was there, any more than she thought he was in the ashes that still sat at the back of her cupboard at home. But it was a focus, a way of telling the universe that she hadn't let him down or broken her promises to him.

Tomorrow she was shopping with Sam, who was hoping to find a dress to wear to a friend's wedding, and Sunday she'd set aside for marking and preparing the lessons for the following week. In the past, she'd resented the way that teaching bled into her weekends and evenings, but for now, at least, she was grateful for the distraction, the way she was able to spend time at home without the loneliness of it closing in on her.

After parking her car in the teachers' car park, she made her way to the staffroom to get a coffee and start her day.

By lunchtime, her upbeat mood had soured. She'd taken on a new English set from a colleague and they had been raucous and difficult. Although she was well used to the ups and downs of the classroom by now, the constant behavioural challenges left her feeling jaded and drained.

'All right?' Pete, one of her department colleagues asked, passing the table where she sat, steaming black coffee next to her, staring off into the middle distance.

'Yeah. Just 11b,' she said.

'Ah,' he nodded. 'Biscuits then?'

'Biscuits,' she said, smiling. He passed a tin to her and she took a few, gratefully. She was always trying to eat healthily, to lose the few pounds she'd gained over the past year: rowing at the gym worked wonders, but she never burnt as many calories there as she had when she was with Will. There just weren't enough distractions in the plain, mirrored room with its various machines – no real distance to cover, no need to keep going if you wanted to get back. Too easy to quit once your muscles started to protest. But somehow, sugar was the only way to refuel after a class like that – there was probably something scientific in it, she thought, stuffing a chocolate digestive into her mouth. Sugar cravings in times of stress, or something. Whatever it was, it seemed unavoidable.

The rest of her lessons passed without incident, but as she went to her car, a light rain started to fall. She briefly considered leaving her visit until the next day, then felt a horrible stab of guilt at having even thought that.

Instead, she climbed into her car and drove the short distance to the little florist that nestled in a line of local shops – a newsagent, chip shop, estate agent – just along from the school. There she bought a bunch of daffodils – the tiny ones that bloomed in white and yellow. Little smiles on stems. Putting them on the seat, she started the car again and drove towards the city centre, through and out again, to the familiar turning into the memorial gardens.

The bumping started almost immediately. Light at first and then more violent, until she was forced to stop. She got out into the wet afternoon air, her face and hair almost immediately saturated by the tiny persistent drops. It was instantly obvious what was wrong: one of her tyres was completely flat, the rim resting on a thin layer of rubber against the tarmac.

'Shit,' she said, looking around to see if there was anyone who might help. But of course, as always, she was alone. She went to the back of the car and lifted out the spare with difficulty, then jacked up the car as her dad had taught her and wrestled with the nuts.

No matter how hard she pushed against them, the nuts would not budge. Tightened by her dad, or maybe even Tom, months or years ago. Designed to keep her safe. But now stopping her from making the repair.

There were moments these days when she enjoyed the feeling of being alone. When she walked along one of the footpaths close to the flats after a busy day; when she could watch whatever she wanted on TV at night; when she could choose what to do without having to check with anyone else. But this afternoon, wet through from the light spring rain, next to a useless car with its sunken tyre and unable to do anything to fix it for herself, she felt only anger. It wasn't fair. Tom should be here, he should be here. With her.

She didn't hear the car pull up behind her, or a man in a black suit get out until he was close. 'Can I help?' he said.

She looked up, her face tear-stained, and wiped an embarrassed hand across her face. 'It's just this tyre,' she said. 'I know how to do it... only...'

'It's no problem, honestly,' the man said, waving to the passenger in his car who, also dressed in black, nodded briefly. He quickly turned the nuts and got the wheel off, putting it in her boot as she placed the spare into its space. Then he was back, tightening things. The whole process took him just ten minutes.

'I hope I haven't made you late,' she said to him when it was done.

He shook his head.

Thanking him again, she climbed back into the driver's seat and drove to the familiar row of the car park closest to Tom's memorial. Climbing out, feeling cold and bedraggled, she grabbed the daffodils and made her way to his stone. She knelt in front of it, not worrying about the damp grass, and traced his name in the grooves of the little plaque with her finger. 'I miss you,' she told him, as she removed last week's chrysanthemums and arranged the daffodils as best she could.

She didn't always cry now when she came here. Sometimes she'd chat to him quietly, share secrets. Other times she'd just stand and look and think. But today she felt hot tears spring from her eyes – a combination of grief and exhaustion and the aftermath of her earlier frustration.

'Why did you have to leave?' she asked the stone bearing Tom's name. 'I'm so alone. So fucking alone.'

She let her head drop, fell silent in her grief. The only noise in the garden was the whisper of grass, the sound of distant traffic.

But then there was something else. The tread of footsteps behind her.

'Sophie?' a voice said.

She looked up and there he was. Will. His eyes full of concern.

'Will! What are you doing here? Not that... it's good you're here.'

He shrugged. 'I come here sometimes. Tom was a mate. I talk to him. Stupid, really.'

'It's not.' She straightened up, rubbing her eyes. 'Ignore me,' she added, trying to smile. 'It's just... it's been a day.'

He looked at her, his blue eyes full of kindness. 'I know the feeling.'

'It's good to see you.'

'You too.' He lifted the umbrella that he was holding to protect her from the rain.

'Probably a bit too late to rescue me,' she joked, looking

down at her sodden coat, feeling her hair hang in rats' tails around her face.

'Coffee?' he asked.

She nodded. 'Thank you.'

Because it wasn't too late at all.

* * *

Sophie smiled now. Loving, dependable Will. Always somehow there, in the periphery of her life. Now at the heart of it, where he so definitely belonged.

52

OCTOBER 2019

'I'm sorry for your loss,' said the man, bowing his head slightly as he shook her hand. Hers was limp and he grasped it with both of his as she looked at him, wondering who he was and whether she cared.

She could stay an hour and that would be enough. Then she'd make an excuse and get home. Sophie couldn't stand being here; the rumble of conversation in the background already making her feel as if people were moving on, the memorial service already in their rear-view mirrors.

She stood in a huddle with Libby, her parents, Sam, Will, some friends from university who'd made an appearance, sipping wine and simply trying to get through it. Once in a while someone she didn't know would clasp her hand and give her an emphatic 'sorry for your loss'; otherwise, people tended to cluster with others they knew and fall into conversation – perhaps about Tom, perhaps about cancer, perhaps about something completely different.

'Have some more wine,' Libby told her, giving her arm a squeeze. 'You've nearly made it.'

And it was true. She'd made it through the service, through the readings and the Humanist sermon that described someone who only half-sounded like Tom. She'd made the journey between there and here, dazed, in the back of a limousine. And now she'd spent almost sufficient time here to be able to call it a day, and slip away to actually start grieving.

It was odd, all the expected protocol of death. She understood it was a chance to honour Tom, to say goodbye. But all it had done so far, in reality, was make her feel very much on the periphery of things. Julie, Tom's mum, was holding court, resplendent in a black shift dress and angled hat. His father, Doug, sipped wine and talked quietly in the corner. They'd become distant, their dealings with her brief and business-like. Somehow as if they resented her. Perhaps because she'd taken Tom from them in his final years.

'Maybe they just can't deal with it,' Libby had suggested when she'd mentioned it. 'Nobody's their best self when coping with grief.'

She'd nodded. 'I suppose.'

'There's no suppose about it! You smashed my best coffee cup the other day, remember? When I said the wrong thing?' Libby's tone was teasing, as light as it could be in the circumstances. She slung an arm around Sophie. 'And it was fine. Because I'd probably do the same. But maybe this is their bad behaviour. Not about you at all.'

Whatever was driving their behaviour, it still made everything feel like a battle. Tom's last will and testament – the hastily drawn-up document he'd made with his solicitor after his diagnosis – named her executor and gave her ownership of the flat, and most of his stuff. Julie had spoken to her after reading it, asked if they could perhaps find a few 'mementoes' of their son.

'Nothing of value,' she'd added – as if Sophie really cared about that.

'Of course. It's important to have things to remember him by.'

In truth, she didn't want any of it, would have happily moved back to her parents' and left the flat for them to sort out. But she'd also wanted to follow Tom's wishes, so she'd dutifully taken the decision to sell the flat and put the proceeds in an account so she could think about it later.

'That's very kind,' Julie had said, her voice stiff and cold. 'Thank you. Although as his parents, we're in no danger of forgetting Tom, don't you worry about that.'

Had she deliberately misunderstood? Been insulted? Sophie hadn't known. But she'd realised at that point that any hope she'd had of keeping a relationship with them – for Tom and because, legally she supposed, they were her family too – was lost.

'Idiots,' Sam had said when she'd told her afterwards.

'I know. It's just... they're my last connection to him.'

'I get that. But if they're somehow blaming you for Tom's death, or treating you as an outsider, then they're not worth it. It wasn't them sitting beside Tom's bedside for all those hours at the end. They probably just feel guilty that they didn't make it in time, you know, to say goodbye properly.'

'Yeah, although his mum said if he'd been at home as she'd wanted...'

'Sophie. He *was* home.'

'Yes, I know. The flat was his home.'

'No, sweetheart. *You* were his home.'

Now, standing with her unwanted drink, she thought again about his last moments. The way his eyelids had flickered open that last time and looked at her. Gone was the desperation he'd had in earlier months, the raging against his fate, the fear about what might happen. Instead, his expression had been kind; serene.

He'd lifted his hand just slightly and she'd covered it with her own, giving it a gentle squeeze. And he'd smiled.

'Love you, Tom,' she'd said.

He hadn't said it back. But his eyes had told her everything she needed to know.

Once he'd gone, she'd sat there for another hour, the nurse hovering, waiting for her to be ready, then laid his fingers gently on the bed as if she might still cause him pain, and left the room.

His parents had booked into the local hotel three nights earlier – despite their actual home only being half an hour away. When she'd called them with the news, his mother had abruptly ended the call. Moments later, she'd called back, apologising. 'I just thought you'd let us know if he was going... imminently,' she'd said. 'It seemed so unfeeling.'

'I didn't know.'

They'd all known it would be only days, maybe hours. But never when. Never quite how. Sophie had offered them the chance to stay in the flat, but they'd declined, not wanting to be too much trouble, apparently.

'It's their own fault,' Sam had told her later.

'Yes, but... I mean, their son died and...'

'Your husband died.'

'Yes.'

'You were there.'

'Yes.'

'They could have been too. You gave them every chance.'

'I know.'

Sam had taken her by the shoulders, made sure she had eye contact. 'Then, Sophie, you have to let them deal with that in their own way. If they're any sort of decent people, they'll be glad he died holding the hand of someone he loved, that he had that comfort in the end. And drop this weird kind of... what? Competitive grief?'

She'd nodded, mutely. Not ready to really accept that Tom was gone, feeling a strange sensation of grief and denial, each fighting the other, and the numbness that came with them both.

53

NOW

Had it been that time in the cafe when she'd first started to realise how much Will had come to mean? Sophie wondered.

* * *

'I've missed this, you know,' she said, sipping her latte and feeling it warm her throat.

The rain still pattered down outside, but in the cafe everything was bright and welcoming. If anything, the dank, cloudy weather outside simply added to the cafe's charm.

'What, coffee?' Will joked.

'Ha ha. No. This.' She paused. 'You.'

His eyes met hers, questioning. 'Yeah?'

'Yeah. Look, sorry about how things went. It was a weird time.'

'Don't worry about it,' he said emphatically.

'It still is, in a way,' she added.

He nodded, taking a sip of his own drink. 'I get that.'

'But it's OK. I've kind of realised that it's always going to be,' she said. 'Weird, I mean. I thought things would eventually start to feel like they used to. But I don't know. It's as if I've lost a limb or something. It's never going away.'

He was silent for a minute. 'Yeah, makes sense,' he said at last. 'But maybe that's OK. Maybe it's good.'

'Losing a limb is *good*?'

'Ha. Well, no, but metaphorically, having that... absence. It's normal that going through something like that would change you. It changed me too. Obviously I wasn't as close to Tom as you were. But he was my friend. He was someone I thought I'd have in my life for years and years. Now... well, things are different.'

She looked at him. 'Yes, I see that.'

They smiled sadly at one another.

'Anyway, how are things going with you?' she asked, determined to change the subject. Once the topic of Tom came up, she'd found conversations almost drifted away – it was hard to bring them back from the life-shatteringly awful to the trivial again. But she needed the trivial – it was what kept her in the moment.

'Ah, OK,' he said. 'Still rowing.'

'Yeah? Still the five o'clock starts?'

He nodded. 'Can't seem to help it,' he admitted. 'It's an addiction.'

'Pretty good addiction to have, as they go.'

'Yep, slightly better than heroin, no worse than crack or cocaine.'

She laughed, the sound bubbling up from within her. 'Yes, I think rowing probably doesn't have its own support group.'

'Oh, I don't know. Do you remember the rowing club lot?' he joked. 'More like a therapy group than a club half the time.'

She laughed again, it felt good. A silence descended, but it was companionable rather than awkward, and they both took a sip of their coffees.

'Remember the party where we first met?' she said. '*A Midsummer Night's Dream* costumes.'

'Yeah,' he smiled. 'I'm still friends with some of the guys on Facebook. It seems like no time since we left, but some of them have got grey hair. Whereas I obviously haven't changed a bit!'

She laughed. 'I know. Neither of us have.' She gave him a friendly nudge.

'Scary, isn't it?'

'What, getting old?'

'Well, old-ER.'

'A bit,' she said. 'But I guess it's a privilege too.'

They were silent for a moment then, 'Sorry,' she added.

'What?'

'Well, bringing the mood down. I wasn't really thinking about Tom when I said it. It's just odd, seeing the years tick by and thinking about where you thought you'd be, comparing it to how things are.'

'Oh, God. Definitely. But you know, I was talking to my grandad and he said he feels the same.'

'How old is he?'

'Ninety-four.'

'So basically, there's no hope for us,' Sophie said, laughing. 'Destined to reach our tenth decades and still wonder where all the time went.'

'The human condition,' he suggested.

'Yeah. If we're lucky.' And there it was again, that dip of sadness. Tom entering the conversation by stealth.

'Do you want to—?' he said, then stopped abruptly.

'What?'

'No, don't worry.'

'Come on, Will. You can't leave me hanging like that. Do I want to what? Have another coffee? Travel to the Congo? Do a bungee jump?'

He grinned. 'I was just going to ask if you fancied giving rowing another go. If you can cope with it, that is.'

She flexed an arm. 'I never really stopped,' she admitted.

'What?'

'Been going to the gym. You know, keeping up with it a bit. It's not the same, but...'

'Oh, that's cool.'

They sipped their drinks quietly for a moment. 'Sorry how I was back then. I wanted to call but...'

He nodded, acknowledging.

'But it would be nice to row again – for real, I mean.'

'Really? Because I'd really like that too.'

'I've missed it,' she said. Then, 'And you. I've missed you.'

She looked at him, setting her cup down in her saucer. Was she really going to say it? 'And you know,' she said, feeling her cheeks get hot, 'I'd like to be friends again, too. If that's OK?'

He smiled. 'Soph, we never stopped being friends.'

'Thank you,' she said.

'For what?'

'Just still being there, while I disappeared. Not minding. Not everyone's like that, you know. Some of the people I... dropped, when things were bad, they've kind of moved on. I'll send them the odd message, email. And they're friendly enough, but it's like they've filled all the spaces in their lives and haven't got room for me any more.'

'That sucks.'

'Yeah.' She stirred her drink. 'Sometimes I think people are afraid of me.'

'What?' he spluttered, almost spilling his drink. 'Because of the bicep?' he joked.

'Because of Tom. Because being around me reminds them that life is short, fragile. And I don't think people want to think about that most of the time.'

He raised a shoulder, a brief shrug of solidarity. 'I get that, a bit. Like the guys from uni – they mention Tom sometimes of course, they raise a pint to him when we meet up. But then it's all chat about jobs and football and house prices. Nobody wants to bring down the mood.'

'Tom would have hated to bring the mood down,' she said, thinking about how much he'd always tried to make people laugh, spread some sort of joy.

'I know.'

'Well, maybe we'll talk about him,' she said. 'Remember the fun parts as well as all the shit that followed.'

'Sounds like a plan.'

'Rowing and reminiscing it is,' she said.

'And coffee?'

'Definitely coffee.'

They clinked their cups together to seal the deal, and Sophie thought back to what Sam had told her when she'd turned up on the doorstep with a hangover and life advice. It had been hard forcing herself to go out. But each time she forced herself into life, things felt a little better.

* * *

Despite still feeling exhausted, shaken from the events of the past two days, Sophie realised, sitting there in the silent room, that she was smiling.

54

JUNE 2024

She'd known it would happen eventually.

She and Will were pushing a cart through Sainsbury's, wondering whether to risk a barbecue in early June, when she saw them, poring over the wine section. She froze, making Will almost bump into her from behind.

'Whoops. Sorry!' he said at their near collision. Then, 'What's wrong?'

'It's them,' she whispered, her voice so low he could barely hear.

'Them being...'

'Look!' she nodded towards them. Will followed her eye.

'Oh.'

It was Tom's dad who looked up first, noticed them.

'Will!' he said, striding forward with his hand outstretched. He noticed Sophie behind the trolley. 'And Sophie! Well, how nice.'

'Hi,' they both said in unison, sounding like a couple of scary twins from a creepy movie.

'Julie, look who it is!' Tom's father said, his tone less subtle than he probably imagined. 'It's Will... and Sophie!'

Julie turned and forced a smile across her face. 'Well, look at you both!' she said. 'Shopping together.'

'Well, yeah,' Sophie said.

Why did she feel that she was somehow in trouble? Julie must have known she'd move on eventually. And it wasn't a betrayal of Tom. 'Well, we'd better—'

'So how have you been?' Tom's father asked Will. 'Still at that little boutique firm?'

'Yeah, I prefer—'

'And Sophie! Still slaving away at the chalkface?'

'Well, still teaching at least,' Sophie replied with a weak smile.

'Well, jolly good, jolly good.'

'Thanks.'

'And you two are...?' Julie said, looking from one of them to the other, despite patently already knowing the answer to this question.

Will put his arm firmly around Sophie. 'Yes, we're together,' he said. 'Must be a couple of years now, give or take.'

'Well,' Julie said. 'That's marvellous.' She turned to Sophie. 'I'm so glad you were able to *move on*! It really is fabulous news.'

'I... um...' Sophie stuttered.

'Actually,' Will said, his voice surprisingly stern, 'she hasn't moved on. Neither of us have. Not completely. But if you're asking whether we've been able to find happiness together, then we have. I love this woman very, very much.'

'Oh,' Julie said. 'I didn't mean to imply...'

'It's fine,' Sophie said. 'Don't worry. Nice to see you.'

She grabbed Will's arm and steered him away down the aisle.

'Sorry, was I too...'

'No! No, it was great. Just... I feel sorry for her. Parents can't move on, can they? Not at all.'

Will nodded. 'I know. But she can't treat you like that either.'

They moved off, Sophie keen to get out of the supermarket as soon as possible. But as they rounded the corner to the bakery aisle, they heard the clip of heels striking swiftly on the tiled floor.

They turned. Julie.

'Sophie?' she said, clasping her hands together.

'Yes?' Sophie braced herself for another snide comment.

Julie looked down at the tiled floor, her blonde hair falling forwards, revealing white roots that made her seem suddenly vulnerable.

'I just wanted to say... Well, I'm sorry.'

'It's OK,' Sophie said softly. 'You don't need to be.'

'Yes,' said Julie, reaching out and holding her arm briefly before dropping her hand. 'I am. And I should be. Tom would be furious if he saw how I spoke to you then.'

'I understand... It's hard.'

'Yes. But... hard for everyone. Hard for you.'

Sophie nodded, overcome. She tried to keep her mouth from faltering.

'And look. I don't blame you. Or resent you. You made Tom happy and... well, I couldn't ask for more, as his mother. I just... when I see you... it becomes overwhelming.'

Sophie nodded. 'I know,' she said softly.

'And I behave appallingly. But somehow, it's the only thing I'm capable of in that moment.'

'Really, I do understand. Honestly.' Sophie felt her cheeks get hot. 'It's all right.'

'It's not. And I will try harder next time. I hope there will be a next time?' her mother-in-law asked. Almost pleadingly.

'I'm sure there will be.'

'Poor woman,' Will said as Tom's mother turned and walked back to her husband.

'Yeah. It's impossible to think she'll ever be OK. Not really.'

'But are any of us OK when we lose someone?'

They pushed their trolley on, half browsing the shelves, half simply moving forward. 'How do you think Tom would feel about our being together?' Sophie asked.

He looked at her. 'Hard to say. I'd like to think we'd have his blessing.'

'Yeah.'

They walked on a little. 'You know, Libby told me once that she'd always thought you and I would get together one day. Right at the beginning, you know? Before I got together with Tom.'

'She did?'

'Yeah.'

He looked at her. 'Well, I always did have a soft spot for you, Sophie Baker.'

She smiled. 'Sometimes I think...' Then she shook her head.

'You think...?' he prompted.

'Well, I wonder if Tom and I had... if things hadn't happened, whether we'd be...' she trailed off, unable to find the right words. 'I love Tom, loved him. But it's... sometimes it's easier with you. Better.'

He gave her a quick squeeze. 'We'll never know,' he said. 'Who can say how Tom might have changed, or you if you'd been with him. What might have happened. We can only really know what's good right now.'

'How did you become so wise?'

'I watch a lot of TikToks – there's some good advice on there.'

'Sounds very lofty.'

'Does it? Maybe I should add that I watch them when on the toilet?'

'That sounds much more like you,' she said, giggling.

Tom's parents passed the end of their aisle, heading for the till, their trolley full of wine.

'And do you?' he asked.

'What?'

'Do you think things are good right now?' he asked.

'Oh, I'd say so,' she said, giving him a kiss on the cheek. 'Things are pretty good right now.'

55

NOW

Sophie sat up. It was time to try to get herself together. She'd taken time off work for the Paris trip. Lying to her head of department about needing compassionate leave for a recent bereavement had felt wrong, but she knew she'd have been denied leave if she'd shared the real reason. It would have been impossible to explain just how important it was.

She fingered her engagement ring as she stood. It had been this that had triggered it all, she was sure of it now.

* * *

It had been shortly after Will's proposal that she'd started to dream about Tom. Healthy, whole, strolling in Paris on her arm. Younger, at university, dressed in that ridiculous tunic. They were happy dreams in many ways, but they always made her ache with sadness on waking. On those mornings, the engagement ring that Will had given her felt cold on her finger, and her heart felt fat and full of emotion.

She'd shake the feeling off as much as possible and get on

with her day. The school had been undergoing an inspection and every other member of staff had seemed both terrified and horrified in equal measure. She'd been a little worried, but also relished the distraction that the additional work had given her.

'You're quiet,' Will would say from time to time.

'I'm fine,' she'd reply. 'Just thinking.'

With Will's career going well, and her salary having increased again a little, they'd been looking for a new place – maybe even a house on the outskirts of the city. Somewhere to perhaps raise a family in, although she'd tried not to think about the hope-and-pain roller coaster that had been her last experience of trying for a baby. Maybe they'd adopt or even foster.

But the ashes had been playing on her mind.

Soon after the funeral, Tom's parents had asked her about them. Whether she'd like to sprinkle them in the memorial gardens – but she'd taken possession of the little pot of his remains, wanting to do the right thing, not ready to let go.

She'd been sure that the right time would present itself, that she'd feel ready. That one day she'd simply know what to do.

She'd pushed the issue to the back of her mind, and the ashes to the back of the cupboard. They'd moved flats with her three times – once to the small, first flat where she'd lived alone, again into her bigger place, and finally into Will's flat closer to the centre. She hadn't been able to imagine taking the urn to their next home, making it part of the furniture there too. It used to symbolise Tom, her memory of him. Now it seemed to have become a symbol of her inability to make a decision.

'I think Tom would be happy wherever you decided to scatter them,' Will had said when she'd mentioned it to him. 'He wouldn't have wanted you to worry about it.'

'Probably,' she'd said. 'But I don't want to regret it. I have to get it right.'

He'd looked at her.

'I know,' she'd said. Neither of them bought into the idea of an afterlife in any real sense, neither was religious. And if that was the case, then why was she so worried about it?

She hadn't been able to explain it.

'Keep him,' Will had suggested. 'Well, get a decent urn. He can come with us.'

But that had seemed wrong too. She'd tried to imagine how she'd feel if the situation were reversed, and it was hard to picture herself living alongside the ashes of her predecessor.

She'd been alone when it happened for the first time. Leaning on the edge of the kitchen sink, her hands in rubber gloves, plunged beneath the foamy water when she'd said aloud. 'I don't know what to do!'

'With what?' someone had said.

She'd turned, expecting to see Will. But instead, there was Tom, standing in the kitchen, looking entirely himself. Except she knew it was impossible.

'I...' she'd begun, feeling the colour drain from her face.

'Happy to help, if you need,' he'd said casually, as if it were perfectly ordinary to be standing in someone's kitchen five years after you'd died, ready to discuss where to sprinkle your own ashes.

She'd lifted her hands from the water and turned fully. But the only sight that had greeted her then was an empty kitchen.

She'd felt her legs buckle, had sunk to the tiled floor with a cry. But a few minutes later when her heart had stopped racing, she'd got up again, got herself a glass of water. The sun had shone through the window reminding her of reality, of life. And she'd begun to wonder whether it had happened at all. It had been easy to dismiss. Overactive imagination. Lack of sleep. A trick of the light.

But the next afternoon he'd been there too, in that hour or so she had in the house before Will arrived home. 'Long time no see,' he'd said, which would have sounded straight out of a horror film if he hadn't been there, looking completely lifelike and smiling at her.

'Are you really here?' she'd asked, feeling stupid for even acknowledging what was clearly some sort of hallucination.

'Far as I can tell,' he'd said, looking down at himself.

'But you're...'

'What?'

'Tom, you're dead. You died.' The words sounded cold, horrible in the afternoon light.

A shadow flickered across his face. 'Yes, I know.' He'd sighed as if it were tedious rather than tragic. 'What a bloody waste of a life.'

'Well, yes.' She was clearly in need of a holiday, she'd thought. A doctor, maybe. A drink.

'Can we just not talk about it?' he'd asked. 'Can we just act as if everything is normal?'

When she'd stepped towards him, he'd been gone.

* * *

When Will arrived home an hour or so later, she was sitting in the spot where Tom had appeared, sipping from a glass of water.

'Are you OK?' he'd asked.

'Yeah.'

'You look sort of pale.'

She smiled. 'Yeah, I feel kind of pale.' She'd looked up at him, not knowing how to put into words what she needed to say. 'Will, I think I might need to see a doctor.'

That had alarmed him; he'd sat at her side and listened

while she relayed the story – how real it had been, how Tom-like his responses had been.

Will had put an arm around her, drawn her to his side. 'OK,' he'd said. 'Well, it's a bit odd for sure, but honestly, I think it's probably just stress. The engagement, work – and you've been thinking about Tom a lot. Well, his... his ashes at least. So...' He'd let his words trail off.

'Yes, that's probably it,' she'd said, but something in the back of her mind wouldn't let her fully feel the truth in her own words.

When she'd seen Tom for a third time, a couple of weeks later, sitting in the early spring light of the garden and waving at her, she'd finally booked a doctor's appointment.

'What can I say is the matter?' the receptionist had asked her.

'I think I might have something wrong with my brain,' she'd said, not knowing how else to put it.

'Any other symptoms?'

'Not really. It's complicated.'

Luckily, she'd been granted an appointment the next day without further questions. And she'd been relieved – whatever happened, at least she could get some answers.

But then, seated in the plastic chair opposite a GP she hadn't seen before, she'd felt suddenly shy. What happened when people confessed they were seeing things? Would she get sectioned or something? Labelled as mad or crazy? Would this end up on her medical records?

She'd taken a breath and explained, as calmly as possible, what was happening. The GP, who'd looked to be about the same age as her, nodded her head. 'It sounds like you're experiencing grief hallucinations,' she'd said matter-of-factly.

Her calm, sensible tone had come as a shock. Because whatever was happening to her couldn't be normal, surely? Were there other people being stalked by dead loved ones? Was everyone talking to people who were no longer there?

'Oh. But he talks to me?' she'd said. 'We have... we have conversations, kind of.'

The GP had nodded. 'I realise it must seem very strange, and I will make a referral for a few tests just to rule things out. But from what you've described, it does sound as if they might be a product of your mind. Usually, they happen quite close to a person's passing. But it's not unknown for them to occur later. When we're overwhelmed with grief, when we want more than anything to see the person we're missing, the brain can play all kinds of tricks.'

'So what do I... how do I...?'

The doctor had tilted her head. 'In all honesty, if they're not causing you any great distress, you'll probably find it's best to let them take their natural course. They will fade off with time. If not, we can arrange some support for you,' she'd said as she rummaged in her drawer. 'There's a grief centre here, and they have specialist counsellors.'

'Thank you.' She'd slipped the card into her bag.

When she'd got to the car, Tom had been sitting waiting for her.

'Do you want me to drive?' he'd said. 'Only joking.'

She'd ignored him, putting the car into gear and making her way out of the car park. Moments later, he'd melted away and she'd been left feeling his absence so strongly that she'd nearly had to pull over. Why was it that just when her life was sorting itself out, just when she was beginning to dare to feel happy, she had to experience this brain glitch, this grief symptom that hadn't revealed itself at all in the early days when – who knew – it might have brought her some comfort?

Once home, she'd called in sick for the rest of the day and keyed in Libby's number.

'Libby Cannings, can I help you?'

It always made her grin when she heard her friend's work voice. But not that day.

'I hope so,' Sophie had said grimly.

After making sure that her friend was alone and had the time, Sophie had outlined what had been happening down the silent phone line.

'Tom's ghost?' Libby had said when she'd finished.

'No. Not a ghost. A hallucination.'

'What's the difference?'

Sophie had sighed; she'd forgotten that Libby was more open to this sort of thing than she was. 'The difference is,' she'd said, 'that ghosts aren't real, but hallucinations are.'

'So you say.'

'OK. Well, ghosts are beings in their own right. Hallucinations come from the mind.'

'So what makes you sure you're not *seeing* Tom?' Libby had sounded intrigued.

'Libby! This isn't helping! What should I do? Ignore them? Get counselling?'

'What do you want to do?'

She'd closed her eyes, leant her head against the wall. 'I'm not honestly sure,' she'd admitted.

'Well, is it horrible?'

'What? Seeing Tom's gh—I mean, the hallucinations?'

'Yeah. Is he, like, mean or, I don't know... dripping with blood or something?'

'Ew! No. He's just Tom. Annoying at worst.'

Libby was quiet for a minute. Beyond her, Sophie could hear

the buzz of the office, the sounds of daily life. 'Well, maybe just... enjoy it?' she'd suggested.

'Enjoy my hallucinations?'

'Enjoy seeing him. If, as the doc says, it won't last, then maybe just enjoy the ride. It sounds pretty harmless.'

'It's weird though.'

'Well, yeah. But this is you we're talking about, Sophie.'

Sophie had grinned. 'Fair point.'

'Have you thought about why it's happening now?' Libby had asked then. 'If it is just your brain kind of firing off? Why didn't it happen earlier?'

Sophie had scratched her nail along the length of the hall cupboard, making a small dent in its varnished top. 'What do you mean?'

'Well, what might have triggered him, I mean... them? Are you happy with Will? Looking forward to the wedding? Feeling OK?'

'Of course!' she'd said, slightly riled.

'Good. Good. Well, maybe it's to do with some unfinished business with Tom. Maybe it's a chance to say goodbye to him.'

'Maybe.'

'Or maybe he's going to haunt the hell out of you and Will and try to break you up?' Libby had said, her tone slightly lighter, teasing.

'Libby!'

'Sorry. But seriously, Sophie, just... try not to worry, OK? I know that's hard for you.'

'I'll try.'

'Atta girl. Oh, and Soph?'

'Yeah?'

'Say hi to him for me.'

56

TWO WEEKS AGO

She thought about Will again as she began to organise her clothes for the following day. Laying out her skirt and jacket, they seemed almost to belong to someone else. It would be odd going back to work – although it had only been a short absence, so much had happened within her.

Will's proposal – the event that she was sure had triggered the hallucinations – had been so different from Tom's. Unexpected. Welcome. Right on time. She hadn't doubted herself for a moment when she'd slipped the ring on her finger that night in their kitchen when he'd got down on one knee.

The only time she'd had a doubt had been two weeks ago when Will had arrived home from work, excited.

* * *

'OK, so close your eyes,' he said, having asked her to sit down on the sofa.

She sat, arms outstretched as instructed, and he handed her what felt like a box.

'Ta-da!' he said as she opened her eyes.

'It's a present!' she said unnecessarily.

'Well, yes.'

She looked at him. 'It's wrapped.'

'Yup!'

'So why the eye-closing?'

He laughed. 'Just for the drama. Now open it!'

She did, and was treated to a bottle of red wine, a teddy with a beret, a book about cheeses, a silk scarf in red, white and blue. 'What's...'

'*Madame*,' Will said in a thick French accent. 'I would be delighted if you would accept a luxurious trip to La Belle France.' He looked at her expectantly.

'No,' she found herself saying.

'No?' he said, slipping quickly out of his accent in surprise. 'You don't want to?'

She shook her head. 'Oh, Will. I'm sorry. It's just it was... well, it was my place with Tom.'

'Oh, not to Paris!' he said hastily. 'The South. Nice, Cannes.'

'I'm sorry. It's not like I never want to go to France again. But... with you, for our honeymoon...' She shook her head. 'I just can't.'

'OK,' he said, 'I should have thought. Sorry.'

'It's OK.'

'I guess I knew about the Paris thing,' he continued, clearly a bit hurt. 'Didn't realise you'd feel that way about the rest of France.'

'Sorry.'

'But it's OK. Now you say it... I do get it.'

'Thank you.'

'Only...' He cleared his throat. 'This is going to sound stupid and self-indulgent, but you do want this, don't you? This life with me?'

'I love *you*,' she said. 'I want to spend my life with you. And I definitely want to go to France, even Paris, with you one day. But it's too... there are so many memories. Some are good. Some bad. All with him. And it just... we can go there another time maybe. But I want this to be just about us.'

He nodded, his face looking slightly less downcast. 'I get it. Stupid of me really.'

'Don't be silly!' She grabbed his face, turning his head towards hers. 'It was a lovely idea. So lovely. Thoughtful. Just... not quite right. Not yet.' She kissed him firmly on the lips.

'OK,' he said.

'We can think of somewhere else, together?' she suggested.

'OK. Ooh, maybe Italy? Greece?'

It was later, when she'd showered and washed and was lying in bed in the darkness, hearing Will's gentle snores next to her, that she began to think of Paris again. She'd never considered that what had happened with Tom would taint her view of France. In fact, she'd thought it might enhance it – be somewhere she could remember him, the good times they'd had there.

But when she'd seen the teddy, the wine, had figured out what Will was getting at, she'd felt a stab of fear, had frozen at the thought of it. And hurt Will's feelings in the process.

* * *

It had been five years since she'd made that last, awful, wonderful trip with Tom. What would it feel like to walk those streets, to see the sights she'd only ever experienced with him? Had Paris died for her when Tom had?

It was only when she woke again to the dull half-light of 4 a.m. that she realised.

She pulled her covers more closely to her and tried to get back to sleep. But her body was buzzing suddenly with adrenaline. Because suddenly she knew what she needed to do. For Tom. For her. For Paris.

Giving up on the idea of getting any rest, she climbed out from under the covers and made her way down to the kitchen. She guiltily rummaged in the cupboard for the cheap metal urn and pulled it out, holding it to her for a second.

'I'm sorry,' she whispered quietly. 'I should have done this a long time ago.'

'Better late than never,' came a voice. She turned, but nobody was there.

57

TWO WEEKS AGO

When Will came down three hours later, she was sitting in the kitchen, the blinds still closed, Tom's urn on the table in front of her.

'Hey,' he said, his eyes taking in the scene and a look crossing his face.

'Hey.'

'Couldn't sleep?'

'Something like that.'

He walked to the sink and ran himself a glass of water, gulping it down thirstily. Then he pulled the blind, flooding the room with light which sparkled off the metallic surface of the sink, the shiny red of the kettle, and seemed to focus on Tom's urn like a spotlight. She watched as he leant briefly on the counter-top, looking out at their rather tangled garden. Then, shaking himself slightly, he made his way to the table, pulled out a chair and sat opposite her, reaching for her hand. 'OK,' he said. 'Shoot.'

'Shoot?'

'Tell me. It's pretty clear something's up. Are you worrying about the ashes again, because I really think—'

'Not worrying as such,' she said, raising her eyes to his. 'Just... I think I know what I need to do.' She felt something fizz in her chest as she said the words, more anxiety than certainty. Not knowing how he was going to react.

After she told him, he sat back, thoughtful.

'Paris,' he said, more of a statement than a question. 'Alone.'

'It just seemed right, suddenly,' she said.

'And you want to do this now? You wouldn't rather wait until after the wedding? I mean, financially...'

'I know. I just think – it feels like something I have to do, Will. It's like...' She spread her fingers on the table and looked at them. Her nails were chipped, her skin rough. Hardly the look of a soon-to-be bride. She'd have to get them done. After. 'It's like I need to put an end to this, a proper end, before we start our life together.'

'Is this about the hallucinations? Are they still going on?'

'Sometimes. And yes, I do think it might put an end to them. Closure, as they say in the States.' She gave a little smile, but he didn't reciprocate. Instead, he looked serious, his brow furrowed.

'And you really don't want me to come with you?'

She flushed a little. 'It just feels... and I hope you don't mind... but it feels like something I have to do on my own.'

'What about Libby?' he asked. 'I get that you don't want me to be there. Why it might not feel right. But what about Libby or Sam? Maybe one of them could go with you.'

It was then she realised, anew, how much he must love her. He wasn't annoyed about the money, or her darting off on a side-quest when they needed to get their plans sorted for their own wedding, their own life together. He was just worried about her.

'I'll be OK.'

He was silent for a moment, watching her. 'OK,' he said at last.

'OK?'

'Yep. I mean, not that you need my permission, obviously. But if you want to go, if you feel this is something you need to do, then I'm on board. I'll help, if I can.'

'Thank you.'

'Have you thought about the legalities?' he asked.

She nodded. 'It's basically illegal,' she told him, making a face. 'I can scatter them in a remembrance garden there, but it doesn't feel quite right.'

'So, what, you're going to break the law?' Will's tone had become sharper.

'No,' she sighed. 'I'm going to bend it a little. And hope that it will be OK.'

She told him of her plan to take her locket – Tom's locket – and place a tiny amount of the ashes in there, then drop it into the river. 'It won't do any harm,' she said, 'if I just use a tiny amount.'

'And the rest?'

She shook her head. 'I think maybe it's time to make peace with Tom's parents.'

58

TWO WEEKS AGO

The first time she entered the number, she cancelled the call before it rang. Then, her fingers shaking slightly, she forced herself to key it in again. They were only people, she reminded herself. And people who, in her day-to-day life, weren't important at all. So if they were short with her, or angry, or abruptly ended the call, nothing much in her life would change. She could do this.

She'd dreaded this moment all day, building it up in her mind as she tried to get children to engage with Shakespeare's sonnets. She simply had to get on with it.

'Hello?' Tom's mother answered with a question. She didn't have Sophie's latest mobile number so clearly didn't know who to expect.

Sophie hoped her voice, her contact, wouldn't shock her too much. 'Hi, Julie,' she said softly.

'Sophie?'

'Yes.'

There was a silence for a moment, as if both of them were

thinking. Then Julie's voice came back more strongly than it had before. 'Well, how are you, dear?'

'I'm OK, thanks.'

'I heard that you're getting married!'

'Oh. Well, yes, I am.'

'Good for you.'

Sophie couldn't tell whether the comment was barbed or not, so she decided to give Julie the benefit of the doubt. 'Yes, thank you,' she said. Then, 'I was actually calling about Tom,' she ventured.

'Oh.'

'His ashes, to be precise.'

Later she wondered how she'd been so wrong about Julie, about her apparent sternness and the way she'd always seemed distant. When she listened to the impact her words had on her former mother-in-law, she felt newly guilty at having kept the ashes tucked away, rather than deal with what had clearly been a traumatic wait for Julie.

Will texted her from work.

WILL
All good?

SOPHIE
All sorted.

She'd booked her tickets, she'd told work she wouldn't be in on Friday, making up a reason. Because this needed to happen, now that she'd decided, and quickly.

'What are you doing?' Tom asked as she tried to prise the lid from his urn.

She jumped, almost scattering him all over the floor. 'Tom! You scared me!' she said.

Every time she thought about the hallucinations in abstract, she told herself that she shouldn't be engaging with them, talking to them. But when he was there, it felt natural somehow to respond. She was drawn in each time, believing on some level that he – his spirit? – was with her, that this very real version of her husband couldn't possibly be the product of her misfiring brain.

'I'm trying to put a bit of... this in my locket,' she told him, finally managing to free the lid and shuddering slightly as she looked inside. 'God, this is awful.'

Somehow she managed to do it, sealing both locket and urn up tightly afterwards and washing her hands vigorously. 'Hey, I could get insulted by that,' he told her.

'Really?' she looked at him and he shrugged.

'You're trying to get rid of me, aren't you?' he persisted as he followed her to the hall table where she placed the urn, ready to be taken to Julie, and made her way upstairs to put the locket somewhere safe.

'What?'

'Scattering my... these ashes. Because you want me to leave you alone?' he said. He seemed quite hurt. She reminded herself yet again that he was only a manifestation of her grief. That Tom wasn't really *there*.

But it was no use. The look on his face forced the words out of her. 'Tom, of course I don't want to get rid of you. I never wanted any of this. But the truth is, you're gone. And it's not fair to keep you here with me any longer.'

He nodded. 'So where are you taking me?'

She smiled then, looked up at the man who'd played such an important role in her life. Had grown up with her, then forced her to go on alone. Who'd made her laugh, shout, smile, cry and pretty much everything in between.

'We're going to Paris,' she told him.

59

TWO WEEKS AGO

The whole journey there, she'd wished she hadn't arranged it. During the rest of the teaching week she'd been able to put it out of her mind. But en route to Tom's parents', she'd felt rigid with anxiety and a kind of anticipatory grief.

Now, hours later and finally home, she was filled with a mixture of relief and the kind of high that only happens when something you've dreaded turns out to be the right thing; cathartic.

But entering the flat, flinging herself on the sofa with a sigh, she felt the tiredness of it all catch up with her.

Will bent down and kissed her softly on the head. 'Tea?' he said, not waiting for an answer but disappearing into the kitchen to boil the kettle.

'How are you feeling?' he asked, his voice filtering through from the other room.

'Yeah, OK,' she said.

'And I wanted to ask. Any... Have you seen him at all? Today? Or since Paris?'

'No.'

'Well, that's good,' he said. She could hear him opening cupboards, selecting cups, carrying out one of the most mundane and ordinary tasks a person could. She tried to feel glad about it too. And she could, almost. But although she'd wanted to let go of Tom, she still missed him, felt the ache of grief that once again she'd had to say goodbye.

Will came in, passing her a steaming mug of tea and a Kit Kat.

'Ooh, chocolate,' she said. 'Jackpot.'

'Knew you were easily pleased.'

She smiled, taking a sip. 'Well, lucky you!' she teased.

'You'll be OK, you know.'

She nodded. 'I know.'

'Proud of you.'

'Thanks.'

There was no need to say anything else.

When they'd dropped off the urn at Tom's parents', she'd seen Julie cry for the first time. His mother had even been dry-eyed at the funeral, despite her obvious grief. Tom's father had slipped an arm around his wife's back and they'd clung together.

'My boy!' she'd said into his shoulder. 'My lovely boy.'

'I'm sorry,' Sophie had said. 'I should have done this before... I...'

Julie straightened, brushing down her clothing as if she could remove the deep creases caused by the hug. 'It's all right, my dear,' she'd said. 'There isn't a best way to deal with grief. No... no instruction manual. We've certainly learned that over the past few years.' She'd looked at her husband and he'd given her an encouraging smile. 'We haven't...' she'd continued. 'We haven't always been fair with you, Sophie, since Tom... passed...'

'It's OK.'

'Yes, but it isn't really. I took it out on you.' Her face had fallen with grief. 'And then I realised we'd lost you too.'

Will's hand had touched her back, a pat of reassurance and a reminder that he was there. Sophie hadn't quite known what to do. Julie wasn't the sort of person you... hugged. She was altogether too formal, too stiff for that.

'Go on,' Will had whispered.

She'd forced herself to step forward, put her arms out, and Julie had stepped into them, hugging her daughter-in-law tightly. 'I'm sorry,' she'd said. 'I'm so sorry.'

'Me too.'

They'd refused an offer of a drink afterwards; it seemed better to leave and let Tom's parents come to terms with their renewed grief. But she had promised to stay in touch. And she would, she decided. Even if Julie never let her guard down again, she'd seen beneath the veneer of coldness that there was a sadness there that made her unexpectedly vulnerable. And it would be no trouble to at least try.

'Thanks,' she'd said, as Will had signalled and pulled away.

'For coming with?'

'No, for encouraging me to hug Julie. You know.'

'The pat on the back?' he'd asked, confused.

'All of it. When you whispered, "Go on" in my ear.'

He'd looked at her. 'I didn't say a word.'

60

NOW

The dress hung in the corner of their room; the bag it was stored in was so long that she'd taken a picture off its wall hook to use it for the hanger, to make sure none of it touched the floor or became tarnished.

'Blimey,' Will had said when he'd seen it. 'Looks like the grim reaper standing there in the corner.'

'Very funny.'

'I hope the dress isn't as scary.'

'Oh, I'm pretty sure you're going to like the dress.' She was, too. Never one for dressing up or making too much of a show, she'd actually embraced the whole wedding-dress-choosing thing this time. Sam and her mum had helped her, and she'd found a dress that was somehow much more 'her' than her previous one had been. When she'd put it on at the last fitting, the folds of the skirt blooming around her ankles, she'd actually twirled.

'Not long now,' he'd said, making a face.

'Hey, this is meant to be the happiest day of our lives!' she'd teased.

'I know. I'm looking forward to after more though.'

'The honeymoon?'

'The marriage.'

She'd hugged him then. 'Softie.'

She'd invested in some new outfits for Mallorca, where they'd finally settled on an indulgent, all-inclusive resort – somewhere to lie by the pool and do absolutely nothing for seven days. Summer dresses, new bikinis, sandals – it had been a while since she'd been on holiday and she was really looking forward to it.

Preparing to pack, she pulled her suitcase from under the bed and unzipped it, taken suddenly by the smell of the fabric, somehow reminiscent of going away – of holidays and excitement.

Unzipping it, she flung back the lid and began to sort through the colourful clothes she'd laid out on the bed, trying to make the most of the space. Then she stopped.

In the netted part on the inside of the case, designed probably to house documents, was a paper bag – the one from Paris, from that trip where she'd sat alone and had her portrait sketched by an artist in Montmartre. She'd slipped it in her bag without even looking at it properly, too overcome with grief after dropping the locket, too full of memories of Tom and what she'd lost to really care whether the artist had captured her good side.

Feeling slightly tearful, she reached for it now and drew the stiff paper from its holding. There she was, on the bench, a sadness on her face that she hadn't realised would be visible to anyone else. The artist had captured her beautifully, in a simple pencil sketch that somehow communicated her sorrow as well as the way she looked. Around her, Montmartre, a jumble of vague figures, easels, stalls, other artworks, tumbled into the background.

It was good.

Then she saw it, bringing the drawing up to her face to get a better look. And she felt suddenly sick. Her hands trembled and she shoved the painting back into the bag, shaking her head and feeling disorientated. Because it simply wasn't possible.

'Will!' she called.

'Yes?'

'Can you come here for a sec?' It was hard to keep the tremble out of her voice.

She heard his quick tread on the stairs and then he was there. 'What's up? Need me to do up a zip or something?'

'No, I've barely started,' she said. 'It's just...'

'What, love?'

Wordlessly she handed the paper bag to him and, with a confused expression, he drew out the picture and looked at it.

'That's lovely,' he said. 'Did you get it when...'

'Yeah.'

'She's... you look beautiful,' he said. 'Shall we get it framed?'

'It's not that, it's...' she indicated with her finger and he looked again at the drawing, the stalls, the artists and their easels, the tourists that populated the square every day.

'Sorry, I can't see...' Then he stopped. 'Bloody hell.'

'Yes.'

'It's him, isn't it?'

She nodded, barely able to speak.

In the picture, the woman sits on a bench, her legs crossed in front. The other seat is empty. But behind her, leaning against a tree, his eyes fixed on her, there is a man. A man with black hair and an easy smile.

'It's Tom.'

And it was. Behind her in the picture as she sat on the

bench, dressed just as he had been in her visions of him, Tom stood and looked at her and smiled.

61

NOW

'Honey, that is *not* Tom,' Libby said later when she'd come over to inspect the picture. She was sitting on the sofa in their living room, sipping from an enormous glass of wine.

'How could you say that?' Sophie cried, picking up the picture and scrutinising it again.

Libby shrugged. 'Sorry, I just don't see it.'

'But he's wearing what he was wearing... you know, that day.'

Libby looked at her kindly. Her face softened. 'Well, then maybe I'm wrong,' she said, brushing a strand of hair back from Sophie's forehead. 'Maybe it's him. Maybe he was there, kind of saying goodbye.'

'It sounds nuts.'

'Yep. But you know, I've heard stranger things, been open to the idea of it,' Libby shrugged. 'I'm just surprised that *you* are, I suppose.'

'It's amazing what a few months of hallucinations will have you believing!'

Libby sat back on the sofa, sipped from her wine. 'And the scattering went OK? With his parents?'

She nodded. Rather than the sterile, somehow impersonal crematorium gardens, they'd chosen to scatter Tom's remaining ashes in the copse at the end of their enormous garden. 'He loved it here as a child,' Julie had told her. 'I think he'd like to be here.'

Sophie had worried a little that they might eventually sell the plot, that it might end up being the site of hundreds of identikit new build houses. But she told herself not to. Because she couldn't control the distant future. Had to just let it happen. And although when people said this sort of thing in movies, it had always sounded a bit corny to her, she had started to realise what they meant when they said that people live on in your heart.

Tom wasn't there in that pile of ash. He was with them. If not in spirit, then in their memories. And that's where she'd learn to cherish him.

Julie had gripped her hand then. 'Thank you. For bringing him so much happiness. He was always a bit of a... worry, Tom. Always a bit too carefree for his own good. But you anchored him. I admit, I didn't like it at the time, his devotion to you. This sudden new version of my son. But I can see now how much... richness you gave his life.'

Sophie had squeezed Julie's hand back. 'Thank you,' she'd said. 'And you don't need me to tell you how much he loved you both.'

They'd stood, Sophie, Julie and Doug, looking at the branches wave on the bushes, hearing the rustle of the grass, the sounds of nature all around. And although they were all crying by the time they turned away, there was definitely a sense of rightness about it all – that they'd come together to say goodbye.

'Well, I'm glad it was OK, everything considered,' Libby said.

'Yes.'

'Do you have your wedding list, by the way?' Libby asked, changing the subject. 'I've lost the link you sent.'

Sophie grinned. 'I'll send it again. But honestly. You don't have to get us anything.'

'Well, we'll see.'

'And you're bringing George?' Sophie kept her tone light, but both of them knew that Libby's bringing him to a wedding was A Big Deal.

'Almost definitely.'

They smiled at each other.

'Look at you, the blushing bride. Again!'

'Your turn next?' Sophie teased.

'Steady on! Yes, George is... well, he's perfect. But it's early. No rushing.'

'Still... "perfect" sounds promising.'

'I'm just saying, though. If you throw that bouquet in my direction, I will high-kick it well out of reach. I'm not even sure if I'm the marrying kind.'

'Fair enough.'

'Never say never, though. Just... I've realised I'll be OK, either way. Maybe that's the wisdom of getting older.'

'Ha. Maybe.'

'And what about you? Are you going to... Have you and Will talked about...?'

It was still awkward, after all these years. Sophie nodded. 'Babies?' she said. 'Yes, we've talked about it. We'd like to. If we... if I can.'

Libby squeezed her hand. 'I'm sure it'll work out this time.'

'I'm not!' Sophie said with a wry smile.

Libby looked at her.

'Well, I'm not! It's OK though, I think. I'm trying to enjoy each day, not worry so much about the future that I spoil the present. I did that, you know. Last time. Wasted it.'

'You didn't.'

'A bit.'

'Well, hindsight is 20/20,' Libby said. 'We'd all do things differently if we could. Probably.'

'You would?'

'Well, I'd work a little harder for a first class degree, rather than settling for a 2.2, for starters,' Libby said. 'And I'd never have plucked my eyebrows into oblivion, if I had my time again.'

Sophie laughed. 'All very serious stuff.'

'It *is* serious!' Libby grinned. 'I have to draw them in with a crayon. I don't think you realise how much I resent that!'

Sophie snorted with laughter, almost spitting out the sip of wine she'd just taken.

'There she is,' Libby said, smiling fondly.

'What?'

'Miss Piggy! The snorter! You always used to laugh like that. A great big oink.'

'Hey!'

Libby touched her arm. 'Seriously, piggies aside, I'm pleased to hear that glorious snort again. I thought you might have lost it, with everything that happened.'

'Really? You missed the snort?'

'Yes. OK, it's not an attractive sound. But it's Sophie's laugh. Sophie's proper laugh when she's happy and properly letting go,' Libby said. Then she made an exaggerated pig sound. 'Ooiiinkkk.'

'Libby!' Sophie said, then without meaning to, she snorted again.

'See! Miss Piggy!' Libby said decisively. 'And you know, I've always thought Will had the look of Kermit about him. You're made for each other.'

'Which makes you...?'

'Ah, no idea. Probably Beaker or something horrific like that.'

'I've got a soft spot for Beaker, if you must know.' Then, 'What *are* we talking about?' Sophie said, laughing again.

Libby was right. It felt good to laugh. Good not to be pulled back into the past, or forward into worries for the future. Neither of which she could control. But just to be here, snorting away, sounding like a Muppet but not caring about that in the least.

EPILOGUE
NOW

The little barn had been decked with small, white fairy lights which sparkled against the bare brickwork and the dark wood, laid by builders centuries ago to house their cattle, and now transformed into a wedding venue with old world charm.

She stood in the vestibule with her dad, smiling in her dress, feeling entirely comfortable and entirely herself. Mum had done her make-up and gathered her hair into a messy up-do, with soft curls that fell against her face.

'You look lovely,' Dad had said when she'd arrived, and she'd squeezed his hand.

She could hear the rumble of conversation from the next room as guests arrived and settled into position. Somewhere among them, she knew, was Will's voice. They'd spent the night apart in some sort of nod to tradition, and she was longing to see him again.

'Do you mind if I...' her father said now, gesturing to the little corridor where the loo was situated.

'Oh, of course. Go ahead.'

Then she was alone in the tiny room with its tiled floor and rough-plastered wall. She set her bouquet – pink and white roses – on a table and went over to the window looking out over the countryside, to the fields dotted with sheep and cows, the cluster of trees on the horizon. She'd waited for this day, in some ways, her whole life – the wedding that she'd always imagined.

But her mind was muddled, filled with joy at the thought of marrying Will, but sadness too at the thought of her first wedding; of Tom.

'Tom?' she whispered into the empty room, half hoping to provoke a hallucination. He'd been absent in the weeks since Paris and that was a good thing. But she missed him too, found herself grieving his absence.

There was no answer.

She closed her eyes, blocking out the view of the countryside beyond the little stone barn, pictured Tom as she'd first known him, dressed as Lysander, or sipping coffee opposite her in that tiny cafe. She remembered their first trip to Paris, their last. Remembered saying goodbye to him. The recent trip to Paris when he may or may not have been there. 'I'm sorry,' she whispered. 'I'm sorry it turned out that way.'

They'd been unlucky. But lucky too. To have found each other, to have had the experiences they'd shared. They'd been through hell together, but had loved each other throughout. Now he was at peace and she had the chance for a new beginning.

She felt a warmth spread through her as she imagined Will standing just out of sight, waiting for her. She imagined Tom too, his face smiling at them both – because he would, she thought, if he could. He wouldn't want her to be alone. And he'd loved Will. Loved them both.

As she straightened the satin skirt of her dress, movement out of the window caught her eye. Out in the courtyard, behind the converted barn she'd walk to a little later for the wedding breakfast, she saw him: a figure in jeans, hands in his pockets, back to her, black hair shining in the sun. Almost iridescent. There was something about the way he was standing, the set of his shoulders. She felt something shift inside her.

Slowly he turned, and although he was several metres away, she recognised his face; the intense eyes, mouth giving way to an easy smile.

Something inside her dropped. Because it couldn't be, could it?

Looking again, her eyes locked with those familiar eyes of his and she felt a shiver as, smiling, he gave her a single nod, as if, somehow, he was telling her to go ahead, to live. She leant closer to the window and—

'Are you ready, kid?' said a voice.

Her father had returned and was standing near the door, holding out his arm. 'You all right?'

She turned back to the window, saw the soft sunlight illuminating the cobbled space between her and the building. Her eyes darted, looking for the man. For Tom. But there was no one there.

She took a breath, filling her lungs with oxygen, with life. And she felt her past fall away, the future stretch before her.

'Yes,' she said, turning with a smile, her eyes shining with moisture. 'I really am.' And she slid her arm through her father's and stepped out of the door towards the courtyard and the place where she'd be shortly saying 'I do.'

ACKNOWLEDGEMENTS

As usual, I have so many people to thank. And I'm completely paranoid that I'll forget someone important. So here goes: to Isobel Akenhead who is always enthusiastic about my work and is brilliant at bringing out the best in every story, and to Boldwood Books for their support and brilliant promotion, especially Nia, Jenna, Issy, Claire and Wendy. To Debra Newhouse for her meticulous and thoughtful editorial input.

My agent Ger, who goes above and beyond to support me.

To Hannah Furness who provided valuable insight into caring for a patient with pancreatic cancer.

And to the brilliant authors including Nicola Gill, Heidi Swain, Clare Merchant, Jenni Kerr, and Linda McEvoy who've taken time to read my work, turn up to events and support me in so many ways. To the D20 authors, all of whom were published during 2020 and who have become a supportive network.

I'm so grateful, too, for the online book community, including the groups on Facebook who make writing feel less solitary: The Fiction Café, The Bookload, Chick Lit and Prosecco, and so many others.

And of course, to Paris. The city that took my own heart over twenty years ago.

ABOUT THE AUTHOR

Gillian Harvey is an author and freelance writer who lives in Norfolk. Her novels, including the bestselling *A Year at the French Farmhouse* and *The Bordeaux Book Club* are often set in France, where she lived for 14 years.

Sign up to Gillian Harvey's mailing list for news, competitions and updates on future books.

Visit Gillian's website: www.gillianharvey.com

Follow Gillian on social media here:

- facebook.com/gharveyauthor
- x.com/GillPlusFive
- instagram.com/gillplusfive
- bookbub.com/profile/gillian-harvey

ALSO BY GILLIAN HARVEY

A Year at the French Farmhouse

One French Summer

A Month in Provence

The French Chateau Escape

The Bordeaux Book Club

The Riviera House Swap

The Little Provence Bookshop

Midnight in Paris

BECOME A MEMBER OF THE SHELF CARE CLUB

The home of Boldwood's book club reads.

Find uplifting reads, sunny escapes, cosy romances, family dramas and more!

Sign up to the newsletter
https://bit.ly/theshelfcareclub

Boldwood

Boldwood Books is an award-winning fiction publishing company seeking out the best stories from around the world.

Find out more at www.boldwoodbooks.com

Join our reader community for brilliant books, competitions and offers!

Follow us
@BoldwoodBooks
@TheBoldBookClub

Sign up to our weekly deals newsletter

https://bit.ly/BoldwoodBNewsletter

Printed in Dunstable, United Kingdom